"Good. How about Casey's Diner?"

"Not there." Kelly cleared her throat. "I mean, there's no reason to go there when we're only getting coffee."

"Okay." Tony dragged the word out as he studied her. "You have something else in mind?"

She waved her hand, but her elbow remained rooted near her rib cage. "There are plenty of coffee shops around."

"You pick, then. You lead. I'll follow your car."

She nodded and continued to her car. What had made her so nervous? And why did she want to avoid the diner? Those were just some of the questions among many he had about Kelly Roberts. At a time when he should have been focusing on his final case and preparing to walk away from the task force, he was too curious about a young police officer who seemed to be hiding something. Too curious for his own good.

* * *

If you're on Twitter, tell us what you think of Harlequin Romantic Suspense! #harlequinromsuspense

Dear Reader,

I am so excited to share Kelly and Tony's story with you. I wanted to explore a romance in the context of an FBI joint task force, where I could peel through the layers of the internet and where the hunters and the hunted are one and the same. I hope you find the ride as exciting as I did.

Her Dark Web Defender is the second story in the True Blue series for the Romantic Suspense line, but it is also connected to the books I wrote for the now-closed Harlequin Superromance line. True Blue tells the stories of the brave men and women from a Michigan State Police post.

If you love Kelly and Tony's story and want to get to know some of the other members of the Brighton Post community, check out *Shielded by the Lawman* (Romantic Suspense) as well as *Strength Under Fire* and *Falling for the Cop* (Superromance).

I love staying in contact with readers, no matter how you choose to connect. Learn more about me and sign up for my newsletter through my website, dananussio.com; connect with me on Facebook, Facebook.com/DanaNussio, or Twitter, Twitter.com/DanaNussio1; or drop me a line on real paper at PO Box 5, Novi, MI 48376-0005.

Happy reading!

Dana Nussio

HER DARK WEB DEFENDER

Dana Nussio

HARLEQUIN®ROMANTIC SUSPENSE

Recycling programs
for this product may
not exist in your area.

ISBN-13: 978-1-335-66224-8

Her Dark Web Defender

Copyright © 2019 by Dana Corbit Nussio

All rights reserved. Except for use in any review, the reproduction or utilization of this work in whole or in part in any form by any electronic, mechanical or other means, now known or hereafter invented, including xerography, photocopying and recording, or in any information storage or retrieval system, is forbidden without the written permission of the publisher, Harlequin Enterprises Limited, 22 Adelaide St. West, 40th Floor, Toronto, Ontario M5H 4E3, Canada.

This is a work of fiction. Names, characters, places and incidents are either the product of the author's imagination or are used fictitiously, and any resemblance to actual persons, living or dead, business establishments, events or locales is entirely coincidental.

This edition published by arrangement with Harlequin Books S.A.

For questions and comments about the quality of this book, please contact us at CustomerService@Harlequin.com.

® and ™ are trademarks of Harlequin Enterprises Limited or its corporate affiliates. Trademarks indicated with ® are registered in the United States Patent and Trademark Office, the Canadian Intellectual Property Office and in other countries.

Printed in U.S.A.

Dana Nussio began telling "people stories" around the same time she started talking. She has been doing both things nonstop ever since. The award-winning newspaper reporter and features editor left her career while raising three daughters, but the stories followed her home as she discovered the joy of writing fiction. Now an award-winning fiction author as well, she loves telling emotional stories filled with honorable but flawed characters. Empty nesters, Dana and her husband of more than twenty-five years live in Michigan with two overfed cats, Leo the Wondercat and Annabelle Lee the Neurotic.

Books by Dana Nussio

Harlequin Romantic Suspense

True Blue

Shielded by the Lawman
Her Dark Web Defender

Harlequin Superromance

True Blue

Strength Under Fire
Falling for the Cop

Visit the Author Profile page at Harlequin.com for more titles.

To my Writer Wednesday crew: Kathy Steck, Jacqui Gretzinger, Karen Kittrell, A.J. Norris, Greg Mahr, D.A. Henneman, Kathy Wheeler, Jeanne Tepper, Cheryl Smith and Liz Heiter. (Also, to Isabelle Drake, who's going to make it one of these days.)
Your love for your stories and your dedication to the craft inspire me.

A special thanks goes to Kim Moore, a retired FBI special agent who also just happens to be a childhood friend. I appreciate your opening your world to me. And thanks again to Michigan state police officer David Willett, who continues to take too many texted questions and still hasn't blocked me. You are both real-life American heroes at a time when we really need them. My characters would salute you, and so do I.

Prologue

"Emily's tongue was bluer than mine," Kelly Roberts blurted in the back seat of the police car, the stinky blanket scratching her bare shoulders.

Why she'd thought of the raspberry slushes they'd been slurping just before *it* happened, she wasn't sure, just as she couldn't figure out why the lady cop sitting next to her kept patting her arm like she was her mom or something. That itched, too. And made her want to jump out of the car and run.

"You sure you're warm enough?"

"I'm fine." But she couldn't stop shaking, even if it was the hottest day in June so far. She would never be warm again.

She let the officer pull the awful blanket high enough on her shoulders to cover most of her freckles and pressed her cheek against the window to get a better look outside.

Past the yellow tape that had been strung between two trees, Emily's new lime-green mountain bike lay abandoned across the sidewalk. It had crashed there when the scary man leaped from behind the bushes and yanked her off the seat. Her cup was on its side, the melted drink a blue puddle on the concrete.

Something was clogging Kelly's throat, and her eyes burned, so she shifted her head. If only her own purple, hand-me-down bike didn't have to be in the next spot she looked. On the grass farther down the sidewalk. The exact same place where she'd dropped it when she'd unfrozen enough to scream. Once she'd started, she couldn't stop.

"Your parents will be here in a couple of minutes. Do you think you can give a description... I mean tell us what the man who took your friend looked like?"

"Yes," she whispered.

As if she could ever forget anything about him. The closed-lipped smile. That raspy voice and his tight jaw while Emily had kicked and scratched to escape, her black ponytail whipping from side to side. A movie villain come to life, with wild eyes and hairy arms. And the only person who could have helped her friend had been too scared to do anything but watch.

That strange lightness she'd had inside her belly a few times in the past half hour floated up again. Was that relief? What kind of friend was she to take comfort in the fact that the bad man had grabbed Emily instead of her? Was that why her eyes were dry when she should have been sobbing by now? Why the officer kept patting her arm and sneaking peeks at her face? No one could ever know the truth. That she was a bad person. That she cared only about herself.

"Don't worry, sweetie. We're going to find her."

Kelly jerked her head to look back at her. She was nine. They couldn't fool her. Police officers were supposed to tell the truth, and the lady was lying. How did she know, anyway? She hadn't seen the meanness on the guy's face. Or the fear in Emily's enormous chocolate-colored eyes.

Stay quiet, or I'll be back for you.

Kelly had skipped telling the police that part. If she had, it would have made what the man said real. She'd already disobeyed his instructions by calling for help. Telling the police about it, too, might make him keep his promise.

She turned to the window again, just as another police car, an ambulance and a truck that looked like her mom's pulled up along the curb. They could ask all the questions they wanted to. They could search for clues and turn on their sirens and pretend that they could make everything better. But Kelly already knew the truth.

Emily was gone forever.

Chapter 1

Special Agent Anthony Lazzaro shoved open the door to the plain brick building and tromped to an office with the vague name, Arch Computer Consultants, Inc. He stabbed in the four numbers of the lock code that changed so frequently he sometimes forgot it and had to call one of the other team members to get inside.

Soon he wouldn't have to remember it at all. The thought should have brightened the drab office walls, just as his formal request should have dulled the stark realities that the two rows of cubicles and the boards of photographs represented. He was finished with agonizing over his decision to transfer from the Innocent Images Task Force of the FBI Cyber Division. No more staring every day at this slimy underbelly of society. No more pretending it hadn't changed him over the past six years and made him feel older than thirty-eight. No more lying.

Too bad he was stuck in purgatory a little longer.

"Hey, Tony. Ready for another day in the salt mine?"

Tony snarled at Eric Westerfield, but the younger man only grinned as he hurried toward him. The local deputy, who'd joined the task force a year earlier, had so much spring in his step that his coffee swilled over the brim of his paper cup. Wasn't the guy ever in a bad mood? But the rush of cool air hitting Tony's face told him Eric had already cranked the air-conditioning, which, by afternoon, would barely challenge the mid-July heat. At least he was good for something.

"Got my pickax and headlamp ready, so sure." He patted his briefcase, where he'd concealed his .40 caliber Glock 22 in its padded holster with a thumb break for the trip from his rental car to the office. Out of habit, he immediately withdrew the weapon from the bag and locked it and the separate hip holster in his bottom desk drawer.

"Special Agent Dawson told me we're getting a new task force member today."

"I heard."

He'd been livid, too. It was bad enough that Will Dawson, the administrative special agent on the task force, had refused to sign off on his transfer until they'd closed the current case. It centered on the murder of two eighteen-year-old girls and possibly involved cybercrimes. Now the team would be saddled with breaking in a new member during the most high-profile investigation they'd conducted in three years. And his last case on the task force.

"It's a trooper from the Michigan State Police Brighton Post, since both victims were from Brighton. They referred the case to us in the first place."

"Heard that, too."

Tony strode toward the galley kitchen, where the office coffeepot served up hot sludge in daily doses. Though he hoped Eric wouldn't follow, he did.

"I won't be low *man* on the totem pole anymore."

"Don't worry." He didn't bother looking back as he poured. "You'll still have your spot near the bottom."

He didn't miss the deputy's emphasis on the word "man," since they both were aware the new officer was female. Men and women were different on the job. Not better or worse, just different. He wasn't looking forward to a changing team dynamic during his last few weeks in that office.

"Are we really going to use her *voice* for this case?"

"Guess so." Another argument Tony had lost. The regular chats would have sufficed, but the others wouldn't listen to his reasoning.

With a wave to Eric, he carried his stained Detroit Lions coffee mug past four cubicles, each equipped with laptops and external monitors and hard drives. Near the far window with blinds always kept closed, he sat at his own cramped square, where he could slip on his headset, enter the parallel universe of the Internet referred to as the Dark Web and pretend to be alone. He could do this. Just one more case, and he would be free.

But would he really be? The answer was as clear as all those faces painted on his memory. Some even smiled back at him from photos pinned to the bulletin board on his cubicle wall. A few of his failures, despite all his fancy computer equipment, education and supposed know-how. It was cruel punishment that he would work his final weeks alongside a task-force rookie probably still starry-eyed with convictions that justice could prevail and good could overcome evil. Things he used to believe.

"Do you think she'll be ready for this?" Eric called from his own desk.

Tony had just fired up his computer and launched the Dark Web browser called Tor, but at his colleague's question, he pushed in his chair.

"Are any of us?"

The click of the door saved either of them from having to answer that question. He stood and stepped outside his cubicle to get a better look. And there she was, entering the office with Deidre Elliot, the administrative assistant. She couldn't have stuck out more in that navy-blue uniform shirt, lighter blue pants with a dark stripe, gray tie and the *badge*.

She probably tied her light-brown hair back so tight to look older, but nothing could mask that youthful blush that contrasted her ivory complexion. She didn't appear much older than the girls whose deaths they were investigating. Legally, they were women, he guessed. Old enough to know better but too young to realize that their search for adventure could get them killed.

Deidre led the other woman toward them. "Hey, guys. I'd like to you meet our newest team member."

"You must be Officer Kelly Roberts."

Wide dark brown eyes stared back at him. She cleared her throat, her tongue slipping out to moisten her deep pink, full lips. Was she surprised that he knew the identity of the new team member? Well, she wasn't the only one who'd received a shock just then as her simple, nervous reaction had jabbed him below the belt. What was that? He'd never had inappropriate physical reactions to female agents or officers before. He didn't notice women at all.

Not anymore.

"Trooper."

He cleared his throat and forced whatever *that* had been from his thoughts. "Excuse me?"

"It's *Trooper* Roberts."

"Right. I knew that." Damn. He sounded as nervous as she appeared. This wasn't a blind date. It was a case, and he owed it to the young women who'd lost their lives to focus on it and track down the suspect. "I'm Special Agent Anthony Lazzaro."

She reached out her hand, but he nodded at her instead, so she lowered it.

"What's with the uniform? How are we supposed to fly under the radar here with you showing up dressed in blue?"

He was being a jerk, but that was easier than telling her she filled out that boxy uniform in all the right places. He was looking for a transfer, not forced early retirement.

"Sorry. I didn't know. I was just told where to report."

"We're plain clothes here." He indicated the slacks, dress shirts and ties he and Eric wore.

"I see that. What about a weapon? Aren't you required to carry one? I am."

"Weapons are required but must be concealed when entering and leaving the office and can be worn or locked up when inside it."

She nodded and continued to scan the rented office space that looked like hundreds of others in Livingston and nearby counties. Her gaze paused on the bulletin boards covered with photographs from current cases and a poster of the "FBI Ten Most Wanted Fugitives" list. Then she turned back to him.

"This is it?"

"Yeah, not much to speak of, is it?" Eric said as he stepped closer. "I'm Deputy Eric Westerfield of the Livingston County Sheriff's Department."

This time the two law enforcement officers shook hands, and Tony was almost sorry he hadn't done the same. Almost.

"The FBI field office in Detroit rents this office space for us," Eric continued. "But no one is supposed to know this is a task force office, and no one without specific business with us is even allowed inside."

"Business with Arch Computer Consultants?"

"One of many fake names the FBI gives for its task force offices," Eric explained.

"Are there just going to be four of us? I thought the task force was supposed to be—"

Tony shook his head to interrupt her. "Ten in all." He pointed to the same number of cubicles. "Two FBI special agents and representatives from area law enforcement, Homeland Security and then administrative staff like Deidre."

He hated having to explain information she already would have known if she'd just read the file.

"Where are they?"

"Some are catching a few hours of sleep since we're working around-the-clock on this case."

"Oh." Her gaze flicked to Eric and then back to Tony. "Well, good. We need to stop this guy before he strikes again."

"Are you saying we're tracking a serial killer? Because we have no evidence to confirm that yet. We don't jump to conclusions here. Our work is meticulous. Precise. We follow the evidence, and we don't make stupid mistakes."

Her jaw tightened. "I'll keep that in mind. Anyway, I'm not saying I *know* anything. But we can't just sit on our hands and wait *in case* he strikes again, can we?"

Touché. Her heavily lashed eyelids lifted, and she glared up at him.

Deidre chuckled as she headed to her own desk, closest to the door. "It's good that we're all getting to know each other better."

Eric gestured toward Tony with his thumb. "Don't

worry about him. He's all grumble with no fangs. He's always tough on the new guy, and lucky for me, you're it."

"Yeah, lucky me."

"All of us bring something new to the task force," Eric said. "The special agent here also happens to be a veritable computer genius."

"It's my job."

Eric brushed away Tony's comment with a wave. "And I might look mild, but I'm seasoned in pursuing human traffickers. So, what's your superpower?"

Tony was careful not to look interested, but he wanted to know the answer, too. The details they'd been given about her were sparse.

"Besides being first on the scene when the victims' bodies were discovered along the Brighton Mountain Bike Trail, I guess it's my voice."

Tony's back teeth clenched before he could stop them, but at least the others weren't looking his way.

"Oh, that's right," Eric said. "That was Special Agent Dawson's idea. Something to sweeten the deal while we're trolling for online predators. Special Agent Lazzaro wasn't a fan of the plan."

Her gaze shifted to Tony, and she seemed to dare him to look away first.

"Most suspects prefer the anonymity of text-only chats."

"You do kind of sound like a kid, though," Eric said.

"Thanks, I think. I've never been hired for my voice before."

She laughed then, a sound like the smoothest whiskey pouring on ice, and the sensation that sluiced over Tony and headed south couldn't have been more different from the jab he'd felt earlier. With a laugh like that she could have worked as a phone-sex operator. He was tempted to tell her so, but the door opening again cut them off. Good thing for that.

Special Agent Dawson entered the way he always did, coffee in one hand, a plate with a Danish in the other and a collapsible umbrella handle strap looped over his wrist.

"I see you've already met," he said as he introduced himself.

"We're old friends now," Eric answered for all of them.

"Well, let's get this done." Dawson dropped his Danish off in his own cubicle and continued toward them. "The sooner we close this case, the sooner my wife and girls can sleep again. The trail's already going cold."

"You're sure we're headed in the right direction?" Tony asked.

"I'm not sure of anything. But we already know that one of the young women was computer savvy and was hanging out in chat rooms. I don't think this was the adventure she was looking for."

Two other team members had followed him into the office, and Dawson asked them to introduce themselves.

"Robert Golden, Homeland Security," the graying one with the paunch told her.

The guy with a crew cut and a gym body lifted his hand in a wave. "Don Strickland, Detroit Police."

"Trooper, tell the team a little bit about yourself," Dawson said.

Kelly shifted her feet. "I've worked with the state police for three years, assigned to the Brighton Post. I'm usually alone in my own patrol car, so you'll need to give me a few days to get used to working in an office."

She might have said something else after that, but Tony couldn't get past the thought that she'd been a police officer that long. She wasn't a rookie, though nothing could prepare someone to work on this task force.

"One more thing. I'll do whatever it takes to get this guy. It's personal for me. I mean, I *live* in Brighton."

Dawson's gaze narrowed. "Are you sure you're not too close to this?"

"No, I'm fine."

Tony wasn't certain of many things. He definitely wasn't sure this officer's voice would help them locate the suspect who'd murdered these victims or even if they'd met online before the attack. But he was convinced of two things at that moment. The first was that he wanted to get this guy—and in statistical likelihood the suspect was male—as much as the trooper did.

His second certainty concerned him more, though. With that gut sense law-enforcement officers hone over time, he knew that the state trooper who'd just marched in there to mess up the task force's equilibrium had also just lied to the team. What he didn't know was why.

Chapter 2

Kelly slid her chair closer to the edge of her cubicle, so she could see the office door. She could shoot out and be back on Interstate 96 on her way to the Spencer Road exit and the Brighton Post in ten minutes flat.

At least she was wanted there.

A report lay open on her desk, but the words and the grisly crime scene photographs swam on the pages in front of her. This was a mistake. She shouldn't be there, and it went beyond the special agent who clearly agreed with her on at least that.

She'd believed she could do this. That eighteen years was enough time. Enough distance from those bicycles. That creepy smile. She'd been wrong. Shame filled her, heavy and familiar. The uniform that she wasn't supposed to be wearing seemed to be the only thing preventing her from splintering into thousands of pieces.

But she had to keep it together, for Emily's sake. She took several deep breaths and focused on a pushpin on her bare bulletin board instead of the file. Finally, her rapid heartbeat slowed.

She'd hoped for an opportunity to make up for the

mistakes she'd made following her friend's abduction, and now she was balking. Yes, it would require her to work with someone who clearly didn't want her there, but atonement wasn't supposed to be easy.

What was Special Agent Lazzaro's problem with her, anyway? He must have thought that those Italian good looks of his—the kind that a sculptor's knife would have loved and a sonnet or two had already mentioned—gave him an excuse to be a jerk. Not that she'd noticed the olive skin, that strong jaw, the dimple in his chin or those blue-gray eyes, anyway, but none of those things made the way he'd spoken to her okay. What had she ever done to him?

Eric had said the agent was always hard on new team members, but she couldn't help thinking it might be something more. That she was a woman? Well, tough crap. She'd proven herself to her fellow troopers by working harder than any of them. If he thought rudeness from one curmudgeonly FBI agent would be enough to scare her off, then he was about to find out how wrong he was.

"You about ready?"

She nearly jumped out of her seat as Tony leaned in to speak to her. The cubicle's walls had prevented her from seeing his approach, but he'd caught her thinking about him. She didn't have time to worry about him or anyone else when they had a double murder to investigate.

"Uh. Ready?" Could she have sounded any less like she was about to prove something to him? And why did his eyes have to smile like that, before his lips even moved?

"I just wanted to know if you're finally up to speed on the case so we can get started. You know, on the voice recordings."

"For the record, I was already well informed about this case. I was first on the scene, remember?" She took a breath so she wouldn't tell him where he could shove all his assumptions. "Now what did you say about recordings?"

"You didn't think you were going to do all of this live, did you?"

The corner of his mouth lifted in a way that was beginning to annoy her. As a matter of fact, she *had* believed she would always be speaking live, but she wouldn't give him the satisfaction of having her confirm it.

"I figured at least some of it."

"Then you were right. Here, let's go back to my computer to make the recordings."

He strode to his desk without looking back at her. She grabbed the binder of case overviews that Dawson had given her and fell into step behind him. Inside his cubicle, Lazzaro had already turned his straight-back visitor chair so that it was right next to his. Too close for Kelly's comfort, but the microphone cord wasn't long enough to reach across the room.

Nothing about the special agent's cubicle surprised her, from the obsessively straight collection of pencils in his top desk drawer to the line of photographs—some children, some adults— in the bottom corner of his bulletin board. All about a half inch apart. Just like the crisp creases in his slacks and dress shirt and his perfectly knotted tie that weren't supposed to be parts of a uniform, Tony Lazzaro was all about preciseness and control. Her arrival must have thrown off his perfect balance.

She rested the binder on the corner of his desk, pulled the seat back and sat. A masculine amber scent filled her nostrils. She'd never been a fan of cologne, but this one was almost pleasant. Distracting.

But she didn't get distracted. By anyone. If she'd never allowed male-female nonsense to disrupt work with her fellow troopers, even the hotties, she should have no trouble ignoring a surly law enforcement officer. Especially one who had a sprinkling of gray in his black-brown hair that made him look at least a decade older than her twenty-seven.

Tony obviously had no trouble tuning *her* out as he focused on his laptop and clicked through several screens. Then he moved the standing microphone closer to her. She didn't miss his frown when he noticed the binder, out of place on his orderly desk.

"Now we just need to record the early stuff. The greetings," he said. "That way you can practice the flirtation."

Her breath rushed out in a choked sound. "Are you saying that some victims *flirt* with their eventual offenders?"

The thought of it made her stomach roll. Emily's attacker had required no enticement. No encouragement at all.

"I guess some potential victims think they're supposed to talk more like grown-ups would when they're in online chat rooms," he explained. "Seventy-six percent of underage victims first encounter their offenders in chats."

Kelly blinked away images from her past to focus on details of the current case. On offenders they might have a chance to stop.

"But don't victims in chat rooms believe they're talking to someone their own age and not some guy in his sixties with a double chin and a second mortgage?"

"Maybe potential offenders aren't that specific, but most tell their victims they're older when they initiate contact."

As he spoke, he scrolled through a website with a series of conversations rolling down the screen.

She leaned forward to get a better look. "That's where you'll have me hanging out? In chat rooms like that one?"

He closed the browser, whether to keep her from seeing what he was looking at or to move on, she wasn't sure.

"Not *you,* really. Just an online identity to which you'll be lending your voice. You won't always be the one at the keyboard, either. It can be any of us. The screen name will be INVISIBLE ME."

"Because victims are often looking for someone to pay attention to them and actually listen to them?"

"That's right. Some of them get more than they bargain for."

"Especially kids like Sienna and Madison."

She expected him to say something about her referring to the recent murder victims by their first names instead of calling them "Miss Cottingham" and "Miss Blackwell," but he nodded at his screen.

"What does all this have to do with the Dark Web?" She hated asking so many questions, but he seemed knowledgeable, and she needed to catch up quickly. "I don't know as much about that as I should. I spend most of my work time investigating traffic accidents and issuing citations."

He slid a glance her way and then launched another browser, one she didn't recognize.

"Most people don't know a lot about it. The Dark Web is just a small part of the Deep Web, that part of the Internet that includes email accounts and bank records. Only the *Dark* Web is different. You access it using a software that makes you anonymous by disguising your computer's IP address. Then visitors can participate in illegal activities without being tracked. Drugs, weapons, assassins…"

"Porn?"

This time, he turned to face her. "That and human trafficking. Those two things are almost always linked."

"Do you think our victims visited sites on the Dark Web?"

"Probably not. It requires too much computer know-how since the sites aren't indexed. It's more difficult to do a search there." He closed the screen and held his hands wide. "But the suspect might hang out on the Dark Web as well as chat rooms in the Surface Web."

"Then it makes sense to look both places."

"Particularly now that he's had a taste of murder. His cooling-off period between the two girls and his next victim might be decreased. If this is even his first time."

Was he watching her because he was discussing the possibility that they were dealing with a serial killer when he'd criticized her earlier for jumping to that same conclusion? Or did he expect her to race out the door after the details he'd shared with her? He put his headset around his neck, handed her a second one and pointed to the microphone.

"Ready?"

She straightened in the chair. "We're going to record stuff right here?"

"Why? Can't turn on your charm with an audience present? Hate to tell you this, Trooper, but we can't provide you with a private sound booth."

The patronizing way he said *trooper* made pinpricks form on the back of her neck. He might as well have said *sweetheart*, and she was not okay with that.

"Hello," she said into the microphone.

"Don't say it like you're about to try to sell him a houseful of vinyl windows."

"Give me a minute. I haven't done this before."

"No kidding. And you thought you were going to do all of this live."

Her glare wasn't as effective as it would have been if he'd looked at her.

"By the time you have a voice conversation with a suspect, you won't be strangers, at least in that world. You'll even tell him your real name is Mackenzie. But if you don't think you can do it, I'll be happy to approach Special Agent Dawson and tell him his idea is a bust."

"Not necessary," she ground out.

It didn't matter that Kelly was so far out of her comfort zone. This jerk had underestimated her, and he should know it. She wouldn't allow him to make her forget why she was there, either. She'd come to track a killer, and there was nothing he could do to stop her. She gripped the microphone and pushed the button to speak.

"Hi there." That voice didn't even sound like her. So smooth. A sexy laugh formed with words. "I'm so glad we finally get to speak to each other. I've wondered what your voice would sound like."

She released the button and, as she pulled her hand away, she peeked over to catch him watching her. He quickly turned back to his computer screen.

"How was that?"

He cleared his throat but didn't look her way. "Fine."

"Good. What else do you need me to say?"

"How about I just ask you some questions, and you answer them the way you would've at about thirteen?"

"You mean with a giggle and maybe a snort?"

"You snort?"

"Not anymore. Well, not much."

He gave her a few more phrases to record.

"Hey, gotta go. My mom's coming upstairs," Kelly said,

recording the last. In her own headset, the words sounded exactly like teenage Kelly would have spoken them.

"Okay, we're done." Tony cleared his throat again. "Good job on those."

"You don't need anything else?"

He shook his head.

She stood and pushed the chair to the open spot in the corner of the cubicle and grabbed her binder. She opened the book to the page she'd been reading before he'd interrupted her: an open case involving a missing teenage boy.

"Just staring at those photos isn't going to get us anywhere."

"You don't think familiarizing myself with these other cases can help? I have fresh eyes. Maybe I'll see something that others have missed." She gestured toward his laptop. "Anyway, how are you so sure that whatever you do on that computer will help more?"

She braced herself for his hot retort. He hadn't disappointed her all morning. When he didn't answer, she lifted her gaze to find him staring, not at her but at that straight line of photos on his bulletin board.

"Looks like you have some pictures of your own. Are those some of the people you've helped? Do you look at them when you need a pick-me-up?"

"No."

At the low tone of his voice, she regretted asking. Something told her that Special Agent Lazzaro was the type of guy who recorded his defeats. Not his victories.

"You don't have to answer," she rushed to say.

But he appeared lost in the photos and the stories that must have clung to them. When he finally turned back to her, his eyes were suspiciously shiny. He quickly lowered his gaze to his desk.

"Those are the ones we didn't help. They're there to remind me just what is at stake."

Chapter 3

Cory Fox gripped the video game controller with both hands as he navigated the danger-filled path on his computer screen to save Princess Amelia from the evil dragon. Usually, he would have scaled those walls and leaped the obstacles with ease in his new favorite game, *Rescuing the Royals*. Not so much this morning. He'd already fallen through the earth twice, and he hadn't even made it close enough to the dragon to try out his super-power lightning flashes.

He was never going to get out of Level 26.

Cory rested the controller on the desktop as he dragged his feet off the desk. He was just too distracted to play. He had to do something to fill the time, though. His four-hour shift at the grocery store wasn't until after lunch, and he was already too hyped up to sit still.

On his desktop, he clicked open a folder he'd placed there a week before, and a list of links appeared on the screen. He clicked on the first.

Bodies of 2 local teens discovered.

His stomach roiled as it did each time he read the articles. If only he could stop looking at them. Or thinking about it. Or remembering.

He set his elbows on the desk and lowered his head into the cradle of his hands. Even with his eyes closed, he could still see it. Blood made him queasy, and there'd been so much of it. He hadn't even been able to drag them far from the bike path where they'd met, so their bodies were discovered the next morning. He'd only brought that pocketknife in case she needed convincing to get in the van with him.

"Why did you have to lie?"

He automatically looked over his shoulder though, as usual, he was alone in his basement apartment. It had been an accident. It was all FUNNY GAL's fault. Make that "Sienna." She was supposed to have been fourteen. Not *eighteen*. And she sure as heck wasn't supposed to bring a friend with her. Was their meeting a joke to her? She was supposed to be his betrothed, his princess, and she'd been a dragon instead.

He closed the file and then the folder, his finger poised to the delete the whole thing. But he couldn't. Instead, he launched a browser and typed the beginning of a website address for one of his favorite chat rooms. The full name showed up in the results box below. Obviously, he'd visited there a lot.

Of course, he needed to avoid chat rooms right now. He should be lying low and staying off the Internet. At least for a while. One of those articles had even mentioned that the girl had been in contact with "men" online. Men? Not just him? His hands curled into fists, his nails digging into his palms.

No, he wouldn't visit the chats while the police were sniffing around. Anyway, time always slipped away from him when he played online, and he'd promised Mom he would keep his job this time. That was the deal he'd made so she would agree to keep paying his rent. He'd given someone else his word that he would stay out of trouble, and he'd already broken that promise.

He moved his mouse in a circular pattern on the mouse pad and then let the arrow hover over the link. His decision came with a click.

And he was there again, that wonderful place where multiple conversations moved at a rapid clip. Introductions were made, connections formed, and screen names vanished with the lure of private chats.

Cory wiped his sweaty upper lip with the back of his hand as he scrolled through comments. There were so many lonely girls, just waiting to be his special friends. Still, he needed to be patient to find the perfect one.

He'd be more careful this time. Courting was a delicate process, after all. But with such sweetness ahead, how could he not continue the search for a princess with whom to share his castle home?

He clicked on the dialogue box. Then he typed the line that could be the beginning of something wonderful: Hi!

A knock on the outside of his cubicle brought Tony's head around with a jerk that made his neck ache. His vision was already blurry from hours of fruitless searches through some of the more popular Dark Web sites. He'd buried himself in his work to get that earlier conversation with Kelly out of his thoughts, and he'd almost succeeded. Until now.

The woman he'd been trying not to think about stepped into the doorway, her hands shoved into her uniform pockets.

"May I help you?"

He was proud of himself that he'd sounded almost civil, especially when he'd hoped not to have to face her again for the rest of the day.

"Sorry to interrupt you, but—"

"But you're finished reading about all the other cases that aren't the one we're investigating?" So much for being nice.

She frowned. "I have finished that, but Special Agent Dawson wants me to observe you putting out regular text communication in the chat rooms."

"Why? Haven't you ever done a chat before?"

"As a matter of fact, I haven't."

His next brusque comment died on his lips. Why couldn't he stop baiting her? She was doing her job, just as he was trying to do.

"Fine."

He gestured toward his guest chair though the last thing he needed was to be close to her again. He'd been trying to get the scent of her shampoo—light, flowery and carefree—out of his head all afternoon.

"How about instead of observing, we give you a chance to practice? I'll make my comments verbally, and you can type your responses on my keyboard."

"Sounds okay."

He stood and slid by her to grab the seat she'd used earlier. She took his place in front of a blank word-processing document.

"Would your friends say you're pretty?" he asked.

She blinked several times. He had to hold back a smile. Of course, they would. Not to say so would have made them liars.

Finally, she started typing.

I don't know. I guess so. They probably would say I have a cute face.

"Are you trying to say you're a bigger person? Would anyone say *that* about you?" he asked.

I'm bigger than some of my friends, I guess.

He had to remind himself that she was creating a fictional character since the woman sitting next to him looked perfect to him. Too perfect.

"You're probably just curvier. They're jealous," he managed to say.

How can you say that? You haven't even seen me.

"We could fix that. You could send me a picture. I'm already sure you're real pretty."

But I hate my braces.

At the second reminder that their conversation had been only role playing, he sat taller in his seat. He'd given her easy questions, and he couldn't explain why. Was it because of that compassion in her eyes after he'd explained the photos on his board? Did he believe she was too tender-hearted for this work and felt compelled to shield her? What business did he have trying to protect anyone from this world when he hadn't been able to shelter himself?

Instead of continuing the mock conversation, he reached for the keyboard and slowly pulled it to him.

"Why are you doing that?"

"You'll do fine. You're a natural. At least for the easy stuff."

"I really was a thirteen-year-old girl once. An awkward, misunderstood and, yes, *larger* teenager. I was in the public speaking club. Not the cheerleading squad."

She'd surprised him. People rarely did that anymore. Kelly Roberts wasn't who he'd expected her to be, from her biography or from her knockout good looks. He knew better than to prejudge people, anyway. That was how the wolves fit in among the unsuspecting sheep in their investigations.

"Some things happened, and I ate for comfort and gained some weight," she added when he didn't respond right away.

"Looks like you figured things out." Immediately, he wanted to take that back. It sounded as if he'd been watching her, and he had. Now they both knew it.

She cleared her throat and pointed to the screen again. "If the conversations online are like that, they sound so benign."

Relieved that she'd redirected the conversation back to their work, where it belonged, Tony went with it.

"They start that way, but they can escalate quickly. A chat where a guy tells his victim that he understands why she's mad at her parents over her curfew quickly turns to demands for intimate photos."

"That's awful."

"That doesn't begin to cover how bad it gets. How are you going to be able to handle—"

"I meant for you."

He came to his feet as if something had pushed him out of the chair, and he moved to the doorway of his own cubicle. Just like earlier, her compassion for *him* unsettled him. Why was she being so kind when he'd been rude to her? Worse than that, he was beginning to like her. He wasn't there to make friends. He had to finish the case so he could be transferred. He needed to remember that.

"I mean you have to read and listen to this stuff every day," she continued, as if she realized she'd struck a nerve. "How do you bear it? Do you turn it off when you get home?"

"It's my job."

He would've said it was as simple as that, but nothing about his decision to leave the task force had been simple. Could he really desert the vulnerable people he helped, and if he could, what kind of agent was he? What kind of human being?

"And mine," she said with a nod. "Do you really think our victims were communicating online with their killer?"

"Possibly. But they were connecting with a few different people, so someone might know something."

She stood up from his desk. "I'm ready to do my part to help find Sienna and Madison's killer or killers. I've already said this case is personal for me."

"You need to stop telling people that, or you won't get to stay on the case." He still didn't buy the reason she'd said it was important to her, but he didn't tell her that. "If you can't separate yourself from it, you won't be of any help to us."

"I can. Separate myself, that is."

"We'll see."

Kelly scooted behind him and started back to her own desk. He stood at the doorway, watching her. Near the nameplate that had been added to the bracket outside her cubicle wall, she stopped.

"And Agent Lazzaro, thanks for all your help."

"Don't thank me. If I was thinking about your well-being, I would tell you to get out of here right now."

Chapter 4

Kelly couldn't remember ever being so exhausted as she tromped inside her apartment and dumped her heavy purse on the floor by the door. It was still daylight outside. She barely recognized the place, with light streaming in between the blind slats and dust motes waltzing toward her coffee table. Usually working afternoons did that to a person. Even on her days off, she was too busy catching up on errands to notice.

Now she was too…something else. Tired. Keyed up. Annoyed. Anything but *intrigued* by some jaded FBI agent.

After locking the door, she crossed into her bedroom, already unbuttoning her shirt. Her uniform had nearly smothered her all afternoon in that stifling office, but she hadn't even loosened her tie. Special Agent Lazzaro would have perceived that as weakness. She'd refused to give him the chance after all the potshots he'd lobbed at her.

Now she couldn't shed the layers fast enough. If only yanking on her old cross-country shorts and pulling on a sports bra and tank top could help her put the day's events out of her mind. Even after she'd worked with him all day, Tony still didn't want her to be there.

Of all his rude comments, the last one kept replaying in her thoughts. *If I was thinking about your well-being...* Had he been trying to tell her what the assignment had done to *him*? After the way he'd treated her today, she shouldn't care, but she couldn't help it. He seemed miserable there, which made no sense.

Her cell phone rang, and for once, she considered letting it go to voice mail. Her couch was calling her, as well. But guilt won as it always did, and she hurried to the door and dug around in her purse until her fingers connected with it. She refused to acknowledge that blip of disappointment at seeing Nick Sanchez's name on the screen.

Had she hoped Tony—make that Special Agent Lazzaro—would call to say he was sorry? Even if he had her number, which he wouldn't, he didn't seem like the type of guy who ever apologized. Anyway, if the Brighton Post's current calendar model was calling her, there had to be an emergency. She tapped the button to accept the call.

"Is everything all right, Nick?"

"Sure. It's fine."

"Then why are you calling?"

"You try to do something nice for a person and—"

"Nice? How?" Had they missed her so much at the post that they were resorting to phone pranks?

"I only wanted to see how your first day with the task force went."

"Oh. Okay, I guess."

"And how was it to drive a desk instead of a patrol car?"

He chuckled this time. Someone else laughed in the background.

"Dion Carson, is that you? Are you two together, even on your day off?"

The laughter became a chorus.

"Can we help it if we're the two coolest people around?" Dion asked.

"Yeah, can we?" Nick piped.

"I hate to interrupt your mutual-admiration society, but is there a point to this call? Other than to torture me?"

Nick harrumphed. "We were going to tell you that we're standing right outside your building, with pizzas, but since you're being so unwelcoming—"

"Did you say pizzas?"

She pushed the buzzer to allow them inside and threw open her apartment door. Footsteps pounded on the stairs, and then they both appeared in her open doorway. Nick had a pizza in each hand, and Dion carried two-liter pop bottles under both arms.

Dion shook his head and tsk-tsked. "Now is that a way for a woman to let someone inside her place? You don't know who could be out there."

"But I already knew—"

Both men laughed again, and she gave them a dirty look. These were her friends, the closest people to her in the world. She would take a bullet for any of them, but sometimes—like now—she wanted to pistol-whip them instead.

"You missed us. Admit it," Nick said with his perfect, toothy grin.

Kelly shook her head. Though she couldn't have found two more attractive males to show up in her living room—one tawny skinned with dimples, the other with sepia skin and sultry eyes—neither Nick nor Dion had ever been swooning material for her. But the barely-still-thirtysomething Italian-American she'd met earlier, the one with crinkles around his eyes and a five o'clock shadow before noon? She couldn't allow herself to think about that guy.

"Earth to Kelly." Nick lifted and lowered the boxes a few times. "Where do you want me to put these?"

"Anywhere is fine."

She followed his gaze around the room. There were only three places where guests could put a pizza that didn't involve getting crumbs in her bed: her dinette with two chairs, the coffee table or the living room floor. Nick went for the coffee table, pausing to note the scratches before setting the warm boxes directly on the wood.

Kelly could admit that the place wasn't fancy. More like minimalism on steroids. It was like the task force office she'd spent the day in. Necessities and nothing more. Would Tony have something to say about that, too?

She pushed the thought aside and hurried to the kitchen for plates, napkins and cups.

Soon the three of them sat shoulder to shoulder on the cramped sofa, munching pizza and sipping pop in the awkward silence.

Dion set his plate on top of the box. "So really, how was your first day?"

"I told you it was okay." Sitting between them, she could feel their skeptical glances coming from both sides. "All right, it stank. It was like starting all over as a brand-new trooper."

"I bet it did stink." Nick took another bite and then talked around it. "It's hard working with cops from different agencies, when everyone's as cocky as you are."

"Are the cowboys from the FBI treating you like a rookie?" Dion asked.

Having just grabbed another piece of pizza, she took an angry bite. "Just one. Special Agent Lazzaro. You'd think he'd never met a female police officer before. Mansplained like I was an idiot. He thinks he knows danger when he's probably not been more than ten feet away from a computer screen his whole career."

"That so?"

Dion had opened the pizza box again, but he stopped without lifting a slice. She glanced from one police officer to the other.

"What?"

Nick leaned forward so he and Dion could exchange a look. "I think she doth protest too much."

"This…Lazzaro," Dion said, "is he a sexy Valentino type?"

Kelly came to her feet. "He's just another jerk male officer. You two would probably be fast friends with him. Is everything a big joke for you guys?"

"Do you *know* us?" Nick asked.

Both men burst out laughing.

"Really, we did come by to offer some support." Dion finally picked up the slice of pizza he'd been going for before.

"Well, thanks."

Nick, who'd already devoured three slices, set his plate aside. "You headed over to Casey's Diner later?"

She shook her head. "I'm beat. Are *you* going? Don't you realize how pitiful that looks that you still meet up with the rest of the troopers on your days off?"

"What's your point?" Nick said, grinning.

Dion tapped his watch. "You probably can't stay out late, anyway, now that you're on the day shift."

Kelly didn't bother telling him she wouldn't necessarily be working days for this assignment. She'd been told she would be clocking a lot of overtime hours until they found some leads.

If she told them, they would be razzing her about being with Lazzaro day in and day out. She was worrying enough about that situation. How was she supposed to be of any help in tracking Sienna's and Madison's killer when all she could think about was the special agent who wanted her out of his world?

Tony had just enough time to throw his keys on his counter, pull a beer from the refrigerator and pop the tab before his doorbell rang. One glance at the clock on the microwave and he grimaced. He'd forgotten. He wasn't in the mood to *entertain*.

But, unlike some people, he honored his commitments. Taking two quick gulps of his beer and then turning the can upside down in the sink to drain, he jogged to the front door.

"Did you forget?" Angelena Hayes hurried inside, a toddler perched on one hip and a preschooler holding her free hand.

"Of course not."

Her smile told him how much she believed his lie. He wasn't the only one in their family with good instincts. His baby sister knew him well.

"Well, good. We *need* a babysitter. Date night has dwindled to once a month already. If it drops to every two months, Miles and I are going to be a divorce statistic like Mom and Dad."

"Don't even joke about that." At least she really was kidding. Angelena and Miles were the real deal, unlike their parents, whose marriage hadn't so much dissolved in acrimony as withered away from neglect. For him and Laurel, it had been more like a murder/suicide.

"Are we going to play, Uncle Tony?"

Squeezed between the two adults, four-year-old Tabitha tapped his leg several times.

He bent at the waist to speak to the child at her level. "We sure are. What do you want to play first?"

Tabitha wrinkled her button nose. "You smell yucky."

"You've been *drinking*?"

Angelena's stage whisper was loud enough for the neighbors in his spread-out subdivision of 1970s ranch homes to hear.

"Two swallows. That's it."

"Had better be it."

He nabbed the little girl and tucked her under his arm, her giggles filling the room and that headful of riotous chocolate curls falling around her face. His sister already knew he would do anything to protect these little people.

"I want to play school!"

"Then school, it is."

Tony and Angelena exchanged smiles because Tabitha chose the same activity every time he babysat. Everyone knew electronics were off-limits at Uncle Tony's house.

"Too," the two-year-old man of few words, Carter, called out, extending his pudgy arms to be lifted.

Tony obliged and shifted the boy onto his opposite hip.

Angelena grinned at her brother. "You're the best babysitter ever."

"The price is definitely right."

"Just name your price. You know we'll pay it."

"Now if I'd known that before…"

He didn't bother finishing that since he always refused to take her money. He also loved the two ruffians like they were his own. As close to it as he would ever get.

"Rough day?"

"The same."

"Oh. Your brow looks more furrowed than usual."

Was it so obvious that he was out of sorts? But then Angelena and Miles were the only ones he'd told about his transfer request. "Your description makes me sound super hot."

"Ew. Just ew."

"Anyway, aren't you going to get out of here? Don't you two have reservations or something?"

"That's an avoidance tactic if I ever heard one."

He opened the door for her, but she didn't seem to be in a hurry to leave.

"Well, what's going on?"

"It's just that this new state police officer joined the task force. Bad timing. And she—"

"She?"

His sister had finally started out the door, but she paused and looked back at him.

"Whatever you're thinking, stop. We're not going there."

"You never *go there*, and you should. With somebody. It's been four years."

Tabitha picked that moment to moan and wiggle until he lowered her to the ground. She planted her hands on her hips.

"Are we going to play?"

"Yeah," Carter chimed.

Tony could've hugged them both and planned to as soon as their mother finally left.

"Thanks for your concern, little sister, but I have everything I need right here." He took both kids' hands to make his point. "And, apparently, I need to play now."

He started down the hall with his niece and nephew.

"See you guys later," Angelena called before she left.

Tony blew out a loud breath. Why had he mentioned

Kelly in the first place? He knew better than to speak of women around his sister, even one as inconsequential as Kelly Roberts. He turned left into his guest bedroom.

Tabitha rushed ahead and opened the sliding closet door. Inside, a small desk was pushed against the wall, a tiny chair stacked on top of it. A cardboard box filled with school supplies had been squeezed in next to it. The other closet door hid an easel with a chalkboard.

"Let's get this party started."

Soon his living room had been transformed from its regular man-friendly state to a proper classroom. The buttery recliner in dark leather, matching sofa and the industrial-style wood end tables had been shoved out of the way to make room for the desk, chalkboard and the sheet spread out to cover the floor. Tony had learned the hard way about marker stains on the carpeting.

"Look. This one is a *U*."

Tabitha sat at the desk and held up her paper. Carter lay on his belly on the floor, coloring a huge art pad and himself. Mostly himself.

"Uncle Tony, can you write your letters? In *order*?"

"In order? That's tough. Maybe I could do it if I worked really hard."

"I can help you."

"Help. Too."

Carter popped up from the floor and approached with his purple marker. His "help" was to decorate his uncle's hands.

If Kelly could only see him now. Tony blinked, his fingers automatically closing. Why had *she* come up again? He was off the clock now, and he didn't need to think about work or *her*. Maybe she'd peeked her annoyingly attractive face into his evening hours because he wanted her to see that he wasn't always a jerk.

Why did she get to him? She wasn't the first newbie police officer to join the task force since he'd been there. Eric was just one example. She wasn't even the first female.

So, what was different about Trooper Roberts? Was he trying to scare her off because he sensed vulnerability in her, and his instinct was to shield her from things he'd seen? She was a trained *police officer*. She'd been carrying a weapon all day, for God's sake. She didn't need his protection. She would consider him patriarchal if not downright misogynistic for considering it.

Still, believing this was about his hero complex was easier than acknowledging another reason he might not want Kelly on the task force. It had more to do with sensual lips that could make a man think of all sorts of naughtiness, brown eyes that seemed to take in everything at once and a body that even a police uniform couldn't disguise. Or maybe it was his temptation to pull those pins from her hair, just to watch it tumble down her back.

That wasn't going to happen.

He didn't do office romance. He didn't do *romance*. Once bitten, twice *done*, you might say. He'd already told Angelena he wasn't going there. With his career in a state of flux right now, it needed to be a hell no. His focus had to be of closing this case so that he could finally be transferred. That meant one thing. If he was even tempted to veer toward that on-ramp, he was hitting the brakes and putting that car in Park.

Chapter 5

With his curtains drawn and office door locked, he dropped into the leather executive chair behind his mahogany desk. Usually that gleaming piece of furniture and the built-in shelves with all his favorite books would have soothed his frustrations, even after a long week at his day job. He might even have smiled at the degrees on the wall and the framed photos on his desk—one a family portrait and the other of him in uniform.

But not today. No, nothing could tamp down his irritation as he attached the cable for his external hard drive to his second laptop, kept just for business purposes. It was all he could do not to slam his hands on the keyboard while using the keys and touchpad to reach the even more secretive back door of his already well-hidden website.

He couldn't alert his dear wife to his problems, either. She'd done a fine job of avoiding asking questions for years and had graciously accepted the baubles he'd showered her with as rewards. No sense in crippling a smoothly working system.

With a few more expert keystrokes, he landed on a page showing recent transactions from his Soleil Enterprises customers, all paid for using the cryptocurrency Bitcoin for anonymity. He loosened his tie, smiling at the second-quarter sales figures. Those had already tripled since the same time period a year before.

It was a beautiful business model, providing a wide variety of goods and services for his clients' proclivities and peccadilloes, all at prices they were willing to stretch to afford. He didn't even know why it was called the "Dark Web," when it spelled a brighter future for the secret bank accounts of people like him.

Except that his sunny days might have been clouded recently with a bucket of blood.

He fisted one hand and squeezed it so hard with the other that all his fingers ached. If only it could have been the guy's neck. Of course, he wasn't certain that it was one of his customers who had crossed the line and murdered those girls. It could have been anyone. But the crushed tiara, part of the secret crime scene information that a loose-lipped peace officer had shared with him, had made him wonder.

Tiaras. Princesses. The sinking feeling in his gut told him it was a possibility. He shouldn't have taken a chance on that guy. But greed could trap anyone in its grasp, just as an online supermarket for dark desires kept his clients coming back. Maybe he'd been caught this time.

"If it's you, you're done," he whispered to the monitor.

Leaving his own site, he navigated to a few others that the local FBI task force regularly monitored. Again, it was information he shouldn't have had but did.

He couldn't casually observe the task force's activities any longer. Everyone was searching for answers. He had to find them first.

He closed the Dark Web browser, launched another on

the Surface Web and selected a chat room website that was among his customers' favorites.

Though he rarely joined in on the conversations, he started a dialogue box for his screen name.

MR. SUNSHINE: Today's been hell. Who agrees with me?

A knock at his office door interrupted him just as responses poured in.

"I'm headed up to bed," his wife said from outside. "Will you be working long?"

"You go ahead. I have a little more to do." Then, as an afterthought, he added, "Sweet dreams."

He wouldn't be able to sleep now if he tried, so he continued to lurk, waiting to see who was playing that night.

He'd worked too hard to build his empire, too hard to protect it. No one would be allowed to expose it or him. Not a customer who'd taken his fun too far. Not a task force that could uncover a connection during its investigation.

Would he kill to preserve this good thing he had? In a minute.

Tony braced himself as he pushed open the office door, but all seemed quiet inside. Although a few of the early risers were milling about, most knew better than to seek his input before his *second* cup of coffee.

Instead of going to fill his cup, he crossed to his cubicle. It wasn't his fault he had to pass hers to get there. He was more relieved than he cared to admit that she wasn't at her desk. Though he planned to make nice with her today, it was too early to start.

But as Tony rounded the corner to his desk, the source of his agitation and lack of sleep sat waiting for him in *his* chair. Out of uniform, she looked different. Brown slacks, feminine cream blouse buttoned almost to the collar and sensible, low-heeled shoes. She could have traded places with any female FBI agent he knew. So how did she manage to make even that outfit look sexy?

"I didn't think you'd ever get here." She crossed her arms and settled back into the chair.

"What are you talking about?" He checked his watch. It wasn't even eight o'clock yet. "Mind giving me my seat?"

He rested his briefcase next to his desk. Though she met his gaze steadily, she gave her nervousness away by tucking a loose tendril behind her ear. If only that hadn't drawn his attention back to her hair, tied up the same way she'd worn it the day before. It was looser though, softer, as if she'd been less determined with a can of hairspray this time.

"I thought we could have a chat first."

His jaw tightened, but he'd promised himself he wouldn't let her get to him today, so he dropped in the guest chair at his own desk. All of this without coffee.

"So, what's up?"

"*What's up* is whatever's going on between us has to stop."

Tony blinked. He couldn't help it. He was usually better at hiding his reactions than that, but he'd done a lousy job of it ever since she'd arrived. "Excuse me?"

"Special Agent Dawson told me to figure out what the problem is that you have with me, so we can find a way to work together."

"He said that?" he asked instead of answering a question.

He shot a glance toward Dawson's cubicle, nearer to the office door, but he really couldn't see it through the maze of temporary walls. Leave it to him to piss off the one person who could delay his transfer even longer.

"Well, not in so many words."

She was staring at her folded hands now, using one thumb to snap away from the other the way she would flick a lighter. Maybe this wasn't as bad as he thought.

"Then with *what* words specifically?"

She stared back at him in what felt like a standoff and then lowered her gaze again.

"He said we need to work together."

"And when did he say that?" Come to think of it, had he passed Dawson's umbrella near the front door on his way in? He always had it with him, just in case.

"Yesterday."

"You mean before we had our practice session?"

This time, she didn't answer *his* question.

"Anyway, I know you don't want me here. I didn't ask to be assigned to this task force, either. But now that I have been, I am determined to help track down this suspect and help make connections to any other cases, if they exist. I'll do my job. You do yours."

"Okay."

"You act like you know me, but you know *nothing* about me. And if you want to get rid of me, the fastest way to do that would be to close this case."

What didn't he know about her? The question struck him, though he had no business wondering or even the right to ask. But she'd brought it up. He had to give her credit for her moxie. Kelly was stronger than she looked, and she hadn't appeared all that frail in the first place.

As Kelly tightened her arms across her chest, Tony tried not to notice how this gave her an extra lift that she didn't need and one that wasn't in his best interest to see.

"That's fair."

Tony was relieved that his words came out as something more than squeaks. He wasn't a seventh grader. He was a grown-ass man, and he needed to start acting like it.

"Okay, then."

He could have let it go at that. She'd made it easy for him to avoid answering any questions, but he couldn't accept the gift. Besides, he wanted to close this case as much as she did. Like she kept saying, it was personal to him, too.

"About yesterday, I was just having a bad day. Can we start over?" He stood and extended his hand. "Hi, I'm Special Agent Anthony Lazzaro. Tony, for short."

She stared at his hand instead of lifting hers. He couldn't blame her. He'd made a point of not greeting her properly the day before. Still, she reached out and gripped his hand.

"Trooper Kelly Roberts. Good to meet you, sir."

Her handshake was firm, professional and a mistake, he guessed from his tingling palm as he pulled away. He couldn't worry about that now. He'd told himself he would focus on the case, and he planned to keep that promise.

"Well, if I'm going to get started on *my* job, I will need my seat back."

Cory's cell phone buzzed again as it had been all morning. He'd silenced the ringer and turned it face down on his desk so he couldn't see the display, but it had continued to buzz about every thirty minutes. Mom never gave up when she wanted something. He was like her in that way.

At first, he'd been too focused on the messages scrolling up his laptop monitor to pay much attention to his phone, but the sound was distracting him now. The chat rooms weren't much fun today, anyway. Just screen names he'd seen before, seeming to talk to themselves or each other. No titillating flirtations. No potential Cinderella or Snow White or even a beautiful Princess Aurora from *Sleeping Beauty*.

He couldn't ignore his mother forever. She might turn off the Internet. He couldn't risk that. When the phone buzzed again, he answered.

"What is it?"

"Excuse me?"

"Sorry." He cleared his throat. "I saw that you called a few times."

"If you saw, then why didn't you pick it up? It's not like you have anything better to do. Like go to work."

Cory straightened in his chair just as he would have if she were in the same room instead of in Boca Raton. At least she hadn't video-dialed in this time. He hadn't showered in a day or two. Or three.

He switched to his best cajoling tone. It had always worked before. "Come on, Mom. I told you that job wasn't a good fit for me. Grocery-cart collector? I hated it. I'll find something better. Soon."

"You're right you'd *better*. And I don't care if you like it. Why do you think 'work' is a four-letter word? In fact, I've been considering tapering off my financial support. Clearly, it isn't helping you to get on your feet."

His chest tightened. This wasn't going the way he'd planned.

"Please, I promise I'll find something. And I'll keep it this time."

"You said that last time. And the time before that."

His hands fisted, but he forced his fingers to loosen

and flattened his palms on the desk. He couldn't afford to lose his cool. Not now. This was too important.

"If you could support me for once."

"I've supported you, all right, in more ways—"

"Or believe me," he interrupted.

At that, she stopped. But his pulse pounded as it always did when he even thought of the forbidden topic.

For a long time, a dropped-call kind of silence filled the line. He might have gone too far in dredging up the past, but she'd pushed him, too. It was her fault.

"You know I believe you."

He didn't answer. He didn't have to. They both knew she hadn't always believed him. When it counted.

"One month."

"What?" He at least had to sound like he didn't understand what she was saying, though optimism broke through the shroud draping his thoughts. He'd won for now. But at what cost? The darkness was peeking out again. He would have to bury it before it consumed him.

"You have thirty days to get a job you plan to keep and begin taking over some of your bills."

"Sounds okay, I guess."

"That's my last offer."

His mother, who'd spent the morning trying to get in touch with him, seemed anxious to get off the phone. He was in a hurry himself. Before, he hadn't taken his search seriously. Now he had a deadline.

One month to plan, to woo her, to win her hand. It was terrifying yet exhilarating. The timing wasn't optimal, he decided, as he chose from among his favorite chat rooms. He would have to search more diligently just when he needed to keep a low profile because of *the incident*. But he would be careful. So careful.

He would find her, too. She would be perfect. And young. And his. Then he and his princess could disappear together forever.

Chapter 6

Kelly's eyes burned and her head throbbed from the hours she'd spent staring at the screen, but it couldn't be helped. She'd needed space from Tony after their conversation that morning. Though he'd never told her what he had against her, it wouldn't matter once they found a way to put it behind them.

If only she could get past her odd reactions to him, as well. How was she supposed to keep her edge as a fellow law enforcement officer when she could only think about his long lashes and the way his biceps strained against the sleeves of his dress shirt? He might have been older than she was, but he probably could have taken on most of the guys she'd met. And maybe he could take *her* on in a much more satisfying way.

"Hey, are you available?"

Kelly startled, a humiliating squeak escaping from her throat before she turned back to find Tony standing at the doorway of her cubicle. Why did he always have to show up when she was having off-limits thoughts? Also *available*? Was he a mind reader?

"The conversations get intense, don't they?"

She didn't bother looking at the screen for anything new on the feed.

"I wouldn't know. The chat rooms you gave me have been dead. I even wrote a few notes to draw out lurkers, but nada. Just a lame hello from somebody called STARGAZER. He said, 'Greetings,' and then nothing else. I half-expected him to follow it up with 'Greetings, Earth people.'"

"I told you those boards would be easy. We haven't seen much action on them lately. But things are starting to heat up on a few other chats, so I wanted you to take a look."

She pointed to her laptop screen with its slow-rolling posts. "Are you sure I shouldn't stick with these? You never know. Something might come up. About a spaceship maybe."

He shook his head. "This one's hot, so I could use your help. I might need a voice for this one."

He stared at the floor when he said it. How he'd managed to not to choke on those words, she couldn't imagine. He was trying.

"Since you put it that way."

She exited the chat room, grabbed her notebook and pen and followed him to his desk.

"You're sure I'm ready for this?" She could have kicked herself the moment those words were out of her mouth. How was she supposed to convince him that she belonged there when even she was questioning?

"Only one way to find out."

He'd already arranged a chair next to his, so she sat, and he handed her a headset. He pointed to a printout on the corner of the desk closest to her.

"The conversation so far."

At first it seemed so strange reading the private chat

between INVISIBLE ME and some guy with the unfortunate name BIG DADDY. She had to remind herself that the screen name wasn't her. She was only lending her voice to an online persona, one of a few identities the task force was using. She tried not to be shocked when the conversation quickly turned sexual, just as Tony had predicted.

Hold up. I gotta pee.

Kelly couldn't help but smile as she read the last line. "You make a great teenage girl. That last line is golden."

"You never saw his answer, did you?"

"It wasn't on the printout."

He pointed to the final line from the private chat on his laptop screen.

Don't make me wait too long. Never do that.

The hairs on the back of her neck stood on end, but she somehow managed to sit still. Memories of those bicycles, two little girls and spilled blue slushes pushed forward in her mind, but she ruthlessly shoved them back. She couldn't go there. Besides, she wanted to ask Tony how he could keep returning to these same lewd conversations when the number of creeps online remained static. Now wasn't the time to think about either of those things.

"It looks like he left the chat room."

Tony nodded at the screen as he closed the chat screen. Soon he had navigated back to one of the larger threads.

"But if I'm right about him, he'll find her again."

Kelly appreciated the way he referred to INVISIBLE ME as "her." It reminded her that even if the suspect was pursuing someone whom he believed to be an underage girl, it wasn't Kelly. She needed to remember that those hands reaching out for this imaginary girl weren't the same ones that had grabbed Emily, either.

"He's back."

At least Tony was too busy studying his screen to notice her shifting in her seat.

"He'll pretend to be disinterested for a minute, and then he'll suggest the private chat again."

He typed a hello message back into the public discussion. Responses from three different screen names appeared below it. One even immediately asked her age.

"What are you going to do?"

"Wait for it." He continued to watch the screen. "Wait…for…it."

Then, as if by magic, a comment from BIG DADDY appeared.

BIG DADDY: So, you decided to come back?

INVISIBLE ME: Told you I'd be right back.

Kelly could only stare as Tony continued to type. He could've been writing an email to his mother, as easily as the words poured from his fingertips. Would she ever be that comfortable with all of this? Did she even want to be?

By the next exchange, the suspect had suggested a private chat again. It didn't take long for him to mention how nice it would be if they could have a voice chat. He promised it was all he would ask for, just the chance to hear her voice.

Tony stalled through a few more comments, talking about how INVISIBLE ME didn't like her voice because it sounded like a little girl, but finally he turned to Kelly.

"Ready?" he whispered as he moved the microphone closer.

"Ready as I'll ever be."

He tapped the microphone and mouthed, "You've got this."

She squeezed the button. "BIG DADDY, are you there?"

Nothing. She slid a glance to Tony. He made a circular gesture with his index finger, indicating for her to try again.

She cleared her throat and pushed the button a second time. "Are you there, BIG DADDY? I was hoping to get to talk to you."

A crackling sound from another microphone filled her ears. "Lovely. Your voice is sweet. I knew it would be sweet."

Kelly's breath caught, a scream expanding like a helium-filled balloon yet trapped inside her chest. That voice. Those words. It was *him*. *Sweet. So sweet.* The words replayed in a torturous loop, reminding her of the other time she should've screamed. She'd failed then, too.

"Say something," Tony whispered.

The sounds around her were too loud. The printer in the next cubicle. The buzz of the fluorescent lights. Tony's voice. Her gaze shot to the microphone button, but her clammy hands had already released it.

"INVISIBLE, *sweetie*, are you still there?"

She could only stare at Tony and the microphone by turns, panic building, twisting, maiming. It was him again, and she was frozen, rooted in place by her own cowardice. Just like before.

Tony grabbed the microphone and crinkled the print-out over the top of it. Then he yanked the cord from the

USB port. Immediately, his fingers shifted to the laptop's keys.

INVISIBLE ME: Sorry. My bad. I must have messed up the microphone. I'll have to have my dad look at it.

BIG DADDY: Oh. Okay. You might want to clear your searches and your cookies first.

INVISIBLE ME: Right. :) Wouldn't want him to know anything. None of his damn business.

Tony wound down the conversation, promising to talk again later when her computer was working better. The suspect threw in a parting comment that he hoped they'd get to meet, which Tony volleyed with the promise of "soon."

With that, he exited all the chat rooms open on the desktop. He turned to face her, crossing his arms just as she had earlier in the same chair.

"What the hell was that?"

Kelly stared at her clammy hands as she gripped them together. Her racing pulse refused to slow.

"I'm sorry," she managed to whisper.

"I don't want *sorry.* I want an explanation."

"I can't. Not now. I need a minute."

Without giving him a chance to ask more questions, she hurried out the office door and down the hall to the public restrooms when she could easily have visited the facilities inside the office. She didn't care if someone else saw her ruddy cheeks in the mirror or caught her splashing water on her face. As long as *he* didn't see it.

She had to get away from the chat rooms, from Tony and from the truth. It sounded crazy, sure, but she was convinced she'd just spoken to the man who'd ripped away her childhood and caused her best friend a life-time of pain.

"You're going to have to talk to me eventually."

Tony followed a few steps back as Kelly hurried down the walk to the nearly empty parking lot. She'd barely given Dawson enough time to reach his car and drive off before she made her own escape, leaving Tony behind with the rest of the stragglers. He already would have asked his questions earlier if she hadn't avoided him all afternoon.

"That's how we're going to play it?" He picked up his pace.

This time, she whirled to face him. "Oh, sorry. What were you saying?"

"That you'll have to talk to me," he repeated, though he was positive she'd heard him.

"Isn't that what I'm doing?"

"I meant about what happened this afternoon."

"You mean about the novice freezing up, just like you predicted I would? Or about the FBI agent swooping in on his white horse?"

"Who's giving away white horses? I didn't get one."

His attempt at humor fell flat, but it gave him the chance to watch her. After the call, she'd been terrified. At least her flushed skin and wide eyes had led him to be-lieve that. Now she lifted her chin and pursed her mouth, as if she dared him to question her. But he wasn't going to let her off that easily, even if technically he already had.

"What happened? Really?"

"Does it matter? You probably told Special Agent Dawson your story the moment I stepped out of the of-fice."

"Stepped out? You practically ran—"

"I didn't run. I walked. Anyway, when you did your duty to report that I froze and proved I shouldn't be here, did you also tell Dawson that you've been trying to scare me off since yesterday?"

"No." Though he would have done the team a favor by exposing a possible weak link.

"You didn't share what a welcome committee you've been?"

"I didn't talk to him at all."

"I don't understand."

That made two of them. "I was waiting to speak to you first."

"Now that you have, what are you going to do?"

"I plan to stand here until you answer my question."

She puffed up her cheeks and blew out a breath. "I guess you got in my head. You set my nerves on edge after all those horror stories you told me."

"I was just trying to prepare you."

"Why? Did someone prepare *you* for this assignment?"

"Not really." It was the most honest thing he'd said all day.

"Then I should feel privileged?"

Tony shrugged. He could no more explain why he'd pushed her so hard than he could tell her why he hadn't gone to Dawson over what had happened earlier.

"It's okay, you know. Some people just aren't cut out for this assignment."

"You should know."

At first, he wasn't sure he'd heard her correctly. "Wait. What?"

"You should know that some people aren't cut out for this task force, since you don't want to be here, either."

"What are you talking about? I don't know where you got that idea." He kept his expression neutral, but he swallowed involuntarily. Who'd told her? Would Special Agent Dawson have shared that information with her? No one else at the office knew.

Kelly shrugged and continued down the walk. Could he blame her for not telling him how she knew so much about him? She was right. He'd set her up to fail, and he might have done it on purpose.

"Wait."

She stopped and turned back, her posture stiff.

"What now?"

"Let me make it up to you. For messing with your head."

"You mean 'start over'? We tried that. Guess it didn't take."

He lifted a shoulder and lowered it. "Come on. Let me. Please."

"How?"

"We could go for coffee. I'll buy."

He could see the "no" in her eyes before she moved a muscle or spoke a word.

"That's not necessary."

"I think it is."

"I'm a police officer. Do you think this is the first time I've put up with crap from a male law-enforcement officer?"

"Probably not."

"I'm used to having to do twice as much to be taken seriously. My colleagues respect me because I've earned it."

"Now I really feel like an ass."

The side of her mouth lifted this time. "You'll get no argument from me."

"Please let me buy coffee. As a peace offering."

She blew out a breath. "Fine."

He decided not to analyze why he was so relieved that she'd relented.

"Good. How about Casey's Diner?"

"Not there." She cleared her throat. "I mean there's no reason to go there when we're only getting coffee."

"Okay." He dragged the word out as he studied her. "You have another place in mind?"

She waved her hand, but her elbow remained rooted near her rib cage. "There are plenty of coffee shops around."

"You pick, then. You lead. I'll follow your car." Technically, he wasn't supposed to drive his FBI rental except on duty and to and from work, but this was on his way home. Sort of.

She nodded and continued to her car. What had made her so nervous? And why did she want to avoid the diner? Those were just two small questions among many he had about Kelly Roberts. At a time when he should have been focusing on his final case and preparing to walk away from the task force, he was too curious about a young police officer who seemed to be hiding something. Too curious for his own good.

Chapter 7

Kelly parked in the near-empty lot adjacent to Mill Pond Park just as the headlights from Tony's task-force-issued sedan darted in after her mini SUV. She'd left her own assigned rental back at the office and would have to figure out a way to get it home later. As he stopped next to her, she slid her drink from the cup holder and climbed out. He caught up to her near the playground area, but she didn't stop until they reached a plastic-covered steel picnic table outside the play area's picket-fence enclosure.

"This place is great." He set down his drink and slid on the bench across from her. "I haven't been here in a while."

She wouldn't have come this time if she could think of a better idea to avoid taking Tony to Casey's. After the ribbing the guys had given her the other night, she couldn't show up at the Brighton Post's after-work hangout with a certain FBI agent. Even if there was nothing going on between them.

The park wasn't a much better choice. It was too hot outside and too quiet now, so near closing time. Well, absent of human voices, anyway. The bullfrogs and cicadas were still performing their nightly chorus. The cloud-covered sky caused the streetlights to cast too many shadows as well, making it appear as if they were sitting closer than they were. Too close.

"I still can't believe there wasn't a single coffee shop open after nine."

She'd driven to three, with him tailing her, before he'd passed her car and led her to a twenty-four-hour convenience store. He'd gone straight for the self-serve slush machines once they were inside.

"Slushes were a better idea, anyway." He took a long pull on his straw, with frozen azure liquid flowing up the narrow tube. "It's too hot for coffee."

She sipped her own cherry drink and managed to swallow. At least hers wasn't blue.

"I still can't believe you don't like raspberry. I thought every kid did."

Not every kid. "I'm not a kid," she said instead.

"I know that."

"Anyway, I don't like the way it stains your tongue."

"*My* tongue?"

"You know what I mean."

He grinned, and she tried to ignore the weightlessness in her belly.

"Anyway, red slush stains, too."

He pointed at her mouth, which in daylight would have looked like Santa's suit by now.

"Good point. I'm not really a fan of any flavor."

"Why didn't you say so?"

"How could I when you looked like an excited kid filling up your cup?" Or when he might have asked her why.

"Oh. I forgot." He pulled his wallet from his back pocket and held out a five-dollar bill. "I said I would buy yours."

"It wasn't necessary."

"Yes, it was. *Is*. I always keep my commitments."

His words were a little intense for a promise to buy a drink, but she let him press the bill into her hand.

"Thanks."

"It's the least I could do."

His mouth opened again, as if he might do more than that, like ask her what really had happened that afternoon. She spoke up before he had the chance.

"Why do you want to leave the task force?"

"I never said I did."

Instead of answering, she waited. It was none of her business, just as her reason for losing it that day wasn't his. Still, she couldn't help wondering why someone who appeared to care about his work could walk away from the victims.

"Fine. I requested a transfer. The double murder will be my last case with the task force."

"Can I ask why?"

"Sometimes people need a change."

"Do you know where you'll be transferred?"

He shook his head and looked toward the water, though the fence in front of him probably blocked his view of it.

"Did Dawson mention I was being transferred?"

"No, he didn't say anything."

"Then how'd you know?"

"You just *seemed* like somebody who needed a change."

It wasn't the whole truth but as close as she could get. She could no more tell him the rest than she could share her own experience with a predator and her suspicion that BIG DADDY and Emily's abductor might be the same person. How could she admit that she sensed a desperation in him? Or that the feeling was so strong it squeezed inside her own chest?

"Because I've been grumpy lately?"

"Lately? You mean that isn't just your personality?"

When Tony chuckled, Kelly finally let her shoulders relax.

"If it is my *personality*, then I've been myself in triplicate lately. Dawson won't sign off on my transfer until we close this case."

She settled back in the seat, the picture clearer then. "No wonder you didn't want a newbie like me around. I'm just slowing your investigation, and you're in a hurry."

"I guess you haven't spent much time working with the FBI on a case."

"Obviously, this is my first."

"If you had, you'd know that we don't rush cases. Ever. Our work is all about precision. We follow the evidence, and we build cases. Ones that don't fall apart at trial."

"This case is different."

He shook his head. "It can't be. I can't be any less diligent."

"But the suspect's still out there. And it might be only a matter of time until he strikes again."

"Not on my watch."

Tony blinked, as if his own words had surprised him.

"I'm with you on that one. He doesn't get to do this to anyone else if there's anything I can do to stop him."

"Even talking with creeps online without losing your cool like you did today?"

Kelly planted her hands on the table edge. "Even that. It won't happen again."

"Okay."

His laser focus bored through her, asking questions she couldn't answer, searching for details she shouldn't divulge. She forced herself not to look away. He held her future on the task force in his hands since he could still go to Dawson. She had to convince him she wouldn't let him, or rather *the team*, down again.

When she couldn't sit still any longer, she slid from the seat and grabbed her cup.

"Want to walk for a bit?"

He walked beside her as she started down the boardwalk that curved around Mill Pond. Neither spoke, so their footfalls along the wooden planks added a drumbeat to the symphony the nocturnal creatures performed.

Though she'd seen couples walking together there before, Kelly had never brought a guy there. She refused to acknowledge how right this felt. Refused to notice the heavy, romantic air. This wasn't a date. Wasn't anything close to it.

"I don't usually get to venture out on the boardwalk much when I come here," he said.

Kelly licked her lips, grateful for both his interruption and for proof that his thoughts weren't traveling the same route as hers.

"It's peaceful here."

She pointed at the dimly lit Brighton Village Cemetery on the other side of a wrought iron fence.

"Unless you're afraid of ghosts, I guess."

"I'm not. Usually." She didn't tell him that some of the worst ghosts lurked nowhere near cemeteries.

"Me, neither. Usually."

He was probably joking, but his words comforted her, anyway. She stopped and rested her hands on the wooden boardwalk railing. In daylight, she would have been able to see the fountain in the center of the pond and would have caught sight of a few carp swimming in their murky home, but at that hour, the water stretched out as black as an oil spill.

Tony settled his forearms on the railing next to her. "You're right. It is peaceful."

He was so close that his breath tiptoed up the side of her neck. It didn't bother her as much as it should have.

A small break had appeared in the bank of clouds, finally allowing a few tiny stars and a waning crescent moon to peek through.

"I think it's beautiful," she said.

"Yeah, me too."

Kelly swallowed. Was he talking about the scenery or something else? Like her? Because she wasn't thinking about *anything* else.

"Except for the mosquitoes."

His comment popped the bubble of her trance, forcing all the things she wasn't thinking about to whoosh out.

"What?"

He swatted at the insect that had landed on his forearm with his cup. "We'd better not stay in one place for too long, or they'll carry us away."

"Oh, right. State bird of Michigan."

Only then did she notice that she'd had a couple of mosquito nibbles as well. One was on her shoulder, right through the blouse that felt sticky against her skin. She was getting carried away, all right, with gooey romantic thoughts.

Because she needed to put some space between them, she started down the path again, past trees, benches and the occasional platform that jutted over the water.

"If you don't walk on the boardwalk, what do you do when you come here?" she asked.

"The playground, of course."

"Doing surveillance for creeps?"

"No, *playing.* Except when the ducks are around. Then we have to feed them instead."

"You come here with your *kids*?"

She winced over her last word, which came out as a squeak. He had to be in his midthirties. Of course, he could have children. And possibly a wife. Or a girlfriend. Or both.

Tony chuckled again, a low and deep rumble that made her shiver as if the temperature was dropping instead of holding steady at eighty-four.

"Does it sound so impossible that I would have kids?"

"Oh, no, no. I just didn't know you were married."

"I'm divorced."

"Oh. Sorry." Great. She'd all but admitted she'd been searching his hand for a wedding ring.

"I don't have kids, either. Do you?"

"No husband. No kids."

"For the best sometimes."

What did he mean by that? She would have asked, but he spoke before she had the chance.

"I bring my niece and nephew here. My sister's kids."

"I bet that's fun." Her words sounded lame, but it was better than confessing her relief that he was *Uncle Tony* and not *Daddy.* Why did she care?

"They're great. Carter just turned two, and Tabitha's four and a half going on twenty-five."

"Sounds like you're crazy about them."

"I still haven't recovered after babysitting last night."

"You *babysit*?"

He laughed again. "People aren't always what they seem."

He was right about that. Few things she'd learned about Tony tonight blended with the picture she'd already painted of him. Had it been a poor likeness? Tony smiled when he was away from the office. He even laughed when he talked about his family. He seemed much younger when he laughed.

"Your sister's lucky to have a brother like you."

"I keep telling her that, but she still thinks of me as the overprotective big brother."

"I can commiserate with her over that one."

"You have a brother?"

She held up two fingers. "Bruce and Sam."

"You're the baby?"

"Is it that obvious?"

"I just wanted to know if you were as spoiled as Angelena."

"Yes, I was spoiled. By my brothers." Why was she inviting him to ask more questions?

"Why not by your parents?"

"Dad wasn't around much. Still isn't. An autoworker on midnights. He slept when everyone else was awake. And Mom? She just preferred sons, I guess. They gave her less to worry about, and she had no time for frilly dresses or makeup."

"So, you became a tomboy to gain your mother's approval."

She shook her head as his observations encroached on the truth.

"It wasn't like that. My parents just didn't approve of me going to activities alone, so when my brothers picked up cross-country, and Mom dragged me to all the meets, I became involved, too. I was even good at it."

"Then you became a cop because you were comfortable being around and competing with guys."

This time she chuckled. "You think you've got me all figured out."

"Maybe."

They crossed a section of the boardwalk that backed up to another parking lot and more shops. The path ended without fully encircling the pond, so they turned back. Kelly found herself walking slower. Would they both return to their cars when they reached the playground again? Why wasn't she ready to leave?

"Was working in the Detroit field office part of your plan when you chose a career in the FBI?" she asked him.

"You act as if I had a plan. I never thought I would work with the FBI. I expected to still be making big bucks in Silicon Valley."

"Still?"

"Yeah, after I earned my master's, I worked in California for about six years. Then I saw an ad saying the FBI was looking for people from all kinds of fields. I inquired."

"That's all it took?"

He shook his head. "That and a two-year process that included a background check that went back to age eighteen, a physical fitness test with a seventy-percent failure rate and the new agent training program at Quantico."

"Wow, that's intense. It might not be the same, but I spent twenty-six weeks at Trooper Recruit School."

"I'm sure that's tough training, too."

"It had its moments. What did your family think about your job change?"

"My parents couldn't understand how I could give up a high-paying career, but they were in the middle of a divorce, so they didn't say much about it. My ex was louder with her disapproval, though."

As they approached the playground again and stepped inside the reach of the parking-lot lights, Tony leaned his head back and stared at the pointed roofs above the slides. He pointed to the highest one.

"That's Carter's favorite spot. I made the mistake of taking him on that slide just once. Now he makes a run for it every time we're here. He hasn't learned to be afraid yet."

He continued to focus on that slide as if lost in his memories. With all he'd witnessed on his job, he probably worried enough for his whole family.

"You gave up a lot to help people," she said before she could stop herself.

His shoulders shifted. "No more than anyone else."

"Most of us didn't have Silicon Valley."

"We all gave up something."

Or a debt to pay. But she kept that to herself.

"Anyway, don't treat me like I'm a knight in shining armor or something. The costume would never fit."

"I think an FBI agent who babysits comes pretty close."

"Oh, you think so, do you?"

She felt his gaze on her before she caught sight of it in her side vision. Was he forming a funny comeback or trying to determine if she was serious? But the weight in the humid air must have tripled because it suddenly felt closer around them. *He* was so close. His hand rested lightly on her shoulder as he turned her to face him.

A smile spread on his lips. And then his gaze lowered to her mouth. Kelly froze, her heart thudding in her chest. Tony was going to kiss her. She knew it with the same certainty that she always expected her fellow troopers to have her back. The question was, did she want him to? Forget that. Hell yes, she wanted him to, and the fact that her face was inching toward his told her that she would. Willingly. Enthusiastically.

Warning bells clamored in her head, but she ignored them jingle by jingle. He was the same guy who'd tested her at work, and they did *work* together, at least temporarily. Unfortunately, that didn't make him look any less like he'd been carved out of marble. Or make his appeal any less, well, *appealing.*

He was so close now that his warm breath feathered over her cheek. Just a little closer. Her gaze shifted to the top of the slide again.

"Did you ever think about having kids of your own?"

Where had that come from? She wouldn't have been sure she'd even spoken those words aloud if his head hadn't suddenly jerked back. Then his whole body followed the path his head had taken.

"Why did you even ask that?"

"I don't know." She hugged herself, suddenly chilled. "You were talking about your niece and nephew, and I was, I don't know, curious."

Why she'd asked when they were a breath away from the first kiss she'd craved in a long time, she wasn't sure. Had she said something to stop him from kissing her because she was afraid that she wouldn't want him to stop?

"Not that it's any of your business, but no, I don't want kids."

"Ever?" Why did she keep asking questions when he clearly didn't want to talk about it? She hadn't thought much about the subject herself, so why was she pressing him on it?

"No, not ever. I never want to be married again, and I never want to bring kids into this awful world. Don't you get that? You can't even imagine the stuff I've seen."

She couldn't. That much was obvious.

Tony shoved both hands back through his hair. "Sorry. That was… I don't know. I've got to go."

He turned and rounded the playground on the way to the parking lot. She hurried after him.

"No, *I'm* sorry. I shouldn't have asked."

Tony stopped and looked over his shoulder. "It's fine. Just a sore subject."

"I figured." When he started moving again, she hurried to walk next to him. "You're not going to drive, are you?"

"I will. Eventually. Depends."

"On what?"

"On how long it takes you to get in your car and drive away. There's no way I'm leaving a woman alone at this park."

She rolled her eyes. He was already back to form. "I'm a police officer, Tony."

"And a woman." He clicked a key fob as he approached his car, climbed inside and shut the door.

Kelly didn't get a chance for a comeback, but it was just as well. She could call him out for trying to protect her, but then she would have to explain why she'd allowed him to cover for her earlier. She couldn't do that. Before she did something to make things worse, she climbed in her SUV and started the engine. With a wave that he probably didn't see, she pulled from the lot.

At least she hadn't kissed him. The thought rolled over and over in her mind as she turned onto Main Street and then again on Grand River Avenue. It would have been a mistake, bigger than all of those she'd already made with him. Because clearly no matter how attractive Tony Lazzaro was, and no matter how attracted she was to him, this job had affected him in some way. Whatever he'd seen, heard and absorbed from humanity's darkest side, it had changed him. It had stolen his hope.

So, why did she still long to have those arms around her, to taste those lips that had been enticingly close? Did she think that she might have the power to heal him or secretly hope he could heal her? If she believed either of those things, she'd lost touch with reality, and she needed to run as fast and far as she could from Special Agent Lazzaro.

Chapter 8

"Here's your coffee, sir."

The man hunched behind the PC grumbled his acknowledgment as his secretary set the mug on a coaster to protect the rich walnut desktop. Almost as nice as the one he had at home, but not quite.

"Is there anything else I can get you?"

"No, Donna. That'll be all. And hold my calls."

"Remember, uh, you have that nine o'clock meeting."

Her voice squeaked when she was nervous. He hated that about her. Only he could have hired a secretary who was always nervous, when his office was designed to intimidate guests.

"No interruptions until the meeting, okay?"

"Yes, sir."

She scurried out the door in that mouselike way of hers and closed it behind her.

"I thought you'd never leave," he whispered to the four walls that kept more secrets for him than most people he knew.

Still, he frowned at the door. It wasn't Donna's fault that the information he'd learned that morning mattered more to him than any of the files she brought to him. She also was as loyal, discreet and incurious an assistant as he could have hoped for. He would tell her to buy herself some flowers. On him.

He lumbered to the door and flipped the lock, just in case. On his way back to the desk, he selected a reference book from the floor-to-ceiling bookshelves, but he didn't bother opening it. He rested it on the corner of his leather desk pad and pulled his laptop from his briefcase instead.

Attaching the external hard drive, he signed on to the Internet using the hotspot from an underground account. He was always careful before, but now it was imperative.

"Let's see what you're up to, INVISIBLE ME."

He smiled as he signed into the first chat room. It was a coup that he'd gotten the name of the task force's recent Trojan horse. Thank goodness for those individuals who shared too many details with people they thought they could trust.

Anyway, investigators were naive to believe that suspects would fall for a screen name like that. *No one understands me. Come get me, creepers.* Did they think no one had watched those programs about trapping predators?

His jaw tightened as the words "MR. SUNSHINE has entered the room" appeared on a column to the left of the chat room screen. Why did they always have to announce his arrival like a visitor at the royal court? Those notices made it difficult to lurk. If he didn't join in, he became suspect.

He scanned the single-spaced list of comments, each visitor's words in a different color. The conversations comingled in a typewritten shouting match. Screen names like I CAN HELP, TOO MUCH FUN and FRIENDS 4-EVER scrolled over the screen, many participants conducting multiple conversations at once.

But no INVISIBLE ME. Had his great information just been another round of BS? His molars clenched. The *friend* sharing details better not have been playing him. He could make it awfully difficult for someone unwise enough to do that.

"Wait."

He typed in a web address for another chat site. His chatty contact had given him a list of places to look. He hoped he could remember all of them. He followed the same procedure with another site.

"Dammit, where are you?"

He was already on his fourth chat room, his index finger cramping from scrolling, when the name he was looking for appeared on the screen.

INVISIBLE ME: Only fifteen minutes late, and they grounded me for THREE weeks. I should run away.

Could she have been more obvious? Apparently, not everyone thought so. Screen names responded to her in a swarm like honeybees pollinating a field of lilies. They commented two to three times for each of her responses. If they only knew that the *sweet young thing* they were pursuing was more likely an FBI agent with a bottle of antacids and a receding hairline.

Or was it that young state trooper that his source had mentioned? The one who'd joined the task force after the double homicide. He'd been researching this Kelly Roberts. Her smile couldn't have been wider as she'd stared back from her recruit school graduation photo. Pretty in an effortless way. Built. He might've tapped that himself if he were ten years younger and had more free time and fewer business headaches.

He was in control again. Monitoring his accounts on the Dark Web would remain a necessity. He was growing his fortune there, after all. But he had to continue to watch the Surface Web as well. Now that he knew what to look for, he could track the investigation step-by-step.

It was like a scientist studying a slide under a microscope, oblivious to the truth that he was on a slide himself, under stronger magnification and a larger glass.

As long as the investigation didn't touch him, they were fine. If the search turned his way, well, nothing personal, but he couldn't let that happen. Unfortunate circumstances happened to people who asked too many questions. He'd worked too hard to build an empire to let an overworked task force destabilize its pilings.

Pushing his shoulders back to stretch his sore back, he scrolled further down the page, observing as the participants bobbed and weaved, ran and chased, all playing their roles in the game. He added a few inane comments from MR. SUNSHINE, hoping to get no responses. He got lucky this time.

Just as he started to click out of the chat room, a new comment to INVISIBLE ME caught his eye. If it was possible for blood to freeze a person's veins, his were Type O ice cubes.

Your folks should treat you better. I would treat you like a princess.

The word soured in his stomach. He still wasn't certain. There had to be plenty of guys who got too caught up in *Grimm's Fairy Tales*. But "princess"? Earlier, he'd been certain he was jumping to conclusions. Now it seemed like less of a leap. He should have known better than to share his business with the idiot, even if he'd been good for profits. Would he pay for his greed now?

The buzz of his office phone made him jump so hard his knee banged the desk. He swallowed a curse, rubbed the injured joint and grabbed the phone.

"I told you not to disturb me until—"

"Sorry, but it's already…"

"Give me a minute." He hung up without waiting for Donna's response.

He unplugged all the cords and shoved the laptop back into the case. For good measure, he opened the book to suggest he'd been doing research all along. Then he crossed to his office door, unlocked it and pulled it wide.

"Ladies and gentlemen, come in and have a seat."

Cory whistled the "Heigh-Ho" tune as he packed a third box with food items. Nonperishable, of course. It would be a while before he had the opportunity to shop for staples again.

The box should have been heavy. There had to be thirty cans of tomatoes, beef stew, vegetables and soups in there. But it seemed light. Like everything else today.

All that searching, all those conversations that started out promising, only to fizzle out in private chats, were over now.

He'd found her.

She was perfect. Beautiful, if her photo was real, and he was certain it would be.

Just one short drive across the Michigan-Ohio border, and they could be together forever.

Tony leaned out of his cubicle just as Kelly started across the office to the kitchen area. He had to force himself to wait sixty seconds before he followed her there. He couldn't blame her for keeping her distance from him all week. What had he been thinking? He'd nearly kissed her the other day. Well, it was obvious he hadn't been thinking, at least with anything above the belt.

"Are you going to keep avoiding me?"

"What?" She spun around so quickly that coffee swilled over the rim of her mug. "Ouch!"

"Sorry. I said—"

"I heard you. For the record, I haven't been avoiding you."

He couldn't help but grin at that. Just like he *hadn't* been steering clear of her for days. "So, terribly busy following up leads?"

"Something like that."

He glanced over his shoulder to make sure no one was listening. "Anyway, it wasn't a big deal or anything."

If it wasn't, why had he waited three days to have this conversation? And why couldn't he stop staring at her lips as he waited for her to respond. Would he still kiss her right now if there wasn't a risk of someone walking in and catching them? He might need to plead the Fifth on that one.

"Yeah, it was nothing."

Then why was he disappointed when she said so? He wanted to blame the moonlight. Maybe nostalgia over visiting the playground again. Anything. There was no excuse, then or now, for his arms itching to pull her to him, no reason for his longing to hold her so close that she would have no doubt that he wanted her.

They were working on a case together. There could be nothing more. No matter how tempting he found her.

"Good. Because I thought we would try a couple more

voice interactions today. INVISIBLE ME is like the new girl at a middle school. Her fans are flocking."

"Guess you made her irresistible," she said.

"I can bat my eyelashes with the best of them."

Her gaze caught his for a dangerous microsecond, but then she looked away. Her mug caught his attention as her hand trembled, making the liquid slosh again.

"I thought you said you wouldn't drink the coffee here."

"Have to stay awake somehow." She shrugged and then turned away to take a sip. "Insomnia."

He could relate to that, but his sleeplessness had to do with a woman who looked amazing in a police uniform, regular office wear and, he suspected, would look even better in nothing at all. What was her excuse?

"Share with your fellow insomniac."

He traded places with her to fill his cup, and she started out of the break room ahead of him. She was already at his desk, her chair and the microphone in position when he made it back.

"Ready to try this again?"

"Absolutely."

She met his gaze with a confidence he didn't expect. Was she trying to prove something to him? Trying to convince him that she hadn't needed him to shield her before?

"Okay, let's chat."

The conversation appeared to have slowed during the time he'd gone for coffee, but the moment Tony typed his first line, his admirers were back. Didn't any of these guys have a day job?

It didn't take long before one of them sent a private message at the bottom of the screen. GOOD TIME GUY wasn't all that shy about escalating the conversation quickly, either. Kelly took over the keyboard, and when the guy suggested a voice chat, she didn't even look Tony's way before she accepted.

"Hey, your voice is rougher than I expected," she said into the microphone.

Only then did she glance sidelong at Tony. He nodded his approval. He'd been right to give her a second chance. Dawson and the others didn't need to know about the other day, the part at the office or anything that happened later. Kelly would be great at this.

When the conversation with GOOD TIME GUY didn't seem to be going anywhere, they ended that interaction and accepted another offer for a personal chat. She navigated that one with BOY AT HEART and even another conversation with BIG DADDY, demonstrating the skill of someone who'd been on the task force a year rather than a week.

Her breathing might have been uneven, and she might have tightened her grip on the microphone, but she was powering through, as if determined to tease details from each of the possible suspects that they could use to track them.

He'd been wrong about Kelly Roberts. She was stronger than he'd expected her to be. Maybe even fearless. And he was dying to know what had made her that way.

Chapter 9

Kelly gripped the steering wheel so hard her fingers ached as she rocked forward and backward in the seat of the parked rental car. It was still hot outside, but she shivered, gooseflesh peppering her arms. Her heart pounded in her chest as BIG DADDY's awful voice replayed in her mind.

I can't wait to see you, INVISIBLE ME.

Again. Had he said that word? She couldn't be sure. Had something she'd said given her away? Had he somehow recognized who she was? After all these years, was he coming for her? The words repeated, his leer joining the sound, and then the message changed.

She's mine. Stay quiet, or I'll be back for you.

She closed her eyes and put her hands over her ears to muffle the voice, but that made the images flash brighter in her memory. His hand over Emily's mouth. The spinning wheel on her discarded bike. The despised blue stain oozing over the cement.

No one had screamed. Emily couldn't. Kelly had been too terrified to try.

"Why didn't I do anything? Why?" She leaned forward and bumped her head on the steering wheel twice.

At the tap on the driver's-side window, she jumped, her hand automatically reaching for her hip, where her weapon should have been but wasn't. Her fingers brushed the useless silk of her blouse as she pulled her hand away. Slowly, she turned toward the sound.

Tony was bent outside the window, staring right at her.

"Why what?" he said loudly enough to be heard through the glass.

Kelly swallowed and then reached for the button to roll down the window. How loudly had she spoken, and what had he overheard? If he had grinned and cracked a joke over catching her talking to herself, she would have acted embarrassed and played it off as nothing. His eyes were wide instead, and his jaw hung slack. He looked as if he'd seen a ghost. Hers. The one that had haunted her all these years.

Still, she had to convince him this was no more than minor humiliation. What else could she do?

"It's nothing. Forget it. Long day." Her words were coming too fast, and she couldn't form more than two-word sentences. She cleared her throat. "That's all."

"Stop."

His voice was barely above a whisper, but Kelly's body still shook as if he'd shouted. Gripping the steering wheel as she had earlier, she opened her mouth to try a second time. His withering stare seemed to dare her to try lying again. She closed her mouth without speaking.

"Now tell me what's going on. And don't say it's nothing because I'm not buying it this time."

"Maybe…it's just that you were right. Maybe I'm not cut out for this assignment."

She couldn't look at him then, couldn't bear the heat

of his X-ray vision, searing past skin and sinew to peek into her soul.

"And, maybe, there's more to it than that," he said.

She couldn't help but to look at him then, realizing too late that she'd just confirmed what he'd said.

"It's just. I can't tell you now. Not…here."

She couldn't finish. No matter how tempted she was to give him some abbreviated version of the truth, she couldn't risk it. Worse than having him recommend that she needed to be reassigned from the task force, she worried she wouldn't be able to stop talking once the first word escaped.

"You were doing a great job inside. Far better than I would have predicted. But look at you now. Your hands are shaking. You're sitting as straight as a suspect faced with damning evidence. And, if it were bright enough out here for me to see clearly, I'm guessing your face would be as flushed as a marathon runner's."

She shook her head, as much to deny his words as to push away emotions crashing at her from all directions. "I just… I just need to get home and shake it off. I'll be fine by tomorrow. Just let me—"

"Not going to happen."

She blinked. "What?"

"I can't let you take off like this. You're in no condition to drive, particularly the rental. You're a state trooper, for God's sake. You know better than to let someone *like you* out on the roads."

She wanted to argue. He didn't know anything about what was going on inside her. But he was right. She'd investigated several personal-injury or fatality accidents where the drivers shouldn't have been behind the wheel for reasons that had nothing to do with intoxicants.

"Fine," she said finally. "I'll just wait a while. You can go. I'll be okay."

"I have a better idea."

She breathed in a ragged breath. "What's that?"

"Scoot over."

"What? I don't think—"

But he already had her door open. She frowned up at him.

He pushed the door wide and bent inside the space to be at her eye level.

"I'm not going to kidnap you. I'll just drive you home. Give a guy a break, will you? I just want to make sure you get home in one piece."

"I don't need anyone to take care of me. I'm doing fine on my own."

"You don't look fine."

She couldn't argue with that. If she looked as bad on the outside as she felt inside, well, she didn't even want to picture that. He'd straightened but was still standing inside the open door, refusing to budge. She tried a different approach.

"But you can't just drive me home. You can't drive my rental. Also, how are you supposed to get back to your car? I mean, thanks for the offer, but it's impractical, don't you think?"

"I'm a safer bet to drive the rental than you are right now. Also, you should move into the twenty-first century and remember that ride sharing is a thing now. I'll contact a RideNow from your place and be out of your hair in a couple of minutes. I get to relieve my worries that you'll kill yourself on the roads, and you won't even have to play hostess. Win-win."

She shook her head, but she was running out of arguments. If she was beginning to understand one thing about Tony, it was that he didn't give in easily. She was too tired to fight.

"All right."

"Good. Now scoot over."

She reached down to unlock her seat belt, only to realize she'd never buckled it. Maybe he'd made a good call that she shouldn't be driving. Wiggling around and then moving her feet first, she maneuvered herself into the passenger seat.

Tony slid behind the wheel and immediately reached down to adjust the seat since his knees were crammed against the dashboard. Then he adjusted the mirrors.

Kelly settled back against the cloth upholstery, sweat plastering the back of her blouse to her skin. She pulled her seat belt across her, and her breath caught as Tony's fingers covered hers and guided the male end of the belt into its female home.

Of course, if he was going to the trouble of driving her himself, he would want to make sure she used proper restraints. So why did the gesture seem like something more? Something...safe.

Once her belt was latched, Tony clicked his own in place. Only then did he turn the key to start the ignition.

"There is one more thing you'll need to do before we go," he said after several seconds.

She swallowed. Was he going to demand to know the story she wasn't ready to tell, now that he was in the power position?

"What's that?"

"You need to tell me where you live."

Chapter 10

Tony stepped inside Kelly's neat-as-a-pin second-floor apartment, his eyes adjusting to the glare from the overhead fixture. On second thought, the room looked so tidy because it was nearly empty.

"Nice place." He slid off his dress shoes and set them by the door.

"You don't have to say that. It's a work in progress."

"How long have you lived here?"

From the pristine quality of the walls, none of them marred with pictures or hanging hardware, it couldn't have been long. He'd been surprised when she'd invited him inside at all. After the awkward fifteen-minute drive to her apartment complex, he'd expected her to wave at the door and make him wait outside until his shared ride picked him up. Good thing she hadn't already instructed him to go on his app to schedule it.

Whether she thought she was okay or not, he wasn't ready to leave her alone.

"It'll be three years in November."

"Progress must be slow around here."

"Isn't it everywhere?"

She had a point, but that didn't make her apartment look any less like an extended-stay hotel. Her living room didn't even have a cluttered bookshelf to personalize it.

"Two bedrooms?"

"Just one."

He could only imagine what it would look like. Only a bed and a closet. He swallowed. On second thought, maybe he shouldn't be thinking about her bedroom at all, not when he was supposed to be there to support her. Not to picture her and him taking full advantage of that forsaken bed.

Some rescuer he was turning out to be, trying to protect her from whatever had her so freaked out. Now who was going to shield her from him?

"Want something to drink?" She started into her tiny kitchen without waiting for an answer. Then she leaned out the doorway again.

"I've got fizzy water. Or coffee. Or beer."

"Do I look like the fizzy water type to you?"

"Well, you do look a little...European."

Was that good or bad, he couldn't help wondering. "I guess that's fair. But I'll have a beer if you have one. Neither of us is driving, at least for now."

He'd also already drunk slushes with her and look where that had gotten them. It couldn't get much worse with beer, right? Maybe if she had a couple, it would relax her enough that she could finally tell him what was really going on. She returned, carrying two bottles of good Michigan craft beer.

"What did you expect? I'm not still in college, you know."

"I realize that."

He took his bottle and sat on one end of the sofa. She settled at the other end.

"You sure treated me like you thought I'd left an off-campus party to come to the task force."

He'd tipped up the bottle and had taken a long swig of it, but at her words, he brought it down too quickly, causing foam to pour over the top. Some spilled on his hand with the rest dribbling on the sofa cushion.

"Sorry." He wiped his mouth with the back of his hand and then brushed at the cushion. "But my behavior wasn't that extreme."

"Close."

He shrugged. She'd seemed so young when she'd first entered their office. Or maybe she'd only appeared youthful to him because he felt so old and jaded. Refusing to think about whatever had brought them closer in age than those two extremes now, he downed the rest of his beer.

"You don't happen to have a couple more of those, do you?"

"A few."

Her gaze narrowed, but she set her almost empty bottle on a coaster and disappeared into the kitchen. She returned with two more opened bottles.

"This is the last of it, so don't pour this one out on my couch." She finished her first beer, set the bottle on the floor next to his and lowered her second one on a coaster.

"I'll try not to."

He took one swallow this time, grabbed another coaster and rested his bottle on it.

"Are you ready to talk now?"

"No."

She sipped from her beer, her gaze far away, and then she set her drink aside.

"You said we could talk about it somewhere else."

"I know what I said."

She crossed her arms over her chest as if to shield herself from his questions.

"What do you want to know?"

"The truth. You didn't panic today on the job like you did the first time, but there's something freaking you out every time you interact with potential suspects."

"My friend, Emily, was, uh, abducted when I was a kid."

His throat tightened. If there ever were a partial truth in front of him, this had to be it. His arms started to reach for her all on their own, so he tightened them at his sides to prevent the movement. He wasn't sure if there was an "Emily" at all. Could it have been a code name for Kelly herself, like when someone asked for advice for a friend?

"That's too bad. How soon was she…recovered?" The last word came out in a strangled sound, as if his voice box wanted to ask it, but his brain wasn't sure he wanted to know the answer. If they were talking about Kelly, she had to know she was lucky to have been found at all.

"She was able to escape after a week and found a neighbor to call police."

"I'm sorry this happened to *your friend*. Did she get the help she needed afterward?"

Now he folded his hands together to keep from reaching out to her. Many families pretended that nothing had happened and only compounded the trauma on their children. Could Kelly's family—or her friend's—have been like that?

"I think she was in counseling for the last few months before she moved—"

"Moved?"

"Chattanooga, if I remember right. Why does that matter?"

"I thought you were talking about yourself. As in *you* were Emily."

She made a tight sound in her throat, and her shoulders lifted toward her earlobes. Tony was just the opposite. The tight muscles in his neck released, allowing his head to dip forward. How could he be relieved that Kelly had been spared when another child had been abducted?

"No, I wasn't Emily. Not even close."

She stared at the blank wall next to the kitchen.

"Then I don't get it."

"What do you mean?"

"You say it was your friend, so why do I still get the feeling that it happened to you?"

"Well, it didn't."

She spat the words and then peeked at him as if to check if he'd noticed. He had.

"What was that?"

"It's just…nothing."

"Tell me, Kelly. I really want to know."

She looked at him then. Really looked, as if she wanted to believe him but couldn't quite make the leap. She didn't speak for so long that he wondered if she would.

"I was there."

"You were with her when it happened? That must have been awful."

She nodded in answer to both his question and his comment. She blinked several times, her eyes too shiny.

He didn't bother stopping his hands this time. They reached for hers then, her fine-boned fingers cradled between his palms. She stared at their joined hands for several seconds and then slid hers away to fold her arms again.

"How old were you?"

"Nine. We both were."

He swallowed. It was a story he'd heard so many times, and yet he couldn't maintain a professional detachment this time. It had happened to Kelly's friend. And Kelly, too, whether she'd been abducted or not. He was tempted to insist that she spill all the details at once, but years of participating in and observing victim interviews had taught him not to rush them. He took another drink of his beer and waited.

"We were out riding our bikes," she said after a long time. "Our parents had finally given us permission to ride without adults as long as we stayed on the sidewalks and remained together."

"A lot of people count on safety in numbers," he said before he could stop himself.

She shifted on the sofa cushion. Would she stop talking now that she'd finally started?

"We thought we were bulletproof. We rode as fast as we could. Didn't wear helmets. Even occasionally rode in the street, but only to get to the next block."

"None of that means that you deserved to be targeted."

Tony pressed his lips together. Why couldn't he stop himself from interjecting into her story? Did he believe that something he would say could fix the past for her?

"I know that."

But she shook her head, contradicting her own words.

"Anyway, we'd gone a little farther that day to buy slushes at the convenience store. Blue raspberry. Emily's spilled all over the sidewalk when *the man* popped out of a hedge and yanked her off her bike."

She shivered visibly, and a faraway look appeared in her eyes.

"I froze. I just stood there watching the whole thing like a bystander at a car accident. I couldn't even scream."

"That must have been awful," he said. "Not knowing what to do. Feeling powerless to help."

She shook her head as if unwilling to accept the excuses he offered.

"He got away with it, too."

"Are you kidding? I figured they got the SOB."

She shook her head. "No arrest was ever made."

"Sounds like the system failed Emily and—"

"I failed her, too," she said to interrupt him.

He didn't bother saying she was a victim as well. She would never believe him. He tried to defend her instead.

"You were just a kid."

"And I kept failing her, even after the police brought her home." She stared at her hands, turning them over and back in her lap. "She was different after that. Quiet. Nervous. No longer *Emily* to me. I convinced myself it was because she knew things that only grown-up women knew, that she didn't want to be my best friend anymore."

"So you pulled away from her?"

"Bit by bit, yes. Then, when her family moved, I just let her go."

"And you never forgave yourself for it."

She shrugged, but Tony didn't need an answer to that.

"This assignment has probably dug up some tough memories for you."

"Yeah. Some."

"Why didn't you turn it down?"

"It wasn't about me. It couldn't be. We were investigating a murder case, and those two girls deserved justice."

She met his gaze defiantly, as if she expected him to argue with her. He couldn't. At least not on that.

"Does anyone at your post know about your history?"

"Some. It's in my file, too. But it was a long time ago, and I never let it affect my work."

Until now, he almost said. But that day, at least, she'd handled herself well with the potential suspects. Only afterward had she allowed herself to fall apart.

"Do you think you can continue to work in this environment, even with your history?"

"I do."

Tony had to take her word for it since he was already in this with her. He'd covered for her, too. If he went to Dawson now, he would have to explain why he hadn't done so earlier.

"Well, we know why at least one of us chose a career in law enforcement," he said.

"What do you mean?"

Her startled expression hinted that she wasn't joking.

"You never considered that your childhood trauma might have had as much to do with your career choice as anything that happened with your mom?"

"Not really. I was a psych major, but when I took a criminal-justice class, I was hooked."

"All I'm saying is there might've been a reason you were drawn to a career where you could serve and protect. Maybe you wanted to give back."

"Since I had a debt to pay?"

"That's not what I meant," he said, though it was clear to him that she believed that. "It's just that our experiences affect our choices in life."

"I suppose." She stared at her hands. "Was it your experience working on cases like Emily's that convinced you not to have kids?"

He blinked, her words catching him off guard. Though he wanted to ask her more questions about the abduction, to get specifics so he could look up the case, he recognized she'd said everything she would on the topic that day. She'd answered his questions, so it was only fair that he answered hers.

"There was more to it than that." So much more than he'd shared with anyone else. Until now. Was it because she'd let him in on her secret that he was unlatching the padlock to his?

"I always wanted kids. Pictured myself with a bunch of them. It's funny how you change your mind about things when your wife aborts your baby."

Her eyes widened.

"Tony, that's awful." She reached for his arm and squeezed. "You couldn't talk her out of it?"

"I didn't even know Laurel was pregnant."

"She terminated the pregnancy without even discussing it with you?"

He shook his head. "She told me what she'd done just before she asked for a divorce."

"That seems so cruel. Why didn't she at least talk to you about it…before?"

Kelly scooted closer, placed her arm around his shoulder and leaned against his side as if she could lend him her strength. It was all he could do not to shake off her compassion, just as she'd pulled away from his touch earlier.

"Maybe she would've talked to me if I'd ever been around to listen. If I'd been a halfway decent husband who paid attention to her occasionally. If we'd had a marriage where there had been emotional and physical intimacy. Or if we hadn't been at each other's throats for months."

Her body stiffened at his words, but she didn't pull away from his side.

"None of those things are good excuses for not telling you."

"Her body. Her choice. I'd always believed that for other women. Still do."

"I believe that, too. But you two were married. Shouldn't that mean you both got a vote?"

"I thought so. I guess I was wrong. Laurel must have figured we were headed for divorce, anyway, and a baby would have tethered us together forever."

"I'm sorry you lost your child, Tony."

A knot formed in his throat. *His child.* No one had ever posed it to him that way, but then Kelly was the first person he'd ever told. Angelena didn't even know. The pain had been too sharp, the loss too great. Anyway, how could his sister ever have looked up to her big brother if she knew how horribly he'd failed?

Had he shared this story with Kelly as a test because he didn't want her to see him as some hero? Why did he care so much what she thought?

"It didn't matter what was going on in your marriage. This wasn't your fault. It ultimately was her decision, and she made it."

"Why is it so easy for you to see me as innocent, when I wasn't, and then blame yourself for your friend's abduction?"

Where before she'd leaned against him to bolster his strength, she pulled her shoulder away, from his words and a pardon she must have believed she didn't deserve.

"Those two things are completely different."

"Yes, they are. You were a little girl. I was an adult. I can be held accountable for my mistakes."

"Youth shouldn't absolve me of any wrongdoing."

"Why not? Youth isn't valued for much. Take what you can get from it."

"Thanks, I guess."

Though she hadn't admitted he was right, he sensed

that something was different between them. He'd thought that sharing his story would push her away, but she was still there, trusting him. Maybe more than she had before. Her story had convinced him that she was stronger than he could have imagined. She'd traveled through a dark tunnel and had emerged on the other side, not without scars, but she'd found daylight just the same.

He could have let the topic fall away, spoken and forgotten, but he couldn't do that. If no one else had already told her and insisted she listen, he was about to try.

"Deep inside you must know that Emily's abduction wasn't your fault. You weren't responsible for being the child who got away, either. Fate or God or whatever you want to call it had a hand in that."

"I know."

"But do you really? I haven't met all the players, but even I know that no one blamed you for what happened. Except you."

"But I should have—"

"Listen to me, Kelly. Nobody blames you. Probably not even Emily."

Her eyes widened as his words hung in the silence between them. Then she did the last thing he expected her to do.

She leaned in and kissed him.

Chapter 11

Fireworks. Or at least a mild electrical storm, where only her lips had been exposed to the most delicious spark. Neither of those things came close to describing the impact of touching her lips to Tony's. Firm rather than soft, with a tickle from his five o'clock shadow at the corner of her mouth.

This was a huge mistake, and she knew it, but when had an error ever tasted this good? Felt this good? He couldn't know what Emily thought about that time so long ago, about a best friend who'd failed her. Yet his words had been so freeing that Kelly could think only of reveling in that moment of escape.

She'd surprised him. That much was obvious from the way his head jerked back and he stared at her, his eyes wide. Her heart must have beat a thousand times in the few seconds that passed as his gaze lowered to her lips and lifted again to her eyes.

"Oh, hell yeah."

Tony bent his head and captured her lips in a move as smooth as if they'd practiced it together for a decade or more. No gentle greeting. No tentative exploration.

He seemed to taste her without apology, and she eagerly shared in his freedom from regret. It was as if the dam of their self-control had given way, and nothing could stop the flood. Good thing because she didn't want it to stop.

She should be cautious, an unwelcome thought suggested, its uninvited twin hinting that more than bodies could be involved this time. She ignored them both as her hands gripped strong shoulders and leaned into the solid wall of his chest.

When she'd moved or kicked off her shoes, she wasn't sure, but suddenly she was draped over his lap, her feet curled into the sofa cushion, her bottom pressed against the fullness of him. It was clear what he wanted from her and what she would happily share with him.

His hands had settled at her lower back and hips, but now they moved past all the places that longed for his caresses to the back of her head, which tingled beneath his touch as well. One hand burrowed into her bun to palm her scalp, while the second mined for bobby pins. He slipped them out, one by one, and tossed them toward the coffee table, some pinging off the wood, some landing silently on the carpet. When most were out, her hair dropped in a mass, and his hands sank into it, tangles and all.

Automatically, both of her hands moved to contain it. "That's got to be a mess."

He reached for one of her hands and laced their fingers together before drawing it to her side.

"It's just how I imagined it."

"You imagined a mess?"

He didn't answer. His lips were too busy continuing their journey from her jaw to her ear. He lingered there, his warm breath sending tingles over her earlobe, while his fingertips skimmed her sleeve from cuff to shoulder.

"Hmm, silk," he whispered.

Then he dabbed his tongue on a place behind her ear that had never been sensitive until that moment but would be from then on.

"Softer than my uniform shirt."

Was nervousness what kept making her say those ridiculous things? No matter the reason, she'd never been so happy to be out of uniform, but even the clothes she wore seemed too restrictive now. And excessive.

Tony brought his mouth to hers again and again, each kiss longer, deeper and more sensual than the last. By the time his thumbs followed the lines of her collarbones to their juncture at her breastbone, she was ready to beg him to touch her in all the places that had warmed and stretched in welcome.

"Is this okay?" he asked as his thumb and forefinger connected with her top button.

"Yes…okay," she whispered because she didn't have the breath to speak the words aloud.

She'd wanted before, but never like this. Though she'd touched and been touched in the past, everything inside told her this time was different.

But instead of ripping all her buttons open, as she hoped he would do, he paused to brush his fingers over the dip in her blouse created by that lone open button.

"Let me." She covered his hands with hers.

"What's the rush?"

He chuckled then, the deep masculine sound washing over her and touching her everywhere, though his hands had yet to oblige.

"This."

She leaned in and took that amazing, perfect chin between her hands and kissed him exactly the way she'd told herself she hadn't been imagining all week. She'd intended to ignite a flame in him but set herself ablaze in the process. She smiled against his lips as Tony's hands fell away from her blouse to grip her hips. She reached for the buttons herself, freeing them with unsteady hands.

"Gorgeous."

His word came on a sigh, though little more of her was visible than the lacy trim of her bra and the flushed skin that peeked over the top. His eyes were darker than normal, his lids hooded with desire. For her. Why did she suddenly wonder what it would be like if he offered more than just sex?

She cleared her throat, pushing the thought from her already muddled mind.

"Here. Let me help you with that."

She yanked his shirttails from the waistband of his trousers and started on the buttons. Tony finished unbuttoning and shrugged out of the shirt just as Kelly lifted the waistband of his white undershirt. Instead of helping this time, he lifted his arms. She tugged it straight up, but her hands stilled as she unveiled a set of abs and a chest as sculpted as his jaw.

"You're not going to leave me here like this, are you?"

He waved his hands in the air, his face still buried, and his elbows still trapped.

"Tough question." She looked from the likely tired arms to the amazing male form she was dying to explore.

The buzz of her apartment's intercom answered the question for her.

As she wiggled off his lap, Tony yanked the shirt back over his head and caught her hand before she could step away from the couch.

"You don't have to answer it."

"I know."

But the intercom buzzed six more times in a doorbell "Jingle Bells" chorus. She pulled her fingers from his.

"I think I do." She spoke over her shoulder and then hurried to the intercom next to the door and pushed the button.

"Hey ya, Roberts!"

"Vinnie, is that you?" Her shaking hands worked on her buttons as she waited for the answer. If Sergeant Vincent Leonetti was standing outside her apartment, chances were, he wasn't alone. Until last week, none of her Brighton Post coworkers had ever visited her home, and now it was becoming a revolving door.

"Sure, it's me. Letting us in or what?"

"Yeah. Just a minute."

Instead of hitting the button to buzz Vinnie and whomever else was included in that "us" inside, she shot a look at Tony. He stood by the coffee table, already buttoning his shirt.

"We've got to hurry." She jogged across the room, tucked her feet into her ballet flats and grabbed her bobby pins off the table. "Invasion of my coworkers."

"They just show up at your place?" He tucked in his shirt.

"Apparently they do now."

He strode to the door. "Okay, go. You can run in and fix your hair, and I'll buzz them in when you're ready."

"Oh. Right." She shoved her hands through her hair, which felt like a rat's nest, as she rushed from the room.

"And, Kelly," he called after her.

She paused and looked back over her shoulder. "What now?"

"Buttons."

Her hands automatically shifted to her blouse, and she glanced down. The front of the garment gaped where she'd missed a button, and the two sides didn't match at the bottom.

"Ah, man." She rebuttoned as she scurried into the bathroom.

She splashed water on her flushed face, wiped at her smeared eyeliner and shoved her hair in the best bun she could manage on short notice.

"You coming out soon?" Tony called from across the room. "We need to buzz them in."

"On my way."

She took one last look in the mirror. The lady in the glass looked like someone who'd been interrupted minutes—seconds—out of bed. The image was spot on. She was grateful for the delay, too, right? Her friends had shown up to save her from danger, even if it was self-inflicted.

So, why did part of her—several parts, in fact—wish they'd picked a different night to pop in for a visit?

Chapter 12

"What took you so long?"

Vinnie's voice beat him through the door as he barreled past Kelly.

"Thought you might be getting *busy* or—"

Even mortified, Kelly couldn't help but grin when Vinnie stopped midstep and midsentence as his gaze caught on Tony. Nothing ever shut up Vinnie Leonetti.

"Hardly," she choked out.

Nick Sanchez followed Vinnie so closely through the door that he bumped into the sergeant when the first man paused.

"Yeah, what was the deal leaving us outside like a bunch of vacuum salesmen?" He leaned around Vinnie to see what had stopped him. "Oh, hey."

Tony leaned back into the sofa cushion, a sock-covered foot crossed over the other knee. He took a sip of his probably warm beer and waved.

Like part of a train veering off the track, Dion stepped out of line. Others crowded around them, six altogether, grinning as if they'd guessed what she and Tony had been up to. Heat rushed up Kelly's neck, and it was all she could do not to cover her face with her hands. Great. So much for the trooper who'd made a statement of avoiding office relationships.

"Let me guess. You're Mr. FBI," Dion said, finally breaking the awkward silence.

Kelly frowned his way. Of course, Dion and Nick would jump to that conclusion after the conversation they'd had the other day. They'd been right, then and now.

Tony set his bottle aside. "I've never been called that before, but I guess it fits. I'm Special Agent Anthony Lazzaro, part of Kelly's team. You guys must be the Brighton Post. The *whole* post."

Delia Morgan-Peterson had been standing behind one of the men, but she slipped around him and stepped closer.

"Not the whole post and, definitely, not all *guys*, but you already must know that." She turned to Nick. "And that's vacuum sales*people* to you, sir."

"Right. People."

With a sly grin, Delia turned back to Kelly. "Clearly, we should have given you a heads-up, instead of descending on you like a SWAT team raid."

"I've missed you guys." Kelly moved through the group, hugging each of her visitors. "It's not a problem. Really."

"Except that these were the last two beers in the whole apartment." Tony pointed to the one he lifted again and then the half-filled bottle on the table. "Kelly had invited me over to have one to decompress. You know. One of those days. Anyway, she discovered she only had two left. So when you all showed up, she was running around, trying to figure out what to serve more guests. I told her it wouldn't be a big deal."

Kelly sneaked a glance Tony's way for a few reasons.

For one thing, she had to know if he smiled when he lied. He'd already said he was part of *her* team, and then he'd weaved a story about her delay in letting her guests in. She also was dying to know what he'd done with their other empties, not to mention the other bobby pins she'd dropped on the carpet.

"Of course, it's no big deal," Lieutenant Ben Peterson answered for them all.

He stepped closer to put an arm around his wife's waist. "Delia's right. We shouldn't have let them talk us into taking a field trip after work tonight instead of going to Casey's."

He pointed to Nick and Dion by turns.

"Since when do you ever listen to them?" Kelly asked, and they all laughed. At least it broke through some of the awkwardness.

Trevor Cole stepped forward and held his hands wide. "Nick said you seemed lonely since the transfer."

Nick and Dion met her frown with sheepish grins.

"I've been fine, but it's definitely different."

"And not even close to ranking with the absolute joy of working at the Brighton Post," Trevor said, his gaze focused on Tony.

"Of course," Kelly assured them.

Tony leaned forward, resting his forearms on his thighs. "From the way she talks about the place, I'm surprised that you don't have to pay the state to let you work there."

His comment drew more laughs, but Kelly shook her head.

"The new assignment has been good, too. Everyone's been really nice and helpful."

She couldn't allow herself to look at Tony, Nick or Dion as she told that half-truth. No, Tony hadn't been welcoming in the beginning, but the other part was true. He'd helped her and challenged her more than he knew.

The lieutenant broke away from the group and crossed to where Tony sat on the couch.

"I'm glad to hear that they've been good to you." Ben turned back to the other officers. "Maybe we should give this guy a break, even if he is one of those FBI cowboys."

Tony stood, and the two men shook hands as Ben introduced himself.

"I sure hope you'll cut me some slack since I'm outnumbered here. And I'll try to keep my spurs in check."

You could take them. Kelly's disloyal thought surprised her. These were her closest friends. When had she become Tony's supporter, as well? When she'd had her tongue in his mouth, that irreverent part of her suggested.

The other officers introduced themselves to the special agent. They were still sneaking side-glances at her and Tony and probably noticing that her hair was messier than usual, but at least no one had continued with the innuendos.

"Why don't you all take a seat?" She looked around the way the others were. "What? There's plenty of carpet here. I'll have to get some folding chairs for the next time you come."

"Or some regular chairs," Vinnie piped.

"Maybe." Certain she wouldn't be able to sit still, she hurried to the kitchen. "Who's up for coffee?"

Several hands went up.

"Give me a few minutes. It's a one-cup maker."

Tony popped up from his seat. "And I'll make myself useful by serving as waiter."

Kelly braced herself for comments about how they were playing a cozy host and hostess, and, as expected, Vinnie gestured toward Tony as he passed.

"Doubt you'll measure up to Sarah, but then nobody ever does."

"Sarah?" Tony asked as he stood in the kitchen doorway.

"A waitress and now co-owner of Casey's Diner. She recently married our coworker, Jamie Donovan."

"Must have been some great coffee."

"Or they were perfect for each other." The words escaped before she could stop them. She turned away, her cheeks burning, tucked the first mug in the coffee maker and popped the pod in the machine.

"You'll need to get a bigger coffee maker if you'll be entertaining all the time," Tony said from behind her. "Do you even have enough mugs?"

"If I use the bunny one and the one that says, 'Caffeine Addict,' I do."

"I take it they don't visit often."

"Until recently, none of them had ever been to my apartment." She set the first mug on the counter in front of him and started the process all over again.

"None of them?" He lifted the mug by its handle. "Even Nick?"

She glanced sidelong at him, but when she found him looking back, she turned to the coffee maker.

"I never date coworkers," she said and then swallowed over the information she'd just revealed. If she didn't get involved with coworkers, what had she been doing draped over Tony's lap?

"Good to know."

Could Tony be jealous of Nick? That didn't seem possible. It was a little late for her to argue that Tony wasn't into her, and guys weren't blind when it came to Sanchez. She held back a smile.

If Tony only knew. Nick's calendar-model looks had

always been lost on her. But a certain FBI agent, with gray at his temples and eyes that still sparkled, despite all that they'd seen, now, that guy could really make her come undone. And had been well on his way to doing that twenty minutes earlier.

Something was different about Tony Lazzaro for her, but she chose not to analyze it there. She would be better off if she didn't investigate it at all.

"Your coworkers really seem to care about you," he said after a long pause. "That's rare. It says a lot about you."

Vinnie leaned around the corner into the kitchen. "Did you two go all the way to Costa Rica for the coffee beans?"

"Almost," Tony said.

He pressed the first mug into Vinnie's hand on the hot side instead of turning the mug to give him the handle. Vinnie winced but didn't call him out for it.

"You have a naughty side," she said to Tony, after Vinnie returned to his spot in the living room.

"I don't know what you're talking about." He leaned out the doorway to speak to her guests. "More coffees are coming right up."

But when he moved back into the kitchen area, he crossed behind her, edging closer in her personal space this time.

"Don't you forget my naughty side."

His whisper wasn't close enough for her to feel his breath on her skin. He didn't *touch* her at all. So why was she tempted to beg him to put his hands on her, even with half of the Brighton Post afternoon shift in her living room?

"Oh. You might want to check under the couch later."

He waited until she looked over her shoulder to add, "The bottles."

The heat in his eyes said nothing about returnables under the sofa but spoke volumes about what they'd been doing on top of the cushions. Every place he'd touched earlier warmed under his gaze, as if brought to life by tantalizing caresses. Those secret places he'd yet to explore preened for his notice.

To busy her hands that were tempted to do a little touching of their own, she switched the mugs again and handed Tony the second one, carefully trading off the handle. "Better get it out there fast or you'll lose out on your tips."

"Wouldn't want to do that."

He hurried to deliver the cup while she tossed the pod and started another round of brewing. They repeated the process several more times.

Soon they were all seated around her living room, sipping coffee and trading stories. She'd tried before not to share Tony with her friends, and now she wondered why. He fit right in with them, despite working in a different agency that wasn't always popular with local police. He laughed at the same jokes and had some of his own ridiculous stories to share.

Conversations splintered then, with several going on at once.

"...need to schedule a ride share back to my car since Kelly drove here," Tony was telling Ben.

"Don't do that," Ben said. "Delia and I will drop you off."

Kelly leaned closer to Delia, who was seated next to her on the carpet.

"How did you and Ben happen to get out tonight, anyway?"

"Grandma asked if she could keep Lydia overnight this time instead of just until the end of our shift," Delia explained.

"And you're not home, uh, *cuddling*?"

"There's time for, uh, cuddling later, but it's nice for us to get to spend time with other adults. Not at work."

"I get that."

"Tony's nice," Delia whispered.

"It's not the way it looks."

"Well, good."

"Wait. What?"

The side of Delia's mouth lifted, but she didn't turn to face Kelly. "I'd hate to think we interrupted some real fun."

Of course, Delia would recognize it. She and Ben had once had their own secret office romance, though technically, Ben had been suspended at the time.

Was that what they were having? A secret office *romance*? Or was it only a tryst? Was she so desperate for someone to tell her that Emily forgave her that she'd thrown herself at him when he had? No matter what it was, maybe it was a good thing they'd been interrupted.

She was supposed to be helping to hunt down Sienna's and Madison's murderer or at least to find out if BIG DADDY was the same man who'd abducted Emily. Why was it that every time she got within twenty feet of Tony, she forgot why she was there and what she was supposed to be doing?

Kelly couldn't help feeling relieved when they all poured out the door, taking Tony with them.

"See you tomorrow," he said.

"See you then."

He only patted her arm when the others had hugged

her on the way out, but her bicep had flexed as if it longed to extend his touch.

She closed the door, only realizing she'd been holding her breath when it came out in a long, full stream. She moved about the apartment, fluffing pillows and loading the mugs in her dishwasher, the first time she'd used it in months. Then, remembering, she crouched in front of the sofa and pulled out the two bottles from beneath it. Her finger traced the rim of the bottle, where his lips might have touched the glass.

She held the bottles away from her as she carried them into the kitchen to rinse. That bottle wouldn't and her mouth shouldn't touch his lips again. Tomorrow she would figure out how to be more helpful in this investigation and how to keep her cool, even if she had to spend an hour talking to BIG DADDY.

But tonight she needed to do one thing first. She had to figure out how to stop wanting things she couldn't have.

Chapter 13

Tony pushed the button, and that same obnoxious sound that had interrupted the best/worst thing that had happened to him in a long time poured from the speaker. He jerked back his hand. It had happened to him? Okay, he'd been practically waving and shouting, "Put me in, Coach," but the rest was true.

What was he doing back here? Ben and Delia had been kind enough to take him back to his rental car. The least he could have done was to stay there when he drove home instead of switching to his personal vehicle and heading out again. He could've treated the interruption as the gift it was and had the good sense to walk away and forget about what had almost happened. No one could have accused him of doing the smart thing.

She didn't answer the buzz. He stuck his hands in his pockets. It was just as well. At least one of them had been listening when the universe blared a warning siren.

"Yes?"

Tony swallowed, his pulse pounding so loudly in his ears that he could hear nothing else.

"Is someone there?"

He cleared his throat and pushed the button to speak. "It's me."

"Tony?"

"Yeah." He glanced over his shoulder to the parking lot. His car was there, waiting. He could still drive away. No harm, no foul. Well, almost no harm. It was like a child's first piece of candy. He'd had one taste, and he couldn't help but to go back for more. "Are you going to let me in or not?"

Nothing. Was he more disappointed or relieved? He stared at the line of buttons for a few seconds more and then nodded. She'd chosen for them both. Then just as he backed away and turned, a click louder than even the buzzer unlatched the door.

He hurried back to the front of the building and yanked it wide. Inside, he skipped a few steps in his rush to reach the second floor, somehow managing not to trip.

Kelly stood in her apartment's open doorway, her hands gripped in front of her. Instead of giving himself time to worry that she might have been having second thoughts, or to wonder why he wasn't, he crossed the distance to her in three long strides. He needed her in his arms so badly that they ached, but he paused just the same and anchored his thumbs through his belt loops to keep from reaching for her.

"You came back," she said in a small voice.

"I did." He waited as she stared back at him, her eyes unreadable. "Is that okay?"

Her tongue darted out to dampen her lips, and his jaw tightened as he tried to ignore his body's automatic response to seeing it. Nothing could make him forget how sweet she'd tasted.

Then those beautiful lips lifted.

"Oh, hell yeah."

Tony barely registered that she'd used his same words from earlier. He reached for her, and she stepped willingly into his arms. Their lips searched for and found each other before he could even crush her to him. Her fingertips pressed into his back.

In an awkward dance, they shuffled into the apartment, neither willing to break that connection of lips, tongues and heated bodies. When the latch clicked and Kelly's behind was pressed against the door, she finally broke off the kiss and drew in a long breath. She rolled her head against the wood and snickered.

"Well, I wasn't going for laughs, but…"

She smiled. "I'm just glad I have the *least* nosy neighbors in the world."

"I like them already." Bracing his hands against the door on both sides of her head, he dipped his chin to taste her again. Gently this time. At his leisure. But she didn't seem interested in taking her time, her kisses desperate, her hands exploring with determination. When he slid his mouth to the side to gulp a breath, she moaned in protest.

He smiled against her neck before tasting that delicate skin again. "Slow down. Have mercy on an old guy, would you?"

Her head lolled to the side. "You mean like how you *slowly* waltzed in here? Anyway, there's nothing old about you. Nothing at all."

His growl surprised him. His hands slid beneath her bottom, and he hoisted her up against the door, nestling himself against her. Was he trying to prove her right? He didn't care. The only thing that made sense to him then was that a want had become a need, and he needed to be as close to Kelly as two people could ever humanly be.

This time when he broke off the kiss, she smiled up at him. "Would you like to see the rest of the apartment?"

Her hint was clear in that he'd already seen every room at her place. Except one.

"Yes, I would."

She turned away then but reached a hand back to him. He laced their fingers and let her guide him to the room with the closed door.

As Kelly flipped on the light, Tony expected to see something that resembled the rest of the apartment. A life in transition. No past to cling to. No future to wish for. Because of his assumption, the lushness of her private space surprised him. Dark wood furniture met a poufy white comforter and a mess of oversize pillows, all covered in a deep red.

But none of those things were as startling as the flow of gauzy netting that started at the ceiling and enclosed the bed on two sides. His mouth went dry.

"Is something wrong?"

"Just checking out the place. It's different in here. Another side of you."

He would have asked about the space that looked like a seductress's palace, but then her hands moved to the buttons of her blouse, the same silk that had gaped when she'd rushed to dress earlier. He forgot his questions. He crossed to her, but instead of taking over the task of undressing her, he observed the unveiling this time.

When her blouse lay open, with little hidden behind the flimsy lace beneath it, she stepped toward him and started on the buttons on his shirt. His fingers ached to caress all that beauty, but he wouldn't, not until some things were said.

"You sure you want to do this?" He asked it just as she'd released the final button, her fingertips skimming the line of his zipper just beneath his shirttails. His breath hissed through his teeth.

She chuckled as her hands moved to his hips. "Are you kidding? I'm the one undressing you."

"Then maybe you'd better ask *me*. I hear that consent is a really big deal these days."

"It always has been."

"I know."

Kelly looked up at him, probably to see if he was serious. She had to know that he was.

"So," she paused, clearing her throat, "where were we?"

"You were about to ask me…"

Her hands went up in surrender.

"Okay. Fine. Do you want to, I mean, are you in agreement, uh, are you *into* this?"

"Oh, hell yes." He grinned at the repeated words, his hands sliding to her hips.

She snaked her arms around his neck and lifted herself to fit intimately to him.

"I'm in, too."

"I can see that."

Tony dipped his head, his lips returning to their sweet spot on hers. He wasn't sure how long they'd clung together, their mouths previewing the act they would repeat with their bodies next and his hands beginning an in-depth exploration. Somehow, though, when he lifted his head again, the backs of her knees were pressed against the side of the bed.

"You need to clear all of the pretty stuff off there?"

She didn't answer at all this time. At least not with words. She grabbed the open sides of his shirt and dropped back on the bed, bringing him with her.

Caught off guard, he extended his hands to catch at least some of his weight on either side of her, but he couldn't prevent her *oomph* when he landed on top of her.

Or the sound of ripping cloth.

The rumble of her belly laugh vibrated through him.

"That didn't go as planned."

He pushed up and looked down at her. "You *had* a plan?"

"Well, a destination." She patted the mattress. "Sorry about your shirt."

"I have others. I wear a uniform, you know."

"You don't say."

He rolled his lips inward, regretting bringing up work. The last thing he needed was for her to have the good sense to change her mind.

"But you don't need a uniform now," she said.

He sighed as she snaked one arm through his and pushed his shirt off his shoulder. To be helpful, he rolled off her, shrugged out of it and yanked his undershirt over his head. Since he was standing, anyway, he unhooked his belt and dropped his dress slacks and slid back onto the bed, wearing just boxer briefs.

Her gaze on him felt like a caress. She lay on her side now, still fully clothed but with lace peeking out from her open blouse.

He swallowed. It had been a while since he'd had any in-the-sack escapades, but this felt different somehow. He wasn't sure how to take it slow when every part of him longed for immediate connection, but he would make this good for her if it killed him. And waiting much longer for it just might.

"I need two things from you right now," he said.

"What are those?"

"First, let's get all this stuff off here. I need more room to work." He reached above his head for two pillows and tossed them out the open side of the canopy. "And, second, we need you out of those clothes."

Both of his needs were quickly met, and after plenty of yanking and wiggling, the cover landed in a heap next to their clothes and the pillows.

"Is that all you want?"

Wearing only that work-appropriate pink lace bra and a surprising black net thong, she smiled up at him, her arms folded behind her head on a regular bed pillow.

"Not even close."

Kneeling next to her, he repositioned her to the center of the bed. Then lifting her foot with those bubblegum pink toes he'd noticed hours earlier, he began a luxuriating introduction to her body. Baby toes. Ankles. Back of her knees. Higher.

He hadn't even reached the taste he craved most when she lifted off the bed.

"Tony, please."

His lips slid away from her skin. "Relax. I'm not even to my best work yet."

With his fingertips tracing her lines and dancing over her curves, he took another slow visual journey over the length of her. Had he imagined anything so amazing when she'd appeared, wearing that uniform? He had, and that was the hell of it. She'd been a flashing light in front of him from the moment she'd marched into the office and onto his radar screen.

"I need you now."

Though Tony had a more extensive expedition planned—more to discover, more to cherish—her words stilled his hands. She didn't just want, hadn't just pleaded for relief from her misery. She wanted *him*.

"Can't disappoint a lady."

He stood, shucked his briefs and sat on the edge of the bed, facing away from her. He'd stopped at the pharmacy for condoms on the way over, so he pulled out the small box he'd stuffed in his back pocket.

"Oh. Right."

"I had...hoped."

She cleared her throat. "Good."

He made quick work of rolling on a condom. "Could this be more awkward?"

They both chuckled for a few seconds, but the sound stopped as he shifted to cover her. He waited for a fraction of a second until she smiled up at him.

"Seems okay now."

He claimed her mouth and brought them together at the same time. For a few seconds, he didn't move. From that first moment of ultimate intimacy, he knew he'd made a mistake. Not that he could have prevented himself from wanting Kelly. That had been as unavoidable as the collision between meteorite and Earth once the pull of gravity was involved.

Following through on that desire, that was his mistake. He could tell it by the humiliating way his insides trembled. Could she feel it, too? He had to be overreacting. He'd been with hundreds of women. Well, tens.

Still, he edged up, needing to see for himself if she recognized his uncertainty. Did it disappoint her? Kelly smiled up at him instead, as if she saw something in him. Something good. Then she lifted to him, both in lips and body. He was lost.

He moved with her, drawing her sighs into his lungs, needing to give and take with a desperation that bewildered him. He didn't want to think about it now, didn't want to take away from this moment. But a worry remained on the periphery of his thoughts: he would never be able to be with another woman without thinking of Kelly.

Chapter 14

The horny investigators were making this way too easy. The driver shook his head as he stared up at the single remaining light in Building Four. Someone might have been a night owl up there, but it was more likely that a couple of law-enforcement officers were forgoing sleep for other, more salacious pursuits.

He'd figured it was time to give the task force members a warning about sniffing too close to things that were none of their business. He hadn't expected to find two of the investigators, who were moving too close to his business of providing prurient services, tucked in for a little slap and tickle of their own.

"He couldn't get inside her building fast enough," he said into the darkness and then jerked his head to see if anyone was close enough to overhear. At least he hadn't opened the car window, though it was hotter than hell with his air-conditioning shut off.

Still, he grinned over that telltale drugstore stop. Those high-and-mighty officers thought they were so different from his clientele. They were all lusty beings in the end, right? To each his own.

Except for the corpses.

He didn't want to believe that his customer might be responsible for that unpleasantness, anyway. Even if the words from that chat-room hero had sounded enough like one of his more memorable clients to raise the hair on his arms, that didn't mean the police had evidence to connect the murder with his business. And he knew more about suspicions and proof than the average Joe.

He didn't have proof, either. The Internet was a huge place, with sites and users all over the world. Just because a participant on a chat room the FBI regularly monitored mentioned princesses and his client also jonesed for minor royalty, that didn't mean they were the same guy. Nor did one crushed crown at a murder scene confirm that either of those guys was guilty.

It didn't guarantee that one of them wasn't, either.

Would his customer be stupid enough to get himself into trouble again so soon after he'd helped him out? Didn't the guy realize that their whole relationship depended on him avoiding run-ins with the police? All he'd been expected to do was stay occupied with the ample entertainment options Soleil Enterprises provided. Had it still not been enough?

"Damn unreliable clientele!"

He slammed the heels of his hands against the steering wheel and then rubbed them together because they hurt. He shouldn't have to deal with shit like this. He offered entertainment, not a disaster-cleanup service.

But because he just might have to provide both, he zipped his dark sweatshirt over his already sweaty chest and pulled his baseball cap low over his eyes. He checked around to make sure there would be no witnesses and threw open the car door. From the trunk, he pulled out the sheathed hunting knife and a pair of dark gloves. It wouldn't do to leave any evidence on either of his stops tonight.

What if you're wrong? He refused to consider that he might be providing an unnecessary warning. Besides, his instincts told him he did have something to worry about. They'd served him well this far.

He jogged across the lot, carrying the case flat against his leg, and crouched behind the car that had been parked there no more than thirty minutes. Pausing only long enough to unsheathe the knife, he plunged it into the tire just outside the hubcap. It only could have felt better if it was a certain person's wiry neck. If he was guilty.

It was time for him to find out for sure. After his adventures tonight, he would pop in for a checkup on his friend, Cory Fox.

Kelly awoke with a start and then shifted again as realization settled in her shadowy room. Though she was in her own bed, she wasn't alone. That weight over her was an arm attached to one slumbering Tony Lazzaro.

She held her breath and lay still, but her mind refused to cooperate, bolting in a half-dozen directions at once. The images were so vivid that when she tried to blink them away in the waning darkness, they bonded with her mind's souvenirs of sweet sensations and sighs. Even now her body warmed and tingled from those memories.

She yanked the sheet up under her armpits, the futility of her effort heating her face even more. He'd already examined, touched and sampled any secrets she could hide, and she'd been delighted to return those favors.

This wasn't about morning-after discomfort alone or even armchair quarterbacking her participation with a level of enthusiasm that called for pom-poms and a megaphone. She'd weathered embarrassing next-day moments before. This was different, and not just because this was the first time she'd ever brought a man into her apartment and her own bed. What did that mean? Was she brave enough to take a chance with someone like Tony?

"Well, that's going to take some getting used to," he said.

"What?"

If only she could have kept her body from jerking again or could have prevented her voice from squeaking.

"You know, waking up with someone who rouses like she's leaping out of a moving car. Do you do that every morning?"

"It's not like that."

How was it that he'd described the way she often burst from sleep, breathless and clawing to escape? And what did it mean that she couldn't remember dreaming at all last night?

"Definitely will take a while to get used to that."

"You're exaggerating."

His chest rumbled with his chuckle. Were her odd sleeping habits something he *wanted* to become more familiar with? Strange how she could see herself regularly awakening with that muscular arm slung over her hip.

Her shoulders curled forward, but his arm only squeezed in a partial hug, his chin resting on her shoulder.

"I'm sorry to have to point this out, but you weren't watching yourself sleep."

Which meant he *had been* watching. For how long? And why? Now his thumb that had rested against her ribcage slid back and forth in the lightest of touches against the underside of her breast. The caress neither advanced nor retreated, only continued until she could think of nothing beyond that simple, repetitive motion.

"How did you sleep?" he asked. "Well, until the last few minutes?"

Sleep. It was the word and not his breath feathering over her ear then that made her shiver. She'd *slept* with Tony Lazzaro. Not just rested next to him as she had with every other guy in her relationship history. A short list and all of them brief, but she'd never slept with a single one. Until now.

"Fine," she answered honestly and shivered again.

"Are you cold? Here, let me help."

He snuggled closer and pressed his bare skin to her back, reminding her again that so much more than sleep had taken place in that bed last night. From the press of him behind her, those were activities he would welcome repeating this morning. Whether it was wise or not, she wanted those things, too. Worse than that, she was torn between wishing he would release her and begging him never to let her go.

"I'm fine. Just waking up. But it's getting late. I need to shower, or I'll never get to work on time."

"Oh. Right. That work thing."

Tony must have received the unspoken messages in her words. She would be showering alone, and she was dismissing him, whether she really wanted that or not. He slid his hand away, seeming to take care to avoid contact with sensitive flesh. A chill spread across her skin from the absence of his touch. She pulled the sheet tighter to her and forced herself to face him. She owed him that much.

As he sat on the edge of the bed and reached for his clothes on the floor, the early light through the blind slats framed the shape of him, from wide shoulders to tapered waist. It was all Kelly could do not to reach for him again. *Join me.* The words were on her tongue, ready to be spoken, but she couldn't force the air from her lungs to give them sound. She needed to think first, had to make sense of all this. The night before had been wonderful, magical, but it hadn't been *her*. She wasn't someone who trusted any man enough to allow him to sleep over at her place, and she'd certainly never let herself become unconscious in anyone's arms before. She didn't take risks like that. She couldn't start now.

Just as Tony pulled his T-shirt over his head and turned back to her, the alarm on Kelly's cell phone beeped. He handed it to her and waited for her to shut it off. Then he flipped on the lamp and grabbed his own cell that sometime in the night he must have set on the nightstand next to hers. There was something oddly comforting about the two phones at the ready in case either of them received an emergency call.

"Well, it's about that time."

He stood and reached for the last item on the table: the box of condoms he'd bought last night. Her cheeks heated again as she noted there would be two less packets inside it now.

"You know," he said, pausing to turn back to her, "we should talk about what happened between us last night. Especially with us working together."

Do we have to? She was a veteran at avoiding difficult conversations, and she would be happy to expand her expertise here. But she doubted Tony would go for it. "Can we make it later?"

"Not indefinitely later."

"Okay."

He must have accepted that because he nodded and stepped to the doorway. There, he stopped again and turned back once more. "For what it's worth, I don't regret it. I hope you don't, either."

Without waiting for her response, he left the room. His footsteps faded down the hall. When the click of her apartment door came, Kelly expected to feel relief. Her chest tightened instead. Her apartment seemed smaller and colder, its bare walls a picture of loneliness. It was as if Tony had finally brushed color over the multiple coats of eggshell paint and then washed it all away when he left.

"I regret it, all right," she whispered in the empty space.

But not for the reasons he would have expected. Like because they worked together. Or because he'd been a jerk to her in the beginning.

She threw back the covers and walked naked into the bathroom. The woman who stared back at her from the mirror had matted hair, swollen lips and smudges of left-over eyeliner. Even the pink marks near her collarbones, where his beard had abraded her skin, gave evidence of a woman who'd been well loved last night. And who just might—

No, she was not falling for Tony Lazzaro. Last night had been about sex and nothing more. Even if it had been the kind of mind-blowing sex that people wrote poems about. She'd messed up and made herself vulnerable by sleeping in his arms, but she'd always been too smart to put her heart at risk. She would be equally cautious this time. She could never let someone have control over her. Not again.

She turned on the faucet and didn't bother waiting before stepping inside the shower. The frigid water should wake her up if nothing else had. As the temperature warmed, she washed away Tony's scent.

In an hour, she would present herself in the office as if nothing had happened. As if nothing had changed. If she had to work beside him today, she would do it with aplomb.

Most of all, she wouldn't allow herself to have any more romantic thoughts about the FBI agent she should have kept her distance from in the first place. She would not fall in love with Tony Lazzaro. But she couldn't ignore the sinking feeling inside her, the one that said she already had.

Chapter 15

Not one. Not two. But all four.

Tony grabbed his head with both hands, forgetting that he held his key fob in one, so it clanked against his skull. Served him right after all the mistakes he'd made in the past twenty-four hours. More so for those he'd made in the past eight. He even deserved the four flats from whichever hooligans had been vandalizing the apartment complex overnight.

"Well, one of us will be getting to work late."

If Kelly looked down from her window then, she would know that he wouldn't be going anywhere this morning. He pulled his phone from his pocket.

As if the wham-whir-thank-you-sir he'd just received upstairs wasn't bad enough after one of the most amazing nights of his life, now he wouldn't even be able to keep his mortification a secret. At least he hadn't driven his task-force-officer rental for an overnighter and had to file a police report, which could have gotten him fired. Still, any report from this address would make his car trouble this morning suspicious. By the time he finally made it to the office, everyone there would have a good idea what he and Trooper Roberts had been up to last night.

He'd told a whopper when he'd said he didn't regret it, but it was better than admitting that he'd hoped having her once would get her out of his system. It had only made him want her more. He should've known better than to let anyone get close to him again, to risk caring. Now he would have to live with the consequences.

He tapped open the screen to dial and touched 9 then 1. But as his finger hovered over the button to dial 1 a second time, a car whizzed past him. Then another. And another. He frowned at the retreating taillights. The drivers were too bleary-eyed and attached to their coffee travel mugs to even notice him. Something wasn't right.

After he tucked his phone back in his pocket, he followed the sidewalk that edged the lot. Several other cars remained in their numbered parking places and under the carport structures. At least from where he stood, none of the other vehicles appeared to have been targeted.

What kind of vandals picked one ordinary car when they could have damaged dozens? Also, why on the targeted car had they gone to the extra effort of slashing all four tires? At first the crime had seemed random, but now he wondered.

Kelly had told him about the abduction in her distant past, but what about more recent stuff in her life? Could a jealous ex-boyfriend be stalking her? The thought of it made him want to do things that would earn him a free ride in the back seat of a patrol car, and he'd only been a one-night stand to her. Would she have told him about another danger she faced if he hadn't been in such a hurry to get her out of her clothes?

Could it have had something to do with the task force? He shook his head, ruling that out as quickly as he'd considered it. Only a select few knew who the members of the task force were. He might even have thought it was a coincidence if he hadn't learned throughout his career not to believe in those.

Because he'd also learned to trust his gut, when he pulled out his phone again, he dialed a different number. A man with a gruff voice answered.

"Do you have a flatbed tow truck you can send out this morning? Four slashed tires."

Tony's favorite mechanic laughed into the phone. "You must have really pissed somebody off."

"Maybe." He would find out who from Kelly later that morning. "But can you pick up my car or not?"

After the man took the address and gave him a time-frame, Tony climbed inside his car and rolled down the windows to wait. That only gave him more time to re-play the events of the night before. It didn't matter that her awkward dismissal this morning made it clear he wouldn't experience those touches again. His fingertips were imprinted with the satin of her hair, the smooth contours of her body. He didn't even have to conjure up the memory of her scent—wildflowers and pure femi-ninity—as it lingered on his skin. How would he ever get her out of his mind?

When Kelly raced out the front door of her building thirty minutes later, dressed in a pink blouse and navy pants, her wet hair tied up, he was tempted to ask her for a ride to work. But how could either of them have ex-plained their carpooling plan? Even though he'd decided not to file a police report, they would have a difficult time keeping this thing between them secret.

She didn't approach his car, anyway. Had he ever no-ticed her taking in her surroundings so obviously before? She appeared to note all the building- and parking-lot entrances. That was probably part of her training, but he'd been too busy checking out her assets to take note of her habit.

Kelly seemed so caught up in her thoughts that she didn't notice him or his car, though he couldn't fault her for missing his personal vehicle when she'd never seen it before. She also could have intentionally ignored him. Well, she wouldn't get the chance to do that at work. He had plenty of questions to ask her now, and no matter how awkward it was, he would insist that she answer them all.

If Tony believed in coincidences, he would have used the scene he found at home as his best example.

He pushed open his front door with a tap of his index finger. An obvious crack showed in the doorframe, the flimsy wood around the sidelight window offering no resistance to the scumbag who'd apparently come at it, foot-first. The doorknob-size hole in the closet door confirmed that his visitor had kicked his way inside.

"Could this day get any worse?"

Then he stepped inside to discover that it could. His house had been ransacked. Tables upended, lamps crushed on the floor, his leather sofa slashed, its stuffing dotting the carpet like a Michigan February snow.

A burglary? Breaking and entering? He was already leaning toward the second. Even his favorite collection of beer steins from the mantel were in a pile of broken pottery.

Like his car that had just cost him a grand for four new tires, this home invasion was all about sending him a message. Someone wanted him to know that Kelly was off-limits. He frowned at the mess that would take hours to clean up. He could have saved the guy the trouble of warning him off. Kelly might have tasted the goods, but she wasn't coming back for seconds.

Way to kick a guy when he was down.

He didn't have time for this. He was already two hours late. A shower and another cup of coffee and he would be out of there, even if the place was a disaster. He continued down the hall, checking for additional damage and mentally weighing the time loss that filing a police report would add.

Strangely, the guest room appeared untouched. The home invader had skipped his room, too. His closet door was closed. No drawers hung open. His half-full ceramic piggybank still waited for a feeding on top of his dresser, a clear sign that the suspect hadn't been there for money.

Needing that shower even more then, he stomped past the dresser on his way to the master bath. Then he saw it. A half-folded sheet of paper lay on his pillow. After putting on a pair of nitrile gloves from a box he kept in his closet, he crossed to the other side of the bed and nabbed it. As he read the words, formed with letters cut from newspaper headlines, something in his stomach dropped.

Curiosity killed the cat…and the girl.

He swallowed, his mouth suddenly dry. At least he had answers to some of his questions now. This had nothing to do with Kelly's dating history. It was all about the task force. His tires and his house had been warnings. This part was a threat, and Kelly was the target.

He shook his head, hard. He didn't care if she wanted nothing to do with him. He couldn't let anything happen to *her*.

After storing the note in a brown-paper lunch bag from the kitchen in case he needed it for evidence later, he hurried to the shower. No time to waste. He had to get to work so he could warn her. Someone thought they were asking too many questions. Or they were getting too close to a murderer.

It was more than that. How had the suspect found *them* instead of the other way around? The task force was supposed to work in secret. Information was only distributed on a need-to-know basis. How had anyone discovered their identities and addresses? Did that mean that there was a leak in the task force, or, God forbid, one of their colleagues was involved?

Killed the cat…and the girl. He shook his head to expel the words that kept replaying inside it. Whoever had left this message not only had his and Kelly's identities and addresses, but he also was aware that the two of them had been together. That person knew that he could get to Tony by threatening *her*.

This game was a different one than they'd thought they were playing in the beginning. The cat was chasing a mouse that had turned rabid. The hunters had become the hunted. He had to stop them. No matter what, he couldn't let anything happen to Kelly. He had to get to her now. Had to warn her. The rules had changed, and new lines needed to be drawn. They could trust no one on the task force. No one except each other.

Kelly's hands trembled as she stared down at the note she held. She'd waited to pull it out of her purse until she'd locked herself inside the handicap stall in the public women's restroom, where no one could see her leaning against the wall.

Particularly not Tony. She'd been dodging him ever since he'd shown up at work late, with some excuse about car trouble. How could she tell him that their night together seemed like a lifetime ago? That no matter what feelings she might have for him, she couldn't worry about them right now.

The words on that paper had changed everything.

Don't ask questions when you won't survive knowing the answers.

As she read the message again, handwritten in block print, her whole body shook. That voice from her nightmares might as well have been reading those words aloud. Her hands were so clammy she could barely hold on to the note.

Someone had not only made it inside her locked building while she slept with Tony, but the trespasser had also left a warning in her mailbox about her work on the task force. Was it from the chat rooms? BIG DADDY. It had to be him. She was more convinced than ever that he was also the man from her childhood.

Stay quiet, or I'll be back for you.

She hadn't stayed quiet. Nor had she stopped looking for answers. Now he'd returned for her, just as he'd promised. This time, he knew where she lived.

A scream built inside of her, and she bent at the waist, swallowing mouthfuls of air to keep quiet. *Stop.* She had to get control of herself. She couldn't let Tony or anyone else on the task force see her like this. Tony already knew part of the truth, and if she told him about the letter and her theories, he would feel obligated to have Special Agent Dawson remove her from the task force.

She couldn't let that happen. Closing her eyes, she wiped her sweaty forehead with her fingertips. All these years, she'd hoped for a chance to track down the man who'd stolen her best friend and her own childhood. Now that she was this close, she wouldn't let anyone else stop her from doing that. Not even the man who'd left her bed only a few hours before.

Tony would think this was about her rejecting him. She didn't want him to believe that, but if he did, he would keep his distance from her. At least then she wouldn't have to tell him the truth.

Anyway, she could handle this alone. She wasn't that little girl the creep had threatened into silence eighteen years before. Maybe the fear of him would never go away completely, but she was stronger now. Smarter. She'd had enough training to be able to take down any assailant. Even him.

Kelly crumbled the note and stuffed it back into her purse, not even caring that she'd contaminated evidence. She couldn't submit it to the lab, anyway, without risking that she would be moved from the investigation for her safety.

She stepped to the sink to wash her hands. "He said he's coming for me. Well, let him come."

Had she spoken those words aloud? She wasn't sure until someone knocked on the women's restroom door. She didn't answer, but she opened the stall and waited.

"Kelly, I know you're in there." Tony said in a stage whisper from the other side of the steel door. "I heard your voice."

She rushed to the door and yanked it open. "Are you kidding me? Are you really following me into the restroom?"

"Nothing else worked. I mean…who are you talking to?" He leaned his head in and peeked around.

She closed the door enough that he had to move or have his head pinched. "Lucky for you, it's empty. Is this the way you go about flying under the radar in a public building?"

"I checked around first. Besides, this is important."

"Fine. We'll talk about it. Later. But not here."

"Guess you only talk to yourself in there."

It was a tiny jab, brought on by hurt feelings that she couldn't do anything about right now. That didn't make her feel any less guilty about it. When she opened her mouth to apologize, he shook his head.

"There are a lot of things we need to talk about, but they'll have to wait."

"You tracked me down here to tell me that?"

Again, he shook his head. "Special Agent Dawson wants us all in the office. Now. There's been another victim."

Chapter 16

A photo of a fourteen-year-old Toledo girl stared back at Kelly from her laptop screen. The circumstances of her disappearance resembled those in the Brighton murders. Rhinestones were found near the crime scene. From a tiara? The victim even had a secret online life.

The smile in the picture remained static, but the blame appeared to intensify in those wide brown eyes. If Kelly and Tony hadn't been too distracted with each other to stop a killer sooner, maybe Harper would have been safely home with her parents. That letter in Kelly's purse, the one that probably wasn't connected to either case, couldn't matter right now. Not when another child was missing.

"You okay?"

She turned back to find Tony watching her from the cubicle doorway, his stark expression suggesting she wasn't the only one affected by the recent development. If there had been any doubt that the case involving the local girls was a federal one, now the abduction of a child, possibly over state lines, all but guaranteed it.

"Yeah. I'm fine. Do you think Harper's already dead?"

"Do you always have to use their first names?"

"Makes them real to me. They *are* real."

Tony nodded but stared at the ground. "It's already been forty-eight hours."

He didn't have to say more to make his point. Like with any abduction, each hour the victim was missing added to the grim likelihood that they wouldn't be able to recover her alive.

"If only we'd been focused on finding Sienna's and Madison's killer instead of…you know," she said.

He straightened and glanced from side to side as if to see if their conversation had been overheard. Obviously, she needed to be more careful. Here and everywhere else.

"Yes, we've been…distracted. But I still need to talk to you."

"Our focus should be on bringing Harper home safely. If it's possible. Can't we just put this conversation off for—"

"No," he said in a stern voice. "We can't."

"What's going on?"

"This is important."

This time, Kelly leaned forward in her seat to see around him. She wasn't the only one speaking as if they were alone.

"I already checked," he told her. "The others must have stepped out to get something to eat."

That made sense. They were all going to be putting in more overtime hours until they found some leads. Or, rather, *if.*

She peeked at the bottom of her laptop screen. It was well after dinnertime. That didn't matter. She couldn't have eaten, anyway. The idea of going home wasn't appealing, either.

"Then what is it?"

"You're in danger."

She swallowed. How did he know about BIG DADDY? Had she given something away? She tried to keep her expression blank, but from his lifted brow, it was clear she'd failed.

"What are you talking about?"

Rather than answering right away, he crossed his arms and continued to watch her. He probably used that same tactic when he was conducting suspect interviews. She didn't want to share anything with him, yet she was tempted to cough up everything she knew.

"What aren't *you* telling *me*?"

She pressed her spine against the chair back. "It's nothing. It's not a big deal."

"*What* isn't a big deal?"

She considered continuing to fight what was becoming a losing battle, but finally she reached down and pulled her purse from beneath the desk. Her hands trembling, she clutched the wadded-up note and handed it to him. He smoothed it out and read. When he looked up at her, he waved the paper.

"Where'd you get this?"

"Someone stuck it in my mailbox."

He flattened his palms against the sides of the cubicle doorway.

"Somebody who was inside your building."

She nodded though he hadn't posed it as a question. "Probably while you…while I—"

"While we were upstairs together," he finished for her.

She crossed her arms, wishing she could protect herself from the guilt that swallowed her. If only they hadn't been in her apartment, doing all those things with vibrant colors that had suddenly lost their sheen, then… What?

Would that have stopped BIG DADDY from finding her before she located him? Could anything stop him?

He tapped the note. "'Don't ask questions when you won't survive knowing the answers.' We shouldn't have put you out there. Like frickin' creep bait or something."

"We're making too big a deal of this. Somebody probably left that message by mistake."

"You mean that threat was intended for someone else?"

She blinked, his words jarring her from her own denials. "That's not what I—"

"Because somebody sure made the rounds last night."

"What do you mean?"

She accepted the letter he handed back to her and then set it facedown on the desk. "You know why I was late for work this morning?"

"Car trouble?" That was the message that had circulated in the office.

He shook his head. "Slashed tires. Four of them. The car had to be towed from your place."

"You were still there when I left? How did I miss that?"

"You were in a hurry. And preoccupied." His gaze lowered to the paper on her desk and then lifted again. "Because of that."

Kelly couldn't keep from trembling. BIG DADDY knew about Tony? Probably knew they'd been together. What did that mean? Would he go after him, too?

"Your tires and my note don't have to be connected. Yours was probably just kids getting into trouble."

Which of them was she trying to convince?

"Awfully coincidental," he said with a shrug. "At first, I thought it was kids, too. Then I wondered if it could have been one of your ex-boyfriends."

Was he jealous? Did she want him to be, even now, when that was the last thing she should be worried about? She couldn't sit anymore, so she pushed past him and paced up the aisle between the rows of cubicles.

"I don't have any jealous exes, if that's what you're asking. They've always been relieved to get rid of me."

"I doubt that."

Her steps slowed, but she didn't look back at him. If she did, all those feelings she'd tucked away since that morning might crawl out again.

"But then I went home, and I changed my mind."

This time, she spun to face him. "What happened?"

"Someone trashed my house."

Her breath caught as he filled her in about his front door and the damage to the rest of his house.

"And then someone left me a warning, too."

He grabbed a brown lunch bag from his desk, slid on gloves and unfolded a piece of paper from inside it. Then he held it up for her to see. The message was on different paper, and the words were cut and pasted instead of printed like on hers, but the message was the same. They'd been asking the wrong questions, and someone wanted them to stop.

"Curiosity *killed*?"

She hated that the last word came out with a squeak.

"Not just the cat, either. He seems highly motivated to keep us from taking our investigation any further."

She couldn't help it this time. She shivered visibly. "He knows where we live, Tony. Both of us. How did he find out that information?"

"There has to be a leak in the office. Otherwise, how could one of our guys have identified us, let alone found our addresses?"

Our guys. Clearly, they agreed that one of the possible suspects from the chat rooms had found them out, but only one of them had a pretty good idea about the man's identity.

"Did you file a police report about the vandalism to your car or house?"

He shook his head and then pointed to her. "About the threat?"

"I didn't, either. What would I have said? That I received a threatening note that I suspected might have come from one of the guys I met online in a joint task force investigation?"

"I see how that would have been a problem."

"How can we keep this from the rest of the task force?"

"We have to. Someone has blown our cover, and we can't afford to let him know that *we* know. We also can't go home."

"That's an unnecessary precaution." But even as she said it, she knew he was right. Deep down, she'd known it all day.

"We'll stop by both of our places, pack bags and move into a hotel tonight."

Immediately, she shook her head. They couldn't stay together. Not after last night. And not after all the discoveries that they'd made today.

His jaw tightened, and he lifted his chin. "We don't have any choice. If someone made it inside your building, he can also get into your place. The door to my house doesn't even lock now."

"I get it. It's just—"

"My note didn't say curiosity would kill the *guy*, and I wasn't the one warned that I wouldn't survive knowing the answers to *my* questions. You're in danger. Not me. There's no way in hell… I mean I can't let you put yourself at further risk just because you're embarrassed about last night."

"It's not that. It's just, well, last night was a mistake. We can't be together. We're coworkers. We should never have taken our minds off the case—"

"Just stop. Pretty soon you're going to say that it was your alter ego and not you in that bed."

"I'm not saying that."

He blew out a breath. "Then we'll worry about your relationship phobias later. Right now, we need to make sure that we both stay alive long enough to close these cases."

She opened her mouth to argue with him, but then it struck her that he'd at least acknowledged that she wasn't the only one in danger. She closed her lips. Whether she wanted to believe it or not, they were in this thing together, and they were in deep.

He frowned, two parallel lines forming between his brows.

"Don't worry. You'll get your own bed, clear across the room." He shoved his hands in the pockets of his dress pants. "And I promise never to touch you again... unless you ask me to."

Kelly nodded, pushing aside the sadness of knowing she wouldn't ask.

"I could always stay with one of my fellow troopers for a few days."

"You realize it could have been one of them who spilled the beans about our work to the wrong person, right?"

"That's not true. None of them would—"

She stopped as it became clear that if one of her friends had given away details, it would have been because she'd shared too much. She would have been the mole. He was watching her as she looked up again. She wasn't alone in recognizing that this all could come back to her.

"The truth is we don't know who told, who they shared information with or what their motive was for doing it," he said finally. "We just can't risk our lives out of some misplaced sense of loyalty."

"Sure, I'm loyal. They're my friends. They've always had my back."

He shook his head. "This is different. We've touched on something that someone really doesn't want us to know about. Something he or she is willing to kill to keep hidden."

"It doesn't make any sense. The suspect in our murder investigation should be on the run. How could he have had time to track us?"

Tony stared down at his gripped hands and then looked up again. "I don't get it, either, but that's the reason we have to keep quiet until we come up with some answers. We might have a suspect who's underground with a bunch of time and unlimited access to the Internet, or it might be something else."

"Something bigger than abductions or murders?"

"Maybe it's not about bigger crimes. Maybe it's more about who's implicated in them. But until we know for sure…"

Something acidic welled in Kelly's gut, threatening to back up into her throat. Could one of their colleagues have provided information to a wanted suspect? Or worse? Could someone they thought they knew be avoiding capture by staying close to the action?

She might have tried to defend her coworkers again, but the click of the office door unlocking drew her up short. Robert and Don were talking as they entered the office, both carrying fast-food bags and supersize soft drinks.

Tony stepped closer to Kelly and spoke in a low voice. "I'll head out now. Follow me in ten. We'll meet up in the lot by Mill Pond Park and then go together to pack our bags."

Don gestured toward them. "Have either of you left the office yet?"

"I was on my way out," Tony said. "Going to get a few hours of sleep."

"I need to finish up a few things, and I'll go, too," Kelly said.

She waved and then retreated into her cubicle, where the note was still on the desk. She tucked it back in her purse. How was she supposed to act as if everything was normal? How was she supposed to pretend that she wasn't suspicious of everyone around her?

We have met the enemy, and they are us. As a version of an old quote repeated in her thoughts, she shook, and the face that reappeared on her screen deepened the shiver. Yes, they had to find Harper before it was too late, but they could only do that if they managed to stay alive.

A few minutes later, she grabbed her purse and headed for the door. Once in the hall, she could finally breathe again. After all this was over, there would probably be hell to pay over her and Tony's choices for going rogue in the investigation, but there was no turning back. Their careers, and possibly their lives, were in each other's hands.

Chapter 17

Tony pulled his too-hot hoodie tighter around his head as he stepped in the side-entry door Kelly held open for him. She'd checked into the economy hotel at least a half hour earlier and waited in her room for his text that he'd arrived. No need for them ever to be seen together in the lobby.

Neither spoke as they took the staircase instead of the elevator to the fourth floor. Only after they were inside, and she'd bolted the door behind them, did she turn back to him.

"Sure you weren't followed?"

"Positive. I even left my car at the park and ride off Interstate 96 and took a shared ride over here like a dude having an affair."

She blinked as if his words had struck a nerve. Well, served her right. They might have spent the past two hours trying to relocate from their homes without being noticed, but that didn't mean her rejection hurt any less. He'd said they would deal with her relationship issues later. Now he had to figure out how to ignore his.

"We were sneaking around like the prey in a bad cat-and-mouse movie," he said.

"I hope we have better luck than those mice. How are you supposed to get back to work, anyway?"

"Aren't you going to drive me?" At her wide-eyed expression, he shook his head. "You'll drop me off at the park and ride, and I'll go pick up the rental. We'll worry about that tomorrow. I told the others I would get some sleep."

Her carry-on and garment bag were already on the bed nearest the door, so he dumped his single duffle on the other bed by the bathroom. She pulled out a few things that had to be underwear from the way she wadded them up to keep him from seeing them. He didn't have to remind her of the intimate items he'd already viewed. They both remembered.

"I couldn't sleep now if I tried." She tucked the first items in one of the bureau drawers.

"Ditto."

Her gaze flicked to him, but she quickly returned to her work, pulling a stack of T-shirts and shorts from the bag.

"Just how long were you planning to stay here?" he asked.

"Not long if you keep picking on me. I'll take my chances at home."

He raised his hands in surrender. "Fine. I'll knock it off."

"Good. Anyway, I can't show up at work looking like I'm living out of a suitcase. So, truce?"

"Truce."

This time she pulled a notebook and two file folders out of that massive purse of hers. "I thought we could try to come up with some theories while we're here."

"You don't happen to have a cheeseburger or two in your *Mary Poppins* bag, do you? We were rushing around so much we forgot to get food, and I can't think until I've eaten something."

"Sorry." She zipped her purse. "The hotel information guide listed several pizza-delivery places."

"Perfect."

Soon they were eating slices of pepperoni pizza on paper plates while sitting on their respective beds. Plastic pop bottles chilled in the ice bucket Kelly had filled from the machine down the hall.

"Better?" she asked.

"Almost," he said, as he polished off his second slice.

At least with one of his needs met, he might be able to bear being so close to her and sharing the same recirculated hotel air without being able to touch her.

She wiped her fingers on one of the flimsy napkins the pizza-delivery lady had provided and then opened a file folder.

"First, let's look at the two investigations. Are they really indicating a common suspect, or are we forcing the connection?"

Tony accepted the file she handed across the chasm between the beds. He opened it and spread grisly crime-scene photos in a line across the overstuffed pillows.

"Those rhinestones are a pretty unusual clue."

"Yeah, that's a different one." She held out her hand, and he passed a photo back to her. "But in the first case, in the autopsy, a few stones were found inside one of the girls' stab wounds. In Harper's case, no blood stains were found anywhere near the crime scene."

"Maybe she was just lucky…at least at first."

"Let's hope she still is."

"We have at least a cursory connection between the

two crime scenes," he began. "Now, what do we have, if anything, that connects those crimes with the letters we received? Because I don't see it."

"We're just missing something."

He grabbed the brown bag from his briefcase, donned gloves and withdrew his note again. After returning to the bed, he held the note near the line of photos but didn't set it with them.

"There's either no connection, or it's not an obvious one."

Kelly opened her purse again, this time pulling out the wadded piece of paper he recognized. She spread it out on the folded maroon coverlet that stretched over the end of her bed. Then she pulled her hands back as if she didn't want to touch it. She sat straighter, seeming more uncomfortable with this note than even the ugly photos they'd been studying.

"He can't get you here," he said automatically and then regretted it.

Her shoulders curled forward again. "I know. It's just…"

Tony waited as long as he could for her to fill in the blank before he demanded, "It's just *what*?"

She shook her head.

"There's something else, isn't there? Something you're still not telling me even after…"

He didn't say the rest, wasn't confident he could without his voice breaking. Hadn't he been humiliated enough today?

She scooted to the edge of the bed and rested her bare feet on the floor. For a long time, she said nothing as she stared at her folded hands.

"It's probably nothing. It's ridiculous, I know. It makes

me sound like I can't tell the difference between real and imagined anymore."

He couldn't bear another moment of not touching her when she appeared so distressed. He sat on the edge of the bed across from her and reached to cover her gripped hands with his.

"Why don't you tell me? I'll help you figure out if it's ridiculous."

Still, she didn't answer. His grip tightened slightly on her hands.

"It was BIG DADDY."

"What makes you so sure of that?"

"Because…because he's the same guy who took Emily."

She lowered her head onto the pile of their hands then. For a few seconds, he sat frozen as so many earlier details lined up like a bulleted presentation. Who had she been chatting with that first day when she'd lost it? BIG DADDY. Who was among those she'd been communicating with yesterday, when she'd been so upset that he'd had to drive her home? Someone using that same screen name.

Carefully, he extracted his hands from beneath her head and gently lifted her shoulders. In her wary eyes, he could almost see that child who'd been too terrified to scream and had never forgiven herself for it.

"What did that man do to you, Kelly?"

At that, she jerked her head up, as if she'd awakened from another bad dream."That's not… I already told you…it wasn't me."

"And the guy you've been talking to wasn't *him*."

She drew her brows together, not buying his words.

"You don't know that. You weren't there." She shook her head. "You can't possibly know who Emily's abductor was or where he is now. He's still out there. He's always been out there."

"What makes you think that the suspect you've been talking to now could be him?"

He lightly rubbed his hands up and down from her forearms to her wrists, but she shifted back as if she didn't want to be touched.

"You don't believe me?"

He kept his hands to himself this time, though his fingers ached to reach out again, to somehow make it better for her.

"I believe that *you* are convinced what you're saying is true."

She shook her head. "No, you're wrong. You don't know. You didn't *hear* him…"

Her words fell away as she shoved her hand back through her hair, messing up that ponytail she'd tied it in when she'd changed out of her work clothes. But she'd started, and he couldn't let her stop now, not until she'd shared the whole story.

"What did he say to you?"

She shook her head but then she spoke, anyway.

"He said, 'She's mine. Stay quiet, or I'll be back for you.'"

"That son of a bitch."

Though it sounded more like a growl than words, she didn't seem to hear him.

"But I didn't stay quiet. I went for help…as soon as I could move."

"You did the right thing. You were a child, and yet you were brave. Because of you, your friend found her way home."

Again, she shook her head, refusing to accept the free pass he offered.

"She escaped. That was the only way Emily ever made it home. He got away and never paid for his crimes."

"You haven't told me why you think BIG DADDY is the guy."

"It's his…voice."

"His voice? It wasn't something he said?"

She shook her head, frowning at him as if he was daft.

"I always told myself I would never forget it, and the moment I heard it again, I just *knew.*"

It all made sense now. She'd fallen apart the moment the guy had spoken in the voice chat. She'd thought she'd heard a ghost. Now she was convinced she had. "You know, it was a long time ago when you heard that man speak."

"I know what I heard."

"And you were probably in shock when he threatened you. From your training, you have to know that even eye-witness accounts from multiple witnesses will be glaringly different."

"It was him. I'm sure it was him. And then the note. He said he'd come and…"

"I know you *want* BIG DADDY to be him. You want to be able to stop him. But it's been how many years? Eighteen? There are nearly 900,000 registered sex offenders in the U.S. alone, and that number includes only those who've been convicted. The odds of you being able to pick a suspect that many years later, just by the sound of his voice…"

"It was him."

Her words were as strong as they'd been earlier, but her tone held questions it hadn't moments before.

"And, remember, Emily escaped. He could have targeted others, maybe even have been caught. This whole time he could have been in prison. Maybe even dead."

Though he hoped it was the last, he'd been in criminal justice long enough to know how rare it was for even convicted felons to receive the justice they deserved.

"I'm sorry, but it's unlikely that the man we spoke to and the predator who hurt your friend are the same person. BIG DADDY could be our suspect in the current case, but chances are, he wasn't the one in yours."

"You're probably right," she whispered and then buried her face in her hands.

If he was right, then why was she crying?

"Sweetheart, it's okay." This time he couldn't hold back. He stood and took her hand, pulling her into his arms.

"It's not okay. It'll never be okay."

"Why?" he whispered, though he suspected he already knew.

"Now I'll never...make it right."

Her sobs against his chest tore right through him, surely touching his core. He ached for the way she'd been hurt, mourned the answer she'd thought she'd found and the fact that the reparation she'd longed for was still out of reach. The ghost from her past would continue to haunt her.

In time, her chest stopped shaking enough for him to loosen his arms. When he pulled away, still loosely gripping her elbows, she stared back at him. Her skin was blotchy, and gray rivulets of mascara trailed down her cheeks.

She cleared her throat. "Thanks."

"Anytime," he said, though he would have given anything he owned for her never to have to cry like that again.

Without asking for permission, he shuffled over to

her bed, moved the files and her purse that remained on it and pulled back the comforter.

"Here, why don't you get inside?"

He expected an argument. She was a strong woman. She didn't need someone to put her to bed. So he blinked back his surprise when she stepped past him and slid between the sheets. As he reached to shut off the side of the lamp directed toward her bed, her hand snaked up and rested on his forearm.

"Would you mind holding me? Just until I fall asleep?"

Good thing she didn't seem to expect him to speak. He wouldn't have gotten a word past the lump in his throat. He started to climb on top of the covers, but she turned them back.

He settled in the bed behind her, slid one arm beneath her and draped the other over her.

"Thank you," she said in a sleepy voice. Earlier today, he'd been convinced he would never have her in his arms again, but here she was, so close he could feel her heartbeat against his forearm. It wasn't the way he'd hoped to hold her, but at least she'd trusted him enough to let him comfort her.

The situation was far from perfect. They still had many questions. The answers might be enough to rip apart the task force he'd chosen to leave but whose mission still meant so much to him. For now, though, they were relying on each other, and it was enough.

"Tony," she whispered.

"Yeah." He traced his fingers through the silky strands of her hair and waited.

"If not *him*, then who else could have left those warnings for you and for me?"

"We'll figure that out. Tomorrow. Rest now."

She either accepted his words, or she was too tired to

argue, as her breathing evened in sleep. He could have returned to his own bed, if he'd been able to remove his arm without awakening her, but he needed that connection as much as she'd needed him.

Tomorrow. He'd promised to find the answers so that she would sleep, but he'd meant it more than she could have known. Yes, someone was coming after them, but he would only be able to reach Kelly over Tony's dead body.

Chapter 18

A circle of aromatic cigar smoke drifted around him in his office, the flavors of honey, coffee and cedar providing fine complements to his general feeling of satisfaction.

He wouldn't even let the MIA status of one Cory Fox bother him. Sure, the guy hadn't been at his crappy apartment either time he'd checked in on him, but it wasn't difficult to find a sniveling momma's boy.

"Hope you like her new condo in Boca," he muttered.

At least that would get him out of his hair for a short while. He'd even keep the creep's secret about sneaking out of town until his probation officer caught on.

No, he wouldn't think about Fox now. Not when the proof of his own genius was right there on the laptop screen. He had *them* on the run this time. The proof came in the two vibrant circles from the tracking devices he'd placed on their personal cars. The digital map showed that both vehicles were stationary now, parked for the night two miles apart.

If Lazzaro thought he'd outsmarted anyone by leaving his car at the park and ride, he'd underestimated his adversary this time. He and his trooper girlfriend probably thought they were taking every precaution to ensure they weren't followed while moving to the no-tell motel. He didn't have proof that they were together there, but it wasn't difficult to guess.

"Nighty night, civil servants. Enjoy your tiny cocoon while you can."

He grinned as the circles of light held steady. Roberts and Lazzaro were now a team of two. They didn't know who their enemy was, nor from where the attack would come. He'd effectively divided the task force since they couldn't report the threats, particularly the slashed tires, without revealing their taboo relationship.

This was a perfect solution. Why had it taken him so long to come up with it? It was like the polar bear hunters, who suddenly found themselves the predator's prey.

Now he only had to sit back, monitor their movements through the tracking device and through the chat rooms and wait for them to make more mistakes. Their first one had been letting him capitalize on their weakness, which turned out to be each other.

He would strike when they were most vulnerable. With one tragic auto accident, he could eliminate them both and bring to light an uncomfortable affair within the task force ranks, as well. Any work the two completed together would be tainted, and any progress on the murder investigation would be lost in a cloud of suspicion.

With a contented sigh, he clicked out of the app. Tiles from several news stories appeared on his desktop, earning barely a glance from him. How could he worry about economic downturns and political unrest when the outlook for Soleil Enterprises was downright sunshiny?

But the last headline on the screen stopped him cold.

Toledo abduction could be connected to Michigan murders

"Dammit!"

He clicked on the link that supplied some of the worst journalism he'd seen in months. Michigan and Ohio agencies had refused to confirm any connection between the local murders and the Toledo abduction, but the local TV news, with its online component, had gone forward with the story anyway. It cited an unnamed source.

This couldn't be happening. He still didn't have any proof. But Fox's absence, which had seemed like a minor inconvenience moments before, had become a possible disaster. Now he would have to send his South Florida contact to Boca to observe whether the guy's mother was really housing a fugitive.

If not, he would chase Fox to hell and back if that was what it took. And if the guy's fingerprints were on this mess, he would send him to the searing flames himself.

"Anything new to report?"

Tony startled at the sound of Special Agent Dawson's voice behind him. Now that didn't look suspicious or anything. He minimized the file he'd been looking at, hoping his supervisor hadn't taken a good look at his screen before he'd spoken up. No reason for anyone in the office to know that his research subject had nothing to do with either of their current cases.

"No. Sorry, man."

He reached back with both hands to rub at the base of his neck. It was killing him after he'd spent the past two hours looking over his shoulder every few minutes. That he still believed someone in the office might be selling information to the highest bidder was only part of the reason.

"What about Golden or Strickland?" he asked to fill the awkward pause.

"No new leads. Still."

"Westerfield or Roberts?"

"Nothing."

Roberts. Just referring to Kelly by her last name seemed wrong to Tony after the night before last. Only a few days before that, he would have sworn that sex would be the most intimate thing they would ever share. He was wrong. Now having slept with Kelly in his arms and receiving the gift of her trust in him, despite the ghosts crowding her memories, that was true intimacy.

It also scared the hell out of him. He wasn't supposed to let himself have feelings like those. He'd promised he would never be that vulnerable again. Yet there he was, a realization that had kept him up all last night, while Kelly slept in her own bed. What was he doing? She'd already rejected him. When it came to women, he never learned.

Dawson cleared his throat. "Where were you? Coming up with some new theories?"

That depended on whether they were talking about their investigation or his personal life. "Something like that."

"I was saying we're well past the first forty-eight."

Tony nodded. They'd both been around cases like these long enough to know that Harper's chances were running out. *The victim's* chances, he meant. More than a few things had changed because of Kelly, even the way he referred to victims in their cases.

"I just wanted you to know that I get it," Dawson said.

Tony straightened in his seat. He'd drifted again. He

had to stay focused, at least there, while surrounded by both enemies and friends.

"Get what?"

"That it sucks your transfer hasn't happened as quickly as you were hoping."

"Right. That."

Good thing his heart rate wasn't on a monitor, or he already would have given himself away.

"I should have just signed off on your transfer when you requested it, but I thought the Brighton case would wrap quickly, and I didn't want to slow it down by—"

Tony held up his hands to interrupt him. "I understand. Really."

Dawson nodded, but then he tilted his head. "Wait. What did you think I was talking about?"

"Hell, I don't know. My eyes are bleary, my brain's turned to mush, and I still haven't come across anything solid to connect the Brighton case to the Toledo one."

"The TV news coverage was premature, but we're going to have to deal with it now. At least the local agencies are having to field the calls instead of us."

"Yeah, good thing."

"Sorry that the Toledo case has to take top priority."

Again, Tony said he understood, but Dawson's apologies seemed extreme. In fact, he couldn't remember the last time the administrative agent had said he was sorry for anything.

"It's just that if you need to make the transfer now, I can…"

"No, it's okay." Tony was careful not to blink or break eye contact. He couldn't show weakness, or Dawson would be obligated to transfer him, whether he wanted him off the investigation or not.

"I agreed to hang around to close the first case, and I always keep my word."

"Never doubted that."

"Then we're good."

There was also no way Tony would leave Kelly alone when they hadn't figured out which task-force member had betrayed them. Could it be Dawson, who was suddenly more willing to put his transfer through? It was exhausting, constantly evaluating all the task-force officers' motivations for everything they did and said.

"Is this the new spot for a coffee break?" Eric asked as he peeked over Dawson's shoulder. "And, if it is, may I join?"

At first Tony frowned, but then he leaned toward Dawson and curved his hand next to his mouth to speak conspiratorially.

"He did say 'may.'"

Eric's strangeness was the first normal thing he'd experienced in the office since he and Kelly had arrived separately that morning. Since they had to do this every day, at least it was on her way.

"Any word on the Toledo victim's computer?" Eric asked.

Dawson shook his head. "The analysts are still looking. She had several accounts and was too computer savvy to reuse a common password or similar screen name for each chat room. She was better at it than half of the suspects we arrest."

"Good thing they're not all that smart." Tony turned to Eric. "How's the activity on the Dark Web this afternoon?"

"Dark and profitable," Eric said with a frown.

That even the jocular deputy was down showed how much strain the task force was facing.

"Why would today be any different?" Tony said.

Dawson shook his head at them both. "You guys have spent too long online. Why don't you take a break?"

"You don't have to ask me twice."

Eric stepped away, waved and then jogged to his desk as if he wanted to get out before their boss rescinded the offer. Tony couldn't blame him. He wanted to get out of there, too. He would do that as soon as Dawson left him alone, so he could find out if the "Emily Nikolaidis" he'd just located in Chattanooga was Kelly's Emily.

But as Dawson backed out of the space, Kelly rushed up behind him, colliding with his back.

Tony had already hopped out of his chair by the time the other agent had turned to face her.

"Whoa, what's the hurry?" Dawson said. "You trying to beat Westerfield out of here?"

Kelly had her hands up like she'd been caught doing something she shouldn't have been, and her eyes were wide as she looked back and forth between Tony and Dawson.

"Sorry. Wait. What?"

Tony stepped closer to the other two. "Never mind him. Did you find something on one of the chats? Did you come up with a new theory to connect the crimes? Is someone trying to establish a voice chat with you?"

To each of his questions, she shook her head, but he didn't give her time to fully answer before he asked the next one.

"Let her speak, will you?" Dawson said.

Tony gestured with a circular motion of his hand for her to continue.

"It's none of those things," she said and then took a deep breath. "It's better."

"Well?" Dawson said.

"What is it?" Tony demanded.

"I just chatted with BIG DADDY. He even brought up again that he wants to get together with INVISIBLE ME. The suggestions he made on the transcript should be enough for an arrest, too."

"Are you…okay?" Though Tony hated that the words slipped out before he could stop them, he couldn't help but search her face for the information she wasn't sharing.

"Why wouldn't she be *okay*?" Dawson turned to Tony instead of the police officer.

"Yeah. Why wouldn't I be?" she said.

Maybe because she'd believed before, and possibly still did, that this was the same suspect out of her nightmares.

Tony had to shove his hands in his pockets to keep from fidgeting, but she appeared calm. Yet another change.

"What did you tell him?"

"That I thought it was time for us to meet, too."

"And when will this appointment take place?" Dawson said.

"Yeah. When?" Tony said. "We need to set up a plan to take him into custody."

"That's the thing." She paused before adding, "He wants to meet me in Brighton. Tonight."

Chapter 19

Kelly tried to keep her shoulders from trembling as she popped the rounded lid on the drink cup and grabbed a wrapped straw from the box. The row of frozen-beverage machines stretched along the back wall, the rainbow of colors and flavors swimming in front of her.

Despite the cranked air-conditioning in the convenience store, her hair felt damp beneath her ponytail, and sweat pooled between her shoulder blades. Was she a fool to believe she could pass for a teenager, even in shorts and a tank top, once the suspect came within thirty feet of her?

"Doing okay in there?"

Tony's voice coming through her earpiece made her jump.

She frowned at the convex safety mirror in the far corner and then checked the second one above the machines. From experience, she didn't count on either of the two surveillance cameras to work properly.

"Other than having no place to put my weapon, I'm peachy," she whispered into the microphone wired beneath her bra and yanked at the hem of her shorts with her free hand.

The middle-aged lady behind the cash register, who was aware a sting was underway, sneaked a peek at her. At least the slush counter wasn't packed with customers the way it was most of the time, or Kelly already would have given herself away by talking about her gun.

"Don't worry," Tony said. "We've got your back."

"That's what I was worried about."

She'd tried to make a joke, but even she couldn't manage a chuckle. It was her fault that this sting had been arranged too quickly and felt disorganized. Even the location was wrong. She should have backpedaled the moment that BIG DADDY had suggested meeting at a convenience store. It had too many windows and few places for backup officers to hide.

Had she done that? Of course not. She'd jumped at the chance to meet with one of their potential suspects and determine whether he'd been involved with the two murders and the more recent abduction. Because of her, they'd scrambled to put the operation together. Tony had worked feverishly to make sure the details were covered, even convincing the nervous store manager to let him set up his surveillance spot just inside the storage-room door.

She shuffled along the slush-freezing units, turning sideways to retain her view of the door while hoping to appear like any other customer choosing from among too many flavors. Cherry, brown cola, lemon-lime and the dreaded blue raspberry.

Again, she suppressed a shudder. Tony had said it was unlikely that BIG DADDY could be *him*. He was probably right, but that didn't make this any easier. Even if she wasn't meeting the ghost from her past, she might be facing off with a predator and a murderer.

"Anyone out there yet?"

"Not yet, but he won't think a girl who keeps talking to herself is strange or anything."

That at least shut him up for a minute on the microphone, but nothing could stop Tony's earlier comment from seeping into her thoughts again. *We can't use you as bait. I can't.* He'd whispered it to her after Special Agent Dawson had hurried to his desk to call the others together.

The look in Tony's eyes had been so startling that she couldn't bring herself to remind him that she'd served as a lure since joining the task force. She'd even been tempted to back out of the meeting. Just for him.

She couldn't think about that now. This was no time to attempt to make sense of Tony's words or his reaction to the haphazard plan, when she needed to be focused on that store entrance. A suspect could come through it at any moment.

As if she'd commanded it, the door flew open, a buzz sounding in the back room to alert the staff of a customer. Kelly took a fortifying breath and stared up into the mirror. Unless BIG DADDY was a woman in her midsixties who'd zipped a sweatshirt over her nightgown for some convenience-store shopping, this was the wrong person.

The woman grabbed a six-pack from the cooler, requested a specific brand of cigarettes when she paid at the cash register and was out the door as quickly as she'd arrived.

"Not him?"

"Her," she whispered.

"Already gone?"

"Yep."

"Take care of yourself, okay?"

"Yeah."

This time her gaze flitted to the glass front of the store. Circles of light from a pair of streetlights covered most of the tiny parking lot, but outside that area, darkness fell like a heavy drape. The other officers hidden behind that curtain were also privy to everything she and Tony said through the microphones.

Just as she couldn't allow them to hear too much when she and Tony still didn't know which team member had betrayed them, she couldn't let herself read too much into Tony's context-void words. That might tempt her to trust someone else fully with her safety, and she could never risk that.

Whether to make a point to Tony or to herself, Kelly shifted further down the line of drinks. She placed her cup under one of the nozzles and lifted the handle. The sweet-smelling liquid flowed inside, its blue color too bright under the fluorescent lights.

Still, she sank her straw through the opening at the top and sipped. Her stomach rolled, but she refused to listen to its warning. Though it was a tiny battle, she'd won it.

A few more customers came and went, even a sketchy-looking guy who wore a long coat despite the lingering humidity. None of them showed any interest in a "teenager" dawdling near the slush machines. Even the creepy guy left with a family-sized bag of chips and some salsa. The buzzing door punctuated each arrival and departure.

"He's late," she whispered.

"He'll come."

Just then, the door opened again. It was all Kelly could do not to roll her eyes at the mirror. The man who entered was probably on his way home from working too many hours at a law office if his custom-made suit and perfectly trimmed hair and beard were any indications.

Like the others, he went about his shopping on the

other side of the store. Probably picking up beer at one of the few places still open this late at night.

"Is it him?"

She bristled at the voice in her ear and would have at least made a negative sound into the mic, if she hadn't sensed that someone had approached behind her. Another peek in the mirror confirmed that she hadn't been watching closely enough. Lawyer guy stood about five feet from her, smiling benignly at the mirror.

Slowly, she spun to face him.

"Oh. Sorry. Do you need to get a drink? I have to go pay for mine."

She started in that direction, hoping her walk appeared less stiff than it felt. If he was the suspect, she couldn't afford to advance first. He needed to be the one to connect cyberspace with real life.

"Wait," he called after her.

She paused, her pulse pounding, as she turned back.

"It's you. INVISIBLE ME, right? I just knew you'd be hot."

He also couldn't tell a full-grown woman from a minor, even at such a close range. That awful blue liquid backed up in her throat, threatening to spew if he said anything more.

"Sorry. You must have me mistaken for—"

"Now don't be coy. I know it's you. I'd know that voice anywhere."

Anywhere? She'd thought the same thing herself. She'd been wrong. Though his voice was familiar from their recent chats, this man clearly wasn't the short, thick-jowled monster who'd once threatened her into silence. But none of that could matter now, even if this suspect's leer caused a shiver to skitter up her spine. She had to know if he could have been involved in Harper's disappearance, the murders or, possibly, the threats against Tony and her.

"And you're?" she asked and waited. He had to be the one to fill in the blank.

"Oh, you know, but you must just need to hear me say it again to be sure. It's me, BIG DADDY."

The door from the storage room burst open then, and, as the poor cashier ducked behind the counter, Tony emerged, his Glock trained on the suspect.

"You'll have to do a little better than that at the booking," Tony said. "They'll need your real name."

The suspect startled and then sprinted toward the door. He came up short as Eric stepped inside, his weapon drawn.

"What's your hurry, buddy? We just wanted to talk to you."

"Yeah, don't go so soon," Tony said.

Eric pointed with his free hand toward the back of the store, and, with a frown, the suspect scuffed closer to the other two again. At a nod from Tony, the deputy handcuffed the suspect and read him his Miranda warning.

"You've got this all wrong," he insisted. "There's been a mistake."

Kelly shook her head at the man, who suddenly appeared disheveled and wide-eyed. "I don't think the chat room transcripts will agree with you, BIG DADDY."

She lifted the waistband of her tank top and yanked out the microphone and recording device.

"You don't have anything on me."

"That will be up to the prosecutor. But you're going to tell us where to find Harper."

"Who the hell is Harper?"

Kelly swallowed. Of course, the guy would deny it,

even if he was involved in the abduction. Still, she hesitated as she turned back to Tony.

"You okay?" he mouthed.

His gaze dipped to the drink in her hands, and then he looked up again. Without words, he seemed to understand that it was about more than a flavor choice.

"I'm good," she whispered.

The suspect's shrill denials and pleas not to tell his wife filled the space as the other task-force officers entered the convenience store and crowded around them. When Tony finally turned away, Kelly sneaked a few deep breaths. Then she closed her lips around the straw and took a long sip of the icy blue liquid.

It didn't taste so bad after all.

This was supposed to be perfect. Why wasn't it perfect? Cory stomped through the overgrown property surrounding the cabin, barely feeling the scratches of the branches and burrs curling out to nab him as he went. He didn't care if it was misting and so hot that mosquitoes were feasting on his bare arms and legs. He had to get away from that tiny building. From the downstairs room that was becoming smaller with every breath he took.

From her.

"Why can't Harper just settle in at the castle like she was supposed to?" he spat and then shook his head so hard his neck ached.

Not Harper. *Aurora.* That was her name now, his favorite among all the princess names since it meant "sunrise." But she was no ray of sunshine like he'd expected her to be. Nor did she appreciate him treating her like a princess.

She wasn't even petite like her screen name, LITTLE BO PEEP, had suggested. She was nearly as tall as he was, and all nails and fists and kicking feet. He couldn't get anywhere close to her. Yet.

She never slept, except out of sheer exhaustion. That amazed him about her. She never stopped screaming, either, no matter how hoarse she became and no matter how many times he explained that there was no one around to hear her.

He hadn't bothered sharing with her that with his grandfather's quality soundproofing in the secret cellar, no one could have heard her, even if they were inside the house. That would have made her holler more, and he refused to give her any attention, or any of that wonderful food he'd purchased, until she behaved. She could have water. That was it.

He squeezed his eyes shut and shook his head. Maybe he shouldn't think about the room that muffled sounds, either. No reason to make himself feel claustrophobic, even outside among the trees that stretched sixty feet into the air.

If only he could go online for a chat. Just for a few minutes. Just to take the edge off. There were downsides to going off-grid. One was leaving his desktop computer behind. That meant no more chat rooms. No more videos, either, at least for a while. He'd brought his tablet, but the solar charger he'd bought with the last rent payment his mother had sent didn't work well in the rain. Even then, he would need to go into another town to use the free Wi-Fi.

He'd already found his princess, he reminded himself. He didn't need to search anymore. And whether she realized it or not yet, she belonged to him. Forever. He had plenty of time for her to come to him and to become his little Aurora.

If she didn't, there was enough space in these woods

for a cemetery. As unpleasant as it was, he would be forced to do what was necessary, again, and begin a brand-new search.

Chapter 20

Tony turned back from bolting the hotel-room door to find Kelly already flopped on the bed near the bathroom. His bed. Even in the roomy sweatshirt and leggings she'd changed into while they processed the suspect at Livingston County Jail, she looked smaller than usual. Fragile.

His whole body ached with the effort to hold himself in place rather than to rush over and pull her as close as she would let him.

How did he even have any energy left to do that? He'd thought it was tiring enough tracking suspects, who were as difficult to identify as single stars among all the constellations. That didn't compare to his exhaustion that night after he'd been forced to stay in the back, helpless, while Kelly had become the bait to catch a suspect.

"I still can't believe that after everything, BIG DADDY doesn't seem to be involved with any of the cases we've been investigating," she said, as she stared up at the popcorn ceiling finish.

"We ruled out a suspect and took a predator off the street at the same time. That's what's important."

Why did he bother lying to her? None of that mattered. At least not to him. She was safe. That was the only thing that came into clear focus in his otherwise jumbled brain. It also demonstrated what a mess he was in. How was he supposed to help recover an abducted teen and help capture a murder suspect, let alone figure out who'd sold Kelly and him out, when he could only think about protecting her?

His stomach clenched just as it had when that other man's voice had filtered through Kelly's microphone and tempted him to skip the door and break through the wall to reach her. The suspect hadn't even touched her, and Tony's hands had shaken with rage as he'd withdrawn his weapon.

Kelly rolled over to face him then, catching him still standing next to the door and staring at the hands that had betrayed him. She propped up her head with her hand.

"I should have known it wouldn't be him. Why would he still have been pursuing INVISIBLE ME when he already had…"

Her words trailed away as the truth must have dawned on her. Of course, a crafty suspect could abduct more than one victim. Especially if one of them was already dead.

"Clive Billingsley's alibis will probably hold." He paused long enough to cross to the other bed and sit on its edge. He tried not to remember how she'd slept in his arms there a few nights before. "He seems like any of the dozens of suspects we've arrested over the past few years."

His gut had also told him that this wasn't the suspect they'd been tracking. Why hadn't he told her before the meeting that it wouldn't help with the current cases?

"An accountant." She shook her head. "A clean-cut,

successful professional. Married. Father of three. He could pass under the radar."

Tony slid out of his shoes. "You mean like Ted Bundy? Appearance. Employment. Those things have nothing to do with it. Predators come from business, politics, clergy from all religions. Even from law enforcement."

"I know. That only makes it worse that I didn't immediately suspect him when I saw him."

"That's just human nature."

"Doesn't make it right."

Why was he making excuses for her? Law-enforcement officers listening to their inherent biases instead of basing their investigations on facts alone contributed to delays in apprehending serial predators.

"No, it doesn't," he said finally. "Still, even if Billingsley isn't connected to our current investigations, he wasn't some innocent bystander. The things he said on those transcripts should have made your skin crawl. The evidence obtained from his vehicle told us he was ready to carry through on his plans."

"You're right. You know, all the team members seemed to have our backs tonight. No one acted strangely or made suspicious calls."

He slid back on the bed until his head rested against the pile of pillows at the headboard. "You wouldn't expect them to be amateurs, would you?"

"I don't know what I expect. Maybe that the good guys would actually *be* the good guys."

He had to give her that. "But if one of them is involved in whatever it is, he's probably been at it for a while and has learned how to avoid discovery. This time we must have stepped too close."

"Probably." She flopped on her back again, drawing

her knees up so that her bare feet rested flat on the comforter. "It wasn't him, either, you know."

Neither needed to identify which *him* she spoke of this time. He was the guy who'd stolen much more from her than a child's belief that the world was a safe place. That man had taken her ability to trust, and Tony wasn't sure if she would ever recover from that loss.

"I'm sorry."

"You don't have to be sorry."

"I know you wanted a chance to stop him. To make things right. Even if you didn't owe anyone anything."

She kept shaking her head on the pillow, as if that would repel his words.

"Maybe I can let it go now."

He wanted to believe that. He hadn't missed the color of the drink she'd been holding in the convenience store. Did that blue slush signal a moment of conversion from self-loathing to forgiveness? That his doubts remained only bothered him more.

"I appreciate your going along with the meeting, even if you knew we were heading in the wrong direction."

"I did no such thing."

"Liar."

Kelly trapped him with her gaze. She had that right, too. He'd been lying to her about lot of things. That he hadn't believed BIG DADDY was involved in either of the current cases was just a minor one, by comparison.

"I told myself I was still searching for Harper's abductor when he invited me into the private chat. I was only being selfish. I had to know for sure that he couldn't be the suspect who took Emily."

"How do you know for sure?"

"Even in eighteen years, no adult can change his basic face structure or grow five inches taller."

"You were young when you saw the suspect. Probably quite a bit shorter, too."

He was pressing her, but he had to know that she was certain. As much as he wanted to vanquish her enemies for her, she would have to conquer this dragon all on her own.

"No memory could be that faulty. It wasn't him. You were right when you said that it couldn't be."

"Just remember that. I'm right about a lot of things."

"And humble."

"That, too."

She pushed herself up until she was sitting crisscross on the center of the bed. "Seriously, though, Sienna, Madison and Harper deserve better than to have me searching for my own answers instead of theirs."

They deserved better than having him wasting time hunting for Emily, too, but that hadn't stopped him. Not so long ago, he couldn't wait to close the case and leave the task force, and now he was finding all sorts of reasons to delay it.

She stretched her arms and blew out an audible breath.

"If only we had a better idea which direction to look. We can't just monitor the chat rooms and track down every local guy who tries to solicit."

"It's just one area of our search. Others are monitoring some of the human-trafficking sites on the Dark Web and—"

"It's not enough."

He didn't say more because she was right. It wasn't close to enough.

"There are so many possible suspects," she continued. "I CAN HELP. SUPER DUDE. TOO MUCH FUN. UNCLE JOE. Just too many. We'll never find them all. Even if we did, that doesn't mean they're involved in either case. We can't waste more time that Harper doesn't have."

Tony couldn't bring himself to remind her that it already might be too late for the girl. He couldn't bear the thought of losing another one, and Kelly wasn't ready to hear it.

"We'll find her," he heard himself telling her. Even that was a promise he shouldn't have made, though he hadn't specified whether it would be dead or alive. Too much time had already passed. If the case involved human trafficking, she might never be recovered.

"I know we will. We have to. There's something we're overlooking. We have to find it."

"It will be clearer tomorrow. We both just need to get some rest. I know I'm tired, and I spent most of my day at a desk, not being forced to dangle myself like a block of raw meat in a lion's cage. You have to be exhausted."

"That was…graphic."

He looked up at her again, realizing he'd revealed more than he'd intended. She was grinning this time. A smile that warmed him in places that had no business being warmed, especially after she'd pushed him away.

"Thanks for not saying that before I had to meet BIG DADDY. I would have been a mess. It was hard enough having to go by my apartment alone to get my *other* clothes for the meeting."

"I didn't even know you had those clothes." He blinked to push the memory of her in those shorts from his thoughts, but it would be a long time before he could forget.

"We all have those things stuffed in the back of our closets."

"What for?"

She frowned again, but her lips finally lifted. "In case we ever have to complete a sting at a convenience store."

They each took turns brushing their teeth and getting ready for bed. Tony changed into fleece shorts and a T-shirt since the room's air-conditioning unit was blowing out heated air. Kelly was still in that sweatshirt and leggings, as if she couldn't get warm enough, as she climbed under the covers of what had been his bed before.

"Good night," she said.

He flicked through the lighting options on the double lamp between them until the room was dark. But it was too quiet, the damp, heavy air suffocating. The sheet he'd pulled over him stuck to his skin, making it impossible for him to get comfortable. Finally, he had to speak up again.

"You sure you're okay?" He hoped she didn't ask him the same question, since he was anything but.

"I am," she said in a sleepy voice. "And Tony?"

"Yeah."

"Thanks. For everything."

"You're welcome."

Her words judged him and found him lacking. He'd wanted to believe he'd been a part of tonight's events only for her, but had he secretly hoped that if she reconciled her past, she could build a relationship with him?

He turned over so that he could stop watching her and wondering if she would sleep when there was no way he would be able to rest. Facing the window didn't help, the outline of the parking lot lights sneaking past the blackout curtains reminding him that they'd been watched. Followed. Warned.

Kelly had been in more danger tonight. Though that suspect was behind bars, another threat remained, one he could neither pinpoint nor dispatch. He couldn't protect her, and it was killing him.

He trained his ears on the sounds of her breathing, hoping she, at least, would get some sleep. As if there weren't enough reasons for him to be restless tonight, his newest discovery had guaranteed he wouldn't be able to close his eyes. He could admit to the darkness what he couldn't say in daylight. He'd let himself fall in love with Kelly Roberts.

Chapter 21

Kelly stood at the side of Tony's bed, careful not to wake him. He was facing away from her, the curve of his shoulder to his waist and then his hip beneath the sheet outlined in the light seeping past the blinds.

Though Tony had turned over several times in the past two hours, his breathing had finally settled in sleep. That was more than she'd managed. How could she rest when so many thoughts and feelings were bombarding her, each declaring its supremacy over the others?

She shivered though perspiration made her clothes cling to her skin. Even dressed, she'd pulled the blankets over her as if they could have shielded her from an attack coming from the inside. So much had changed in the past twelve hours, some things becoming sparklingly clear. How she felt about Tony was one of them.

That didn't make it any easier for her to take this step when she was reneging on the deal she'd made with him. Would he even still want her?

She shook her head, initiating a tremble that continued down her neck, torso and arms. But she'd already proven she was strong that night. Blue-slush strong. Taking this step would serve as more proof.

She reached for the hem of her sweatshirt, yanked it over her head and tossed it on her own bed in one fluid move. Then she unclasped her bra and lowered it into the pile. She could almost breathe now. Her leggings and panties were easier to remove, though she had to balance herself standing on one leg at a time to shed them.

Once she stood there in the dark, completely naked, the air drying some of the sweat on her skin, she hesitated. She wanted this, right? No, she *needed* this. Before she could talk herself out of it, she lifted the sheet and slid in behind him, her arm snaking over his waist.

He didn't startle awake as she probably would have had their roles been reversed, but the slight tightening of his muscles told her he was awake.

"Not okay after all?"

His voice was rough from sleep, or a shortage of it, but he kept his back to her.

"No, it's not that."

"Then what is it?"

As he rolled over to face her in the dark, Kelly's arm fell away, and his hand brushed bare skin. He did startle then and dropped on his back.

"What's going on, Kelly?"

She chuckled. The sound was strange in her ears. Forced.

"I thought it was obvious."

Her fingertips trailed down his arm, past his elbow, and settled on his hipbone. He rested his free hand on hers, preventing it from exploring.

"What I want to know is why? I mean why now?"

"Does it matter?"

"Hell yes, it matters."

She'd pulled her hand from beneath his and would have touched him again, but his words stilled her movement.

"You said we couldn't be together, and then after everything that happened tonight—"

She shook her head, wishing the movement could sweep away memories so clear from the convenience store that night. And fuzzier ones from further in the past. "I don't want to talk more about tonight."

"Well, I can't have you coming to me because you're grateful. Or, worse, because you're just trying to forget the memories that were stirred up tonight."

He leaned over to flip the lamp switch, flooding the room with unwelcome light. Then he sat up with his back against the headboard, the sheet puddled near the waistband of his shorts. The bravery she'd mustered in the shadows faltered. Maybe she wasn't ready for this. Because he appeared to have left the sheet for her, she tucked it around her as she still lay on her side, propping up her head with her hand.

"Is that what you think? That I would use you to forget?"

"Wouldn't you think that if you were me?"

"Maybe."

Had she meant forever or just until the end of the investigation when she'd pushed him away? Even she wasn't sure, so how could she expect him to know? She'd been right to say they couldn't afford to be distracted, and that had been *before* they'd discovered they were targets.

Had it been more than that all along? She could admit to herself now that being with Tony had frightened her because it had been more than just sex. Her heart had been as exposed as her body was.

"I'm sorry. Maybe I…" Kelly didn't know what else

to say. She hadn't thought her seduction plan through, hadn't considered what she would tell him if he didn't take her in his arms without asking questions.

"Now don't get me wrong. I'm interested." He shifted. "More than you can imagine. But I can't be only a way you can block out the past. Not this time."

"You aren't. Never were."

Tony rolled his head against the headboard and then stared down at his hands in his lap.

"I wasn't going to do this again. I wasn't going to be this stupid. Wasn't going to let…"

Kelly's heart thudded in her chest. Why hadn't he finished what he was saying? Didn't he want her? Unable to stop herself, she reached out to him, her fingers curling over his hands.

"What are you trying to say?" she asked him.

Though he didn't pull away, he continued to focus on their hands instead of looking up at her.

"Maybe we'd be better off if we just—"

"What? Walked away. No. That can't be better. It's not better for me. I'm hoping it's not better for you."

"Why?"

This time, he did look over, his gaze boring through, demanding answers she still wasn't sure she could give.

"You pushed me away."

She shook her head. "Not because I didn't want to be with you."

"Then why?"

"I was scared." Her words came out in a rush of air.

His eyes widened, but he didn't ask again. He continued to watch her, waiting for her to explain herself.

She cleared her throat. "You touched me that night in places I'd never been touched before."

His lips lifted slightly.

"I didn't mean it like that. It was deeper than just skin or erogenous zones."

He blinked and opened his mouth but closed it again without responding. If he did answer, he might reject her, so she rushed on before he could.

"And now the idea of living in a world where I can never touch you again seems just...empty."

His tongue darted out to dampen his lips. "Empty?"

"I don't want that life. Do you?"

His gaze lowered to her hand that gripped his so tightly now that her knuckles and the fine bones were outlined against her skin. She forced her fingers to loosen.

"I don't want to," he said without looking up.

"To?" she asked when she couldn't wait any longer.

Finally, he lifted his head, his gaze unwavering.

"I don't want to walk away."

In a rush of movement, Kelly untangled herself from the sheets and scrambled to face him in his lap. He was waiting to catch her, shifting forward so her legs could slide behind him. She was barely settled before he crushed his lips to hers, claiming them with a desperation mirroring the feelings overwhelming her.

His arms encircled her, pressing her so tightly to him with his palms that she struggled to breathe. She didn't care. When he finally dragged his lips away to trace kisses down her jaw, she gulped air.

Tony pressed his forehead to hers, his fingers tracing mesmerizing circles on her back. "Sorry 'bout that."

His chuckle rumbled from his chest against hers. As he leaned against the headboard again, his hand slid forward, bringing a tress of hair with it.

She rolled her forehead against his and drew in a few

more deep breaths before she could speak again. "Don't
ever be sorry."

"Now what?"

"You don't have *any* ideas?" She rolled her bare bottom over his clothed lap, the insistence of him beneath
her hinting he might have a few suggestions.

He drew in a slow breath between his teeth, but his
serious expression jolted her. This would be no playful
seduction, where she could hide her nervousness behind
flirtation and titillation. He deserved more.

"You have to be sure." He cleared his throat. "I *need*
you to be sure."

"I've never been more certain of anything in my life."

That must have been enough for him, as his lips covered hers again, tentatively at first, then with insistence
and, at last, with barely constrained need. She followed
him through the first two steps and took the lead on the
third. She couldn't get enough of him. His taste. His
heated, masculine scent. The roughness of his fingertips
as they glided with mastery over her skin.

She smiled at his grunt of frustration when she pulled
her mouth away to trail kisses over the firm line of his
jaw and that perfectly formed ear. Then she gripped the
sides of his T-shirt and started shimmying it up his torso.

"One of us is wearing too many clothes."

He tightened his upper arms against his sides to slow
her progress. "Too soon."

The sound of frustration came from her this time.

"Patience, sweetheart. I only want to appreciate my
gift for a while first."

"Well, when you put it that way—"

She didn't get the chance to finish what she was saying as he flipped her over in a move that would have im-
pressed wrestling coaches and kneeled above her to make

good on his promise to *appreciate*. Tony seemed to have no other agenda than to explore her body at his leisure, cherish each discovery with his hands and mouth and draw sigh upon sigh from her lungs and heart and soul.

"I need you," she breathed out when even that bliss wasn't enough.

Those words must have reached him as he sat back on his feet, his eyes hooded, a sensual smile on his lips.

"You need me, huh?"

"I do. And now, if you don't mind." Again, she reached for his shirt, grazing him beneath the hem.

He reached for the tag of his shirt and yanked it over his head. After backing off the bed, he shucked his shorts and underwear and stood there nude, confident and utterly male. He lifted the sheet to climb back in but stopped himself and stepped to the dresser. He returned with the partially filled box of condoms from the other night.

As he lay back to cover himself, she settled herself over his legs and began her own thorough exploration. He gently pressed her palms together and brought her hands to his lips.

"But I'd like to return the favor."

He kissed each pair of matched fingertips by turn. "No favor. A gift."

"Then I'd like to give you a gift of my own." She swayed her hips against him, earning another of his coveted gasps.

"Plenty of time for that." He closed his eyes and chewed the corner of his lip. "Anyway, you are my gift."

"Yes, I am."

She lifted herself above him and, her gaze never leaving his, brought them together in a gentle shift. His hands

Chapter 22

"I love you."

Tony's breath caught as Kelly's whispered words punctured the stillness in the darkened room. The silence returned, but he could only exhale in tiny puffs. She'd spoken the words. He shared her feelings, so intensely that his chest ached from squeezing so many emotions into that small space, but she'd put it out there in this room where the air was already dense and had suddenly become heavier.

Was she waiting for him to respond? To admit the truth that she already had to know?

The answer came quickly as her breathing settled into a steady rhythm of sleep. No wonder she'd sounded so drowsy. He chuckled as she startled but didn't awaken. Only a confession made in her twilight period between wakefulness and sleep.

She probably wouldn't be able to recall saying it tomorrow. Maybe she didn't even mean it. Or at least would tell herself she didn't, during her rational daylight moments. He, on the other hand, would never forget it.

From behind her, he reached around and brushed back

settled low on her hips, his fingertips pressing in, drawing her closer and closer still.

Neither spoke again as they moved together, sharing their bodies and their breaths. Kelly had no voice anyway, not with the enormity of feelings blossoming inside her.

Her heart hammered in her chest. Her skin slickened with perspiration, not entirely from the heat the two of them formed together. She wouldn't pull back this time. She wouldn't run the way she always had from anything that pried her from the comfort of numbness. Just for tonight, she would give him everything and take all. She would allow herself to be more exposed than from nakedness, more vulnerable than any threat could show.

Another kiss. Another touch. Tantalizing sensations building until she could think of nothing but Tony. About how the jagged points of her suspended development were so easily completed in him. The crest took her by surprise, rolling her in waves of delight. Tony followed her through the tumble.

Afterward, they lay together, Kelly curled into the curve of Tony's body, his arms still holding her close. She couldn't have imagined a more perfect moment. Tomorrow, outside their cocoon, she might retreat to her corner as she always did. But just for tonight, she would revel in the magic of loving Tony.

her hair from her face. Why did it have to feel like silk? Why did everything inside him still warn him of the risk of loving her, and yet she'd skimmed past his walls as effortlessly as smoke through an open window. He didn't even want to bar her access anymore.

She wiggled in his arms, scooting back against him and probably seeking only warmth. How just the brush of her could still reawaken his passion after their love-making that night, he wasn't sure. He should have been sated by now. Yet he was beginning to realize he would never get enough of her.

He snuggled closer until her hair brushed his face, the satin texture and floral scent enveloping him in a world he could have easily called home. As his eyes closed, an image of another day danced temptingly before him. In his daydream, his hands slid around her again, brushing the frothy white fabric of her nightgown as they settled on the lush roundness of her belly. She carried a child. *His* child.

His eyes popped open, and he blinked several times in the darkness. His hands, which had been rubbing a circular pattern over her flat tummy, froze against her skin. Was this a premonition? Had he gotten her pregnant, despite their careful precautions? His gaze slid to the bedside table, where even now outlines of several empty packets remained. No, that was silly. They'd been smarter than that.

Disconcerting images continued to settle around him, refusing to budge or vanish in respect for his scars. One with Kelly pressing his palm to her abdomen so he could feel his child kicking. Another with a tightly wrapped infant suckling at her breast. Still another with him coaching a team of pint-size soccer players with the pride of knowing one of those children was theirs.

He shook his head, hoping to force away those forbidden images. He'd said he didn't want children, but had he been honest? Had it been just another way to wall himself in and avoid pain? The baby-that-never-was still haunted him, no hypothetical child to him, but a son or daughter who'd been ripped away. Had he always feared the possibility of losing another child, one he'd had opportunity to know?

He smiled into the darkness and shook his head, startling her once more. He brushed her hair again to ease her back to sleep. Knowing it was a mistake to be with Kelly hadn't stopped him from wanting her. Nothing could have. A child with Kelly's eyes, hands or laugh would be like that. Even if the idea of it terrified him, he would want nothing more than to raise the child they would make together.

He was getting ahead of himself. They hadn't even defined what was between them outside of this hotel bed, and he was already decorating a nursery. Kelly would get a kick out of how their gender roles had been reversed on this one, if he ever had the guts to tell her about it.

Still, as he drew her closer against him, and she snuggled with her head in the crook of his shoulder, he released the tight hold he'd had over his dreams. He'd thought that happiness was something he would never have the chance to enjoy again. Then he'd met her. Finally, he could give himself the freedom to believe that there just might be a chance for Kelly and him.

The police report on his computer screen made gooseflesh form on his arms beneath his dress shirt's rolled-up sleeves. That only pissed him off more. Usually, he wouldn't have blinked at an arrest like that one. They were worse than a dime a dozen in his world. Maybe half a penny.

Usually, he would be thinking that someone who'd been busted for those crimes would make a great customer, later, after a good attorney arranged for him to plead guilty to a lesser charge.

This time was different.

Now he had to take time away from his business to study this arrest and other mundane developments through a more critical lens, and it was all their fault. He pounded the side of his closed fist on the keys of his laptop, which only caused the apps screen to pop open and hide the arrest record. Something else he had to deal with, and he was tired of playing fixer because a pair of law-enforcement lovebirds couldn't keep their noses out of where they didn't belong.

He opened his geotracking software and checked on the status of his two subjects. Sure enough, one car was parked again at the park and ride, while the other was back at the hotel, where they were tucked in for the night.

If only he could have ended this little game in a highway accident or hotel fire, but he wasn't an impulsive man. Like in chess, the moves required forethought and strategy.

"All in due time, my friends."

Part of that master plan required him to stay several steps ahead of those who might be moving too close. He clicked back to the police report and read again.

"The suspect, who identified himself by his screen name, BIG DADDY, also addressed the officer serving as a decoy by the name of one of the task force's online personas."

The name of both the female task-force officer and the screen name were redacted in this version, but he could fill in both blanks himself. Trooper Kelly Roberts and INVISIBLE ME. It wasn't as if the highly male task force had a plethora of choices to act as a lure. He rolled his eyes and then studied the report once more.

"Don't think even a good lawyer's going to help you out—" he paused to scroll to the top of the screen "—Mr. Clive Billingsley."

So, the destructive duo had moved beyond monitoring the chat rooms to arresting nearby suspects. Why now? Why when they were investigating two murders and an abduction? Could they have found a connection between the newest resident of Livingston County Jail and those other cases? Somehow, he didn't think so. If they had, he would have at least heard rumblings that an expedited search warrant for the guy's place had been granted.

As it was, he wouldn't even have known about the arrest if he hadn't been sipping a beer earlier at one of area law enforcement's favorite late-night haunts. It was amazing how much information someone could glean when surrounded by those who thought they weren't oversharing.

BIG DADDY… That screen name sounded familiar. Had he seen it while creeping on the boards as MR. SUNSHINE? Was that the task force's plan now? To take down local suspects, one by one, until they located one on whom they could pin those crimes? Sure, it was like a needle in a haystack, but it could work eventually if the pile of dried grass was small enough. Especially if Cory Fox was hiding inside with a bad case of hay fever.

"Where are you?"

The little weasel had yet to resurface. Even in Boca. His friend had come up with zilch while checking for a thirtysomething guest at a certain seniors-only condo complex. No activity in Fox's apartment, either. He'd vanished. Did the idiot think even the laziest probation officer in Livingston County wouldn't pick up on it eventually?

At first, he'd been able to talk himself out of the suspicion that Fox might be involved in the double murder, but his doubts had grown each day the guy remained out of touch. His disappearance was also too coincidental, given the current abduction case. If he was involved with the murders, would he have been stupid enough to strike again so soon? The answer to that question nauseated him. The guy clearly had no impulse control and not enough brains to even try. Worse than that, if he was in some of the chat rooms where the task force was baiting the hook for locals, he would be biting in no time.

"Where the hell—"

He stopped himself as a flash from a few years prior struck him. Why hadn't he thought of that before? He leaped up and rushed to his file drawer. Not the one from the four-drawer filing cabinet pressed up to the wall. Instead, he pushed away the fake rubber tree in the corner and pressed in the section of the square wall paneling where a second cabinet was hidden.

Plenty of suckers had offered him gifts for a little extra help over the years. He'd even taken a few presents, when they'd pleased him. But what was he supposed to do with what amounted to a timeshare of a crummy, deserted cabin in the woods? Keep record of it, of course. Alongside all the others. One never knew when something like that might come in handy.

Like now.

He pulled out an unlabeled file and sifted through the stack of papers until he came to a miniaturized property diagram and a few blurry photos. Nothing more remarkable than any rural central Michigan hunting cabin other than that it was on a huge wooded property that had been in Fox's family for generations.

"I've got you this time."

The words didn't ring true, even as he spoke them, but he needed to believe it was at least something. Fox might not have been the suspect at all and was probably just another of the run-of-the-mill creeps who'd made him rich.

But if he was right? That might even make for a delightful plan. He had a customer who'd drawn too much attention to himself and a few investigators who'd stepped too close to his cyberspace property. Didn't he deserve the chance to employ his version of Michigan's Castle Doctrine in these circumstances?

Maybe it would be a hard sell if his attorney tried to use it as a defense in court, but that wouldn't matter if there was no one around to tell. And a deserted location might be the perfect place for three nuisances to be quieted for good.

Chapter 23

Nothing.

Kelly propped her elbows on her desk and lowered her head into her hands as words on the chat room board continued to scroll on the screen in front of her. None of the conversations in any of the chats they'd monitored had produced even a red flag in more than forty-eight hours. In fact, she'd never seen them so dead.

She couldn't say she was surprised after the article had appeared two nights before on one of those local online newsfeeds. She clicked on the tab where she kept the article open and ground her teeth as the headline appeared on the screen again.

Local teens' deaths connected to chat room play?

The reporter probably thought she was keeping the search for Sienna and Madison alive by bringing to light details collected from the victims' neighbors rather than from police. Kelly was tempted to message her through that link at the bottom of the article and tell her she'd only been telegraphing warnings to potential suspects. They'd gotten the message, too.

As if they needed any more setbacks after her wild goose chase involving BIG DADDY. She would have thought that a bad lead was better than none, but she was wrong.

"Slow day?"

Kelly startled at the sound of Eric's voice and turned back to find him standing at her cubicle doorway.

"The slowest. How about you?"

He shook his head. "Not a thing. Same with Lazzaro, Golden and Strickland. Even the local agencies in Toledo aren't getting any new tips. The suspect who took the victim—"

"Harper, you mean?"

Eric blinked a few times and then nodded. "Whoever took…well, they've had a long time to get far from northern Ohio or do whatever they'd planned."

"We can't give up. Harper needs us not to give up."

That those were the same words she'd spoken to Tony the night before startled her. Tony had coaxed away her worries with tender lovemaking for the second consecutive night, but her misgivings had intensified in the daylight.

Eric was watching her too closely when she remembered to look back at him again. Had she given him some clue that she and Tony were far more than colleagues now, or was it something else? Could Eric have been the one who'd betrayed them? She still didn't want to believe that about any of them.

"I know this is new for you, Kelly, but we don't always win. You came in after the first two victims—"

"You mean after *Sienna and Madison* were *murdered*," she ground out. Whether or not she should be suspicious of him, she couldn't let him whitewash their identities or the truth.

"Yeah." He shifted his feet when he said it this time. "We don't even know for certain that the abductor brought, uh, Harper, to Michigan. And even if he did, they could be dipping their toes in Lake Superior by now."

"Or she could be dead. I know." Her shoulders dropped with her concession. Maybe he was just looking out for her. Maybe he didn't know any more about the threats than she did.

"I just want you to be prepared for the possibility."

"Thanks. I'm good."

It was a bald-faced lie, and he probably knew it. She was nowhere ready to accept that Harper might have faced the same fate as the other two victims. Not if Kelly could have done anything to reach the girl first. Not if she could have found answers sooner if she hadn't been spending all her time falling in love with Tony.

"Well, okay, then."

Eric turned away.

"Hey, sorry, Eric."

He turned back and brushed off her apology with a wave of his hand. "No problem. We all get on edge when the leads stop coming in. Oh, Lazzaro's on his way over. If I don't get to the coffee first, he's going to drink it all, and I'll have to make a new pot. Again."

Eric hurried away, and Tony came to her only seconds later.

"Guess I'll be making coffee," he said when he paused in the doorway.

"Looks like it. Eric said you're stuck, too."

Tony's eyes narrowed as he glanced in the direction the young officer had gone. Clearly, he hadn't ruled out any of their coworkers, and he appeared suspicious of each move they made.

"Yeah. Not even any larger-item bartering on the Dark Web."

Since *larger items* tended to indicate human trafficking, she didn't mind this time that he'd spoken in code.

"Maybe Eric's right. Maybe the Toledo suspect didn't even come to Michigan."

He shrugged. "Could be, but until we've ruled out that possibility, we investigate as if she's in our own backyard."

"I hope we're not wasting any more time."

Kelly started to say more, but her activity watch vibrated against her wrist to signal a text message on her connected personal cell. No name on the watch face. Just a phone number she didn't recognize. The message that scrolled after it had her heart trying to beat its way out of her chest.

He didn't listen!

He? It didn't say *You*? She didn't bother trying to guess who the "he" was or what message Tony had ignored. Both were obvious, and they were about to pay for not heeding a warning. She tried to release the breath she was holding, praying he wouldn't notice.

"Anything important?"

Slowly, she lifted her gaze to find him staring down at her, concern etched in the pair of vertical lines between his brows. He was trying to get a look at her watch, so she was grateful that the words had vanished as quickly as they'd appeared.

"Oh, that? It's nothing."

That she had any voice at all surprised her no less

than how effortlessly she'd lied. To this man who'd gone out of his way to help her deal with her past. This person she loved, whether she'd told him or not. She wasn't sure why she hadn't told him the truth about the text other than that the instinct to shield him had been immediate and overpowering.

The side of his mouth crinkled. "Doesn't look like 'nothing.'"

"I just don't usually get texts on my personal cell. I told you my parents and brothers aren't big communicators."

Instead of giving him time to dismantle her argument, she bent beneath her desk and pulled her phone out of her purse. After turning her office chair so she was facing him and the screen wouldn't have been visible to him, she clicked on her messages and read that one again.

She'd expected more since her watch didn't always show the whole message, but only those three threatening words showed on the screen.

"Mom just got a new phone number. She probably still thinks I'm on the afternoon shift, so she wouldn't know I'm at work now." She clicked out of her text messages and tossed the phone back in her purse.

"You never told her about the change?"

She cleared her throat. "Guess they're not the only ones with communication problems."

"Guess not."

"I probably should give her a call. You know. Catch up."

He gave her another skeptical look but then shrugged. "You want any coffee?"

She shook her head. No way could she keep that down right now.

Tony continued up the aisle, and Eric passed her cubicle again. This time he didn't stop. She scooted her chair to the entry, and after assuring herself that no one else was coming, she dug in her purse again. She nearly dropped her phone when it vibrated in her hand, a similar pulse following at her wrist, before she could even click on the message.

You didn't tell him, did you? He'll be sorry if you did.

A tremble shimmied up her arms, and she curled her shoulders forward. She should let Tony know about the message, but how could she do that? He was the one in danger this time, and she couldn't risk involving him until she knew what she was dealing with.

She swallowed and started typing.

What do you want?

I thought we were talking about what YOU want. A missing girl, perhaps?

Kelly gasped, her chest feeling like a truck was parked on it. But the texter already had her at a disadvantage. She couldn't afford to reveal her hand too quickly.

What are you talking about?

Do you want to bring the Toledo girl home alive or not?

Harper was alive? She gulped down several quick breaths, but her lungs were still starved for oxygen. She couldn't type fast enough to let him know that, of course, she wanted what he was offering. Forget worrying about showing her cards, this suspect held them all regarding Harper's safety and, possibly, Tony's as well.

The next text had no words at all, just a photo of a printed map of rural Livingston County with a star in the middle.

Come here in one hour. Alone.

I'll be there.

If you don't come alone, she dies. If you bring your FBI boyfriend, he'll die first. Then the girl. Then you.

She typed her promise to be there and set the phone on her desk, continuing to stare at the screen. If she didn't go, Harper would die. If she told Tony, he would insist on joining her. That would be like signing his death warrant.

She shot a glance to the aisle to ensure that no one was watching her and unlocked her desk drawer, sliding her weapon and holster into her purse. Then she grabbed the phone again and scrolled through the message thread. Her breath caught again as she read the first one.

He didn't listen!

No, she couldn't take the chance that the man she loved would die while trying to help her with this rescue. Or, worse yet, be killed trying to protect her. She would be a fool not to believe that someone as motivated as this suspect wouldn't make good on that threat.

She considered—for a fraction of a second—calling on some of the others for backup, but even among her state police colleagues, whom would she choose? She still didn't know which of them were friends and which were enemies.

Her purse was already on her shoulder when Tony passed her desk again, glanced over and stopped.

"Where are you going now?"

"I have to do something. Can you cover for me for a little while with Dawson?"

His gaze traveled from her purse to her face again. "Let me get my keys."

She shook her head and forced a smile. "It's not about the case. It's my mom. Something's up, and she needs me to come by the house. I won't be gone long."

"What is it? Can I help?"

"It's nothing serious. But she did ask for me. Not Bruce. Not Sam. Me. You know what a big deal that is."

That it was also an enormous lie with no chance of ever becoming the truth caused a lump to form in her throat, but it couldn't be helped. She needed Tony to accept her story, and this was the only way she could convince him she had to do this on her own.

"If there's anything I can do, call me."

The hurt in his eyes before he looked away made her throat squeeze even tighter.

"I will."

It was another lie, but what was one more? She would do whatever was necessary to keep him safe.

"I'll be back soon."

As she waved and started for the door, she tried not to think about whom she was trying to fool this time. She could be driving into an ambush, but she had no choice. She wasn't that scared little girl who'd watched as her best friend was dragged off that lime-green bike. If there was even the slightest chance that Harper was still alive, she had to reach her. If she didn't make it back, at least she'd protected the man she loved from making the same mistake.

Chapter 24

A pulsing circle filled the screen of Tony's cell phone, Kelly's photo off to the side, as it showed her car's changing location on the map. He zoomed on the circle until the streets were visible, and her movements were displayed, turn by turn. He swallowed and flipped the phone facedown on his desk.

"You can't do this," he whispered, shoving his hand back through his hair.

His reasoning had sounded almost valid the day before when he'd adjusted the settings on her phone to grant himself permission to locate her on the Companions Connect app. He'd invaded her privacy as a precaution, the same excuse he'd given himself to push past his suspicion of Dawson and request that Kelly be reassigned from the case. She was too close to it. They both knew that.

So, what was his excuse for using the app now? When had he become one of those guys who checked up on their girlfriends? Technically, she wasn't even that yet. They hadn't had *the talk*. Was his worry about the threat she'd received enough of a reason? She wouldn't think so. She was a cop. Though they'd been taking care of each other the past few days—in so many ways—she clearly could handle her own safety.

No, he wouldn't be *that guy*. He hated that guy. To decrease the temptation, he pushed the phone farther away on the desk. He would be happy for her that her mother had reached out to her instead of her brothers this time, even if he couldn't help wondering *why now* after the woman had spent a lifetime failing her daughter. He would be grateful that at least one of Kelly's broken pieces might be mended.

"Hey, Lazzaro, could you come out here for a second?" Dawson said from the open area outside his cubicle.

He popped up and hurried out. "What's up?"

Dawson clutched a file folder to his chest. "Have you seen Trooper Roberts?"

Tony shook his head. Of course, now would be the time the special agent chose to announce to Kelly that he'd removed her from the case, instead of yesterday or even this morning, when she'd first arrived.

"She'll be back soon. She said she had to run a quick errand."

"Okay. You'll just have to catch her up when she gets back. I wanted to update you all at the same time."

Only then did Tony notice the others crowding the walkway around them as if they'd all been summoned.

"What's going on?" Eric asked from several feet over.

"There's been a development," Dawson said.

"What's in there?" Tony asked, pointing to the file.

Instead of opening it, he turned to face Tony. "You've still been comparing the list of regulars in the chats from ten days ago to now, right?"

Resisting the urge to grab the papers from his superior's arms, Tony gestured with his thumb toward his desk and the pile of conversation printouts on top.

"Yeah, but there are multiple suspects who drift in and out. Some lie low after relatives discover their extracurricular activities. It might take a while before we have a complete list of those who were active ten days ago and haven't appeared since."

"Keep on doing what you're doing but see if this one rings any bells."

This time Dawson handed the folder to him and then turned back to the others. Tony opened the file and scanned the notes inside, splitting his attention between the documents and his boss.

"A mother in Florida asked the Oakland County Sheriff's Department to do a welfare check on her son, Cory Fox, age thirty-two, in New Hudson. When he didn't respond to their knocks, they entered the premises and found it mostly deserted. The guy has vanished."

"That doesn't necessarily make a connection," Eric pointed out. "A guy in his thirties disappears so he doesn't have to deal with his mother? I can name five friends who would trade places with him."

The frown Dawson gave him suggested that joke time was over.

"Any chance that he just skipped out on his mother?" Tony asked.

"There's always that chance. But it's the stuff he left behind that has local investigators reaching out to us."

"Such as?" Tony prompted, though he was already scanning the pages, searching for the answers himself.

"The desktop computer with all kinds of encrypted material and a random IP generator. The posters of animated princesses papering the closet walls."

Eric lifted a brow this time. "Okay, so the guy liked animation and might like to visit websites where he didn't want his IP address collected."

Dawson kept talking, but Tony had tuned out when he'd mentioned cartoon royalty.

"…couple of tiaras on the top shelf of the closet…more rhinestones in the carpet…was charged with receiving child pornography but convicted of a lesser charge. On probation."

"Hold on a minute."

Tony didn't bother waiting for anyone to acknowledge his comment before rushing back to his desk. He instinctively went to the stack of printouts taken prior to the Toledo girl's disappearance and started shuffling through the papers, barely acknowledging that the others were crowded in the doorway of his cubicle.

"They have to be here somewhere."

He scanned the pages, looking for conversation starters where a potential suspect tried to connect with possible underage girls by asking about their favorite animated princesses. Tony and Kelly had joked about the dude's smooth line. Just the thought of it nauseated him then.

After flipping through a few more pages, he was ready to give up, or at least tell the others to go back to their desks and let him have a few more minutes to find it. Then his gaze caught on one of the lines.

My Briar Rose trumps your little Cinder girl every time.

"I found him. It's got to be him." He pointed to the line on the transcript as the others crowded behind his desk. "FRIENDS 4-EVER."

"How can you be sure?" Dawson said. "We have suspects with all kinds of…interests."

"Here." He flicked divided sheets detailing contacts from the past ten days among his colleagues. He recognized that one of them still might be willing to hide what he found, but he didn't have time to worry about that.

"See if he's been active at all during this time. I'll look at his contacts during the three days prior to both incidents."

He hated how easy it was, how simple it should have been all along, if they'd just known what they were looking for. Even without an in-depth study, they'd already determined that FRIENDS 4-EVER had at least spoken to FUNNY GAL, Sienna's screen name, and that he'd invited her into a personal chat. The evidence connecting Cory Fox to that screen name and to Harper's disappearance was still circumstantial, but they had enough to consider him a person of interest.

Dawson rushed into Tony's cubicle without bothering to knock this time.

"I thought you said Kelly would be back soon?"

"I did." Soon was stretching too long for him, as well. What was going on with her mother? Maybe it was something serious. Maybe he should reach out to help. "I'm sure she'll be back any minute."

"We need her sooner than that," he grumbled. "Fox's mother said he might be a suicide risk. She listed several places he might have gone. One was a cabin owned by her late father. We're trying to locate the place, and we need all hands on deck."

Tony reached for his phone. "I'll call her cell."

"Don't bother. I already tried three times. It just goes to voice mail."

Every muscle in Tony's body clenched, and the hair at his nape leaped to attention. Whether Kelly would have answered for him or not, she always would have responded to her boss.

Unless she couldn't.

"Sorry, man." He couldn't have regretted more that he'd listened to her.

He had to force himself to wait until after Dawson stomped away from his desk to lunge for his phone. His fingers fumbling over the numbers, he had to enter his password twice before the screen would awaken.

Forget minding his own business. Forget worrying whether she would be furious when she found out he'd been watching her movements. Nothing else mattered until he made sure she was okay.

The tiny circle that pulsed again on the screen didn't come close to matching the pace of his heartbeat. If her mother lived in downtown Brighton, what was she doing heading west on Michigan 36 toward Hamburg? But the answer was as clear as if she'd shouted it: she'd gone rogue. He'd known this could happen when he'd asked Dawson to remove her from the case. Why hadn't he already made that change?

"Why did you let her go alone?" he whispered and then shot a look around him to ensure that no one had overheard.

Deep down, he'd known she was lying. Why hadn't he called her on it then? His shaking hands gripped the phone tighter.

Curiosity killed the cat...and the girl. The words from that note several days back sneaked into his thoughts again. His stomach clenched. Who had really sent her the message? It clearly hadn't come from her mother. Had it been from Fox? Were these crimes and the threats against Kelly and him even connected?

Questions filled his thoughts, one after another, but one elbowed its way to the front row, insisting on being heard. What had the texter said to convince her to go in alone? It was a trap. Couldn't she see that?

Checking once more if anyone was watching, he unlocked the bottom drawer of his desk. He made quick work of transferring his Glock, hip holster and extra magazines into his briefcase. He hoisted the bag on his shoulder and hurried to where Dawson was speaking to Golden.

As he stepped close, he gestured for his boss to come over to him.

"Where are you going?" Dawson said in a low tone when he reached him.

Tony lifted a shoulder and lowered it. "I might know where she is."

"Why would you know—"

Then Dawson stopped, as if he'd just figured out why Tony might have more information about the young police officer than anyone else on the task force did. They were involved. His gaze narrowed.

"We can't afford to lose you, too, right now."

Tony braced his shoulders to keep them from shaking. Of course, his boss only meant losing them both as manpower. If he only knew.

"We need everyone on the team." He held his hands wide. "Look. I know where she is, and her phone must be dead. I'll go there and bring her back. Then, at least, we'll be at full strength."

The lies came so much easier than he'd expected. Effortlessly. But he had no choice. He couldn't let whoever had been feeding task force information to the guy give him the heads-up that Tony was coming. Kelly's life might depend on his surprise arrival.

Dawson blew out an exaggerated breath. "Fine. Just get back here twenty minutes ago. We're going to need everyone, once we get the exact location of the cabin."

With a nod, Tony hurried toward the door. He had to

force himself not to run. He was lucky Dawson hadn't asked more questions he couldn't answer. Hell, he was relieved the guy hadn't asked him right then what he'd been thinking to sleep with Kelly.

His hand was on the office door when Dawson called out to him again. He turned back to find the special agent standing ten feet away.

"When this is all over, you'll both have a lot of explaining to do."

Chapter 25

Kelly checked her phone's GPS again and turned into what must have once been a driveway. With the crowded rows of trees on either side and the seedlings and weeds that had choked out most traces of gravel, she couldn't tell for sure. Her rental car crept forward, winding past fallen branches, the unsettling scent of decay creeping in through her slightly cracked window.

She inhaled through her nose and exhaled through her mouth, but it wasn't enough to relieve the tightness in her chest. As she braced her back against the car seat, she tried again. She had nothing to be afraid of there, anyway. The place was deserted. No cars. No tire tracks. Nothing.

"Harper isn't here," she spat.

She probably wasn't anywhere in a hundred miles. If anywhere at all.

Kelly shook her head to push away the thought that was no more helpful than her journey to this rotting property. Never mind Harper, no one else had been to this place in years. What had she been thinking, taking off after receiving that text? She knew better than to go in without backup. Whoever was threatening them had probably been trying to separate the team and leave them vulnerable. What kind of cop was she not to recognize that?

A structure caught her attention peeking out from the lattice of low-hanging branches. More a huge shed than a cabin, the place's wood siding had long since cracked and faded to a dull gray.

She parked, slid on her Kevlar vest and hip holster and debated about her phone. It wouldn't fit in her tiny dress pant pockets, so she left it behind as she climbed out of the car. Since she was already there, she should at least check out the place.

The crunch of sticks beneath her flimsy flats echoed around her, but at least no other sounds joined them. Even the cicadas had chosen this moment to be quiet. The building ahead gave her no reason to worry. The level of crud on the single-pane window all but guaranteed that no one would have been able to see in or out of the place in a decade.

Still, to be safe, she moved closer to try to peek inside. Only as she lifted her foot on the bare wooden porch that stretched the length of the building, something out of place caught her attention in her side vision. Something purple. She jerked her head to get a better look. A beat up, eggplant-colored minivan was parked off to the side.

A deserted old car shouldn't have surprised her in a place like this, but the black luxury car parked next to it did.

As she backed off the porch, she withdrew her weapon and pulled back the slide to load a round. There'd been more than one entrance into this property. She'd obviously chosen the wrong one. With all the mistakes she'd made that day, what was one more?

She shot a look in both directions and then started

around the side of the cabin closest to the cars. A shout and a responding shriek from the opposite side of the house brought her up short. Harper? She was alive? Not for long if that sound gave any indication.

Her ears attuned to every sound, she switched directions and jogged past the window to the other side. As carefully as she could to avoid making it squeak, she stepped up on the porch again and pressed her back to the wood near the corner. Then, with her weapon poised between her grip hand and support hand, she turned toward whatever lay on the other side.

The scene in an open area not thirty feet from the house made no sense. Not a teenage girl, but two *men* grappled on the ground. Or rather, one was trying to kill the other with repeated blows to the head, while the victim made ineffectual attempts to shield his face. He wailed every time a strike connected. Why hadn't she heard them before? Had the fight just started?

Kelly turned fully away from the house, planted her legs wide and braced arms.

"Stop! Police!"

Her legs were shaking so much she was surprised she could even stand, let alone walk, but the men kept rolling and punching, so she continued forward. She didn't have time to worry that there were two of them and one of her. She had to make this stop, or she would be witnessing a murder.

"Step back from each other. Now! Lie face down and put your hands behind your head."

One of the guys could barely wiggle out of the fetal position he'd rolled into, but the other shifted off, as if he planned to comply. Only when he should have stretched out on the dirt, he sprang up, dragged his opponent in front of his knees and pressed a handgun that hadn't been visible before to the guy's head.

"Oh, I don't think so, Trooper Roberts."

"What?"

Of course, if he'd managed to obtain her cell number and had sent that text to get her here, he knew her identity. Who was *he*? Maybe the adrenaline was messing with her senses, but something about the guy's imposing frame, salt-and-pepper hair and cockeyed wireframe glasses struck her as familiar.

She didn't recognize the frail younger guy with strawberry blond hair at all, but he probably looked different without blood all over his face and an eye that was nearly swollen shut.

"What's going on here?" she said in a stronger voice. "Where's Harper?"

The man in the power position smiled.

"Now, slow down, my friend. We're just having a little off-line party, but I can't tell you more about it until you get rid of that." He slid his gun away from the other man's head and pointed with it toward her weapon.

That barrel and the firepower behind it should have been the only things on her mind then if she had any survival instinct, so why couldn't she stop thinking that she'd heard his voice before? Hadn't she learned from the BIG DADDY fiasco that her auditory recall couldn't always be trusted? The man who'd been slumped against him jerked into a seated position. At least one of them recognized the danger.

"I meant now!" the older man barked.

"I can't do that." The other guy's life depended on it. Maybe Harper's. Certainly, her own. She held her weapon steady, refusing to tremble.

"Do you want me to splatter his brains right now?"

The younger man shrieked as the metal touched his head again.

"No. No. There's no need for that."

She swallowed as she considered her options. She had none. While pointing the barrel downward, she disconnected the clip. Then she rotated the weapon to its side, pulled back the slide and dropped the cartridge into her left hand.

"Always a good cop, following proper gun safety rules." He chuckled. "Throw it and the round in the brush. Your cell phone, too."

"I don't have it."

"Then take ten steps forward and sit on the ground."

As useless as her unloaded weapon, Kelly followed his instructions. She needed to buy time, and she had nothing to bargain with to even *rent* a delay. If only she hadn't quit carrying her second weapon in an ankle holster when she'd stopped wearing her uniform. She was defenseless.

"Now, that's better," he said once she was settled.

"Let's talk about this," she said. "You don't really want to hurt this guy, do you?"

"How do you know that I don't *really* want to tear my little friend's head off?"

She wasn't sure how to answer that, but the other guy's yelp spoke for them both.

"Well, you wanted me to come," she managed. "I'm here. Now tell me why. And tell me who you both are and where Harper is."

She couldn't think about where the girl might really be. Instead, she calculated the momentum she could gain in the short distance between them and his reaction time if she tried to overpower him.

"You don't recognize me, Trooper?"

She did. That was the worst part. Even if he hadn't answered her question about Harper, he'd keyed in on her confusion. If only she could recall where she'd seen him before.

His chuckle was slow, low and creepy enough to make a shiver play her spine like a clarinet.

"I guess I look different without my robe. And gavel."

She swallowed and blinked several times. "Judge… Stevenson?"

Why she posed it as a question, she wasn't sure. Now she couldn't imagine how she'd failed to recognize Luther Stevenson before. What did a powerful judge of the Livingston County Circuit Court have to do with the murder of two local girls or the abduction of one from out of state? And why had he been trying to kill the other guy?

"Yes, but my friends online call me MR. SUNSHINE."

"You're MR. SUNSHINE?" Some investigators they were. Though the screen name was familiar, it hadn't even made their list of possible suspects. Yet here she was.

"The name is a play on Soleil Enterprises. You know. *Sun.* That's my highly successful online business venture. More profitable than any job on the bench."

"You mean all of this is about a business?"

"Well, not *all* of it." He glanced at the man next to him and then looked over her shoulder. "Where's Special Agent Lazzaro? You were supposed to bring him with you."

"But you said—" She stopped herself because it was so obvious what he'd expected. *If you bring your FBI boyfriend, he'll die first.* She was a cop. Even if she'd agreed to come alone, he'd known she would bring Tony. It would have been the only smart thing for her to do.

Stevenson had tested her emotions against her training, and she'd failed that test.

"How do you know he isn't on his way right now?" She shouldn't have bothered lying any more than she should have tried saying that she and Tony weren't together. No way would Stevenson ever believe her.

"Oh, I know."

He also had to be aware that if any others were coming to her aid, they would already have arrived by now.

"Don't worry. I'll come up with a plan B," he added.

If only she had one.

"Are you...could you be...INVISIBLE ME?"

Next to Stevenson, the injured man had perked up again though a powerful hand still rested on his shoulder. He was studying her with his good eye, while she had both of hers focused on him. How did he know her? How did he know her screen name? At first, he'd appeared to be Stevenson's victim, but if he knew about INVISIBLE ME, he was somehow involved, too.

"Good guess, Cory?" Stevenson answered for Kelly as he transferred the gun from his dominant hand to the other. "Too bad you couldn't put it together earlier that the trooper here carried a gun. And would never wear a crown."

A *crown*? Something clicked in her memory, but it kept misfiring instead of offering answers.

Then, as quick as a shot, Stevenson grabbed the smaller man's arm, twisted it behind him and then pushed it even higher, using the gun barrel for leverage.

"Stop!" she called out too late.

A sickening snap fractured the silence. His captive cried out like a wounded animal and then collapsed into a heap, whimpering.

"Why did you do that?" She was surprised that she

was able to make any sound at all as tightly as the vise around her lungs squeezed them. This was what Stevenson did to people who crossed him. If she'd had any doubts that at least two of them were going to die today, those were gone.

"Oh, that's right, Trooper. I was being rude. You don't know our friend. Please allow me to introduce Cory Fox. Like you and I, we met in court. Only he was in the defendant's chair."

"Defendant?"

"You probably called him FRIENDS 4-EVER."

As dozens of conversations replayed in her thoughts, acid scrambled up from her stomach. FRIENDS 4-EVER had made the suspect list. Sure, he was the guy who talked about princesses all the time. What had been found at the murder scene? Tiaras. How had they missed it? If she hadn't been so preoccupied with tracking BIG DADDY, would that screen name have been moved to the top?

Fox had managed to sit up then and was cradling his limp arm against his body. He shrieked as Stevenson pressed the gun barrel into his elbow.

"You said I wouldn't want to hurt this guy. Let's see how you feel about it now that you've guessed what he's done."

"Harper?" The word slipped from her lips in a squeak.

"Why don't you ask him about the two girls first?"

Bile backed up in her throat.

"Sienna and Madison? What do you know about them?" she demanded of the man rolling on the ground. "Was it you?"

She ground out the words in the last question. It was several seconds before Fox answered in a whine.

"It was an accident."

"You *accidentally* murdered two girls?"

He was shaking his head hard. "No. That's not right. It was their fault. They came together. There shouldn't have been two. And FUNNY GAL, she was…old."

"You sick mother—" She managed to stop herself before saying what he really was, but just barely. Though this wasn't the way she was trained to question a suspect, she didn't care. This case was too personal for her. It always had been.

"You see?"

Stevenson was grinning when she lifted her gaze to meet his again. "You want to hurt him, too. He was one of my best clients at my company, at least for a while."

"Clients?"

"Soleil provides a specialized form of entertainment to grateful customers."

"Pornography? Human trafficking? On the Dark Web?" She waited for his confirmation though she already knew she was right.

"I'm just a businessman providing a service. Light sentences equal a built-in audience of grateful and *loyal* customers. A beautiful business model."

Greed. That was what this whole mess—well, at least the part involving threats against Tony and her—had been about. Not right and wrong. Not human lives or even common decency. Just money.

"You're as sick as he is."

"No. I'm just rich."

"Come on, Judge," Fox called from the ground. "Please don't revoke my probation. I've learned my lesson."

Kelly could only stare at him. How could the guy be worried about his probation? Didn't he see the gun? Did he believe that his broken arm was the only punishment he would receive for murder? Or that the judge would let him go after he'd risked his business? Just how deep had Fox fallen into the well of his fantasy world?

"You know it's not that simple," Stevenson said.

"I'll say I fell when the doctors reset my arm. I promise. Just let me go, and I'll—"

"I can't do that, Cory."

"But I promise I'll stay out of the chat rooms. For real this time."

Instead of answering, Stevenson jammed the gun barrel into Fox's elbow again, causing him to scream and writhe on the ground.

Kelly cleared her throat, reaching inside for calm she didn't have. "This…situation…can't be good for business."

She hated using sanitized words for repulsive crimes, but she had to use terms a sociopath with no sense of empathy would understand.

"Just like your investigation isn't good for my business, so I needed to shut it down." He shook his head, smiling. "I was right about you, Trooper. Beautiful *and* smart. Well, except for coming here alone. That was stupid. Still, it's hard to blame Lazzaro for throwing his career away to tap all that."

She shivered visibly then; she couldn't help it. But she couldn't think about Tony now. Couldn't worry that she'd never get a chance to say goodbye to the man she loved enough to make this horrible mistake. Her time was running out, and she had to focus on what she came here to do.

"Tell me where Harper is."

She watched Fox as she said it, but Stevenson answered for him.

"How do you know Cory even has her? Or *still* has

her, anyway. Maybe you shouldn't ask questions when you can't survive knowing the answers."

He must have expected her to recoil when he said those words, so close to the ones he'd written on that note stuffed in her mailbox, but she refused to give him the satisfaction. She straightened her shoulders and planted her hands on her thighs.

"You said she was alive."

"No, I asked if you wanted to *bring her home* alive. I never said you would. Big difference."

The judge was right about that. He'd made no such promise. She'd thrown herself out there as target practice for nothing. If she had to die now alongside a worthless human being like Fox, she would find out where he'd hidden Harper's body first. She would figure out a way to leave clues about the location for the task force when they came for her. If they ever came.

"I still need to know where she is."

"Sorry. I can't help you. And even if I could, I still wouldn't."

Impotent fury flooded her veins, and her hands fisted, though her target would gun her down before she ever reached him. It wouldn't serve his purposes for the girl to be found, so he would never tell her what he knew. If he felt anything about that, it didn't show as he withdrew his phone from his pocket. With the adept skill of a teenager, he typed something with only one thumb, still holding the gun in his other hand.

"Harper was no princess!"

Kelly jerked her head to look at Fox, whose outburst didn't appear to be directed at her. He'd sat up again, and his eyes had taken on a faraway look. Stevenson was staring down at him as well, his jaw tight.

Was? Had he just given confirmation that the girl was

dead? She could barely constrain herself from rushing over to him and shaking the rest of the information out of him.

"She isn't my Aurora, either," Fox continued in his conversation with himself. "She was just LITTLE BO PEEP. That's all she was."

He'd referred to the teen three times in the past tense, but one time he'd used the present. Was she dead or alive? And she didn't know what the reference to "Aurora" was about, but LITTLE BO PEEP was familiar to her. It was Harper's screen name, kept out of the media but added to their investigation report a few days before. She now had proof that Fox had at least taken Harper.

"Where is she, Cory?" She used her gentlest voice, the one she tried during suspect interviews when she hoped to get a confession. She had to this time. Their time was running out.

"Just tell us where you put her. It'll be okay. She just wasn't a…princess."

The last she had to force out, but her words sounded strangely measured in her ears. Fox met her gaze as if he'd only now realized he wasn't in the conversation alone. Did he believe she understood some part of his delusion?

"She's—"

"Sorry, buddy, but you're too much of a liability. Soleil can't have more scrutiny. Or any more bodies. At least any that can be found."

Before Kelly recognized what Stevenson had planned, he returned the gun to his captive's temple and fired. Fox's brain matter splattered over the grass and onto nearby trees, and his body collapsed in a heap for the last time. Whatever response he'd been giving, whether a true answer or just another riddle, died on the ground with him.

"No!"

Kelly leaped to her feet and rushed at Stevenson with an adrenaline that seemed to come from somewhere outside of her. Everything around them disappeared, leaving only his face. His lips moved, and his voice registered, but his words were like white noise. A message intended for someone else.

"You killed him!"

In what felt like a slow-motion sequence, he aimed and fired.

Her arm stung, at first in those tingles, like a foot that had fallen asleep. But as she kept coming toward him, while covering her arm with her hand, blood seeping between her fingers, dozens of needles seemed to be puncturing her skin in unison.

"Stop or I'll shoot again!"

For some reason, his words penetrated this time. But by the time she froze, she was close enough that his gun brushed her chest. Fox's body lay not five feet away, a dark red puddle forming around what was left of his head.

Stevenson pressed the barrel against her sternum, drawing her attention back to him.

"Now, look what you made me do. I had no intention of hurting you. At least not yet. Now get back on the ground. Over there."

He pointed to a spot farther from the body. She shuffled over and lowered herself awkwardly. Even if she'd ever had a chance of overpowering him, that was gone now that she only had the use of one arm.

"Why would you kill him?"

"How can you even ask me why?" he said when she was seated. "You know you wanted to do it, too. You should just be grateful that I relieved the earth of a freak like him."

She gritted her teeth so hard her jaw ached. "He knew where to find her body. And I know it probably isn't true, but what if she's alive? Now we'll never find her."

"That's unfortunate, but we can't have more loose ends. It's just business. You understand."

"No, I don't understand."

"That's why you're the one with skin blown off your arm, and I'm the one holding the gun."

As she shifted her shoulder, the needle pricks she'd experienced before transformed into an almost unbearable fire. She lifted her hand away briefly and spread her fingers, congealed blood forming sticky weblike shapes between them.

"It's just a surface wound. You'll be fine. For now."

Her gaze lowered to her hand, still pressed to her injured arm. Then she turned back to him and lifted her chin.

"Why didn't you just kill me?"

"In due time, Trooper. I'm waiting for your boyfriend to get here to witness it. Then, if he cares about you at all, and I'm thinking he does, he'll be ready to die right along with you."

Kelly shook her head, refusing to believe that she could lead Tony into this trap. From the drawstring backpack he carried, Stevenson produced several nylon ties. Because it was too difficult to secure her injured arm behind her, he cuffed her wrists together in front of her.

"Can't have you helping him out when he gets here."

"He's not coming. No one is. You were right. I'm a lousy cop. I came here without backup."

"That's where you're wrong."

He showed her his recent text messages. There was

no name of the recipient at the top, but she recognized the number. Tony. Like in that message to her, the first text only featured a map. The second was just part of a message she recognized, and one Tony would find familiar as well.

Curiosity killed the cat...

Then he scrolled to the last words the man she loved would read about her before he had the chance to watch her die.

Come alone or INVISIBLE ME will vanish altogether.

Chapter 26

Tony parked his car a few hundred feet from the purple van and the black car. Sure, the map the texter had sent him showed the drive on the opposite side of the property, five acres over, but since the email he'd just received showed the same plot of land had two entrances, he opted for the element of surprise.

If Cory Fox was holding Kelly, the guy would have nothing to lose. This might be their only chance to make it out alive.

He paused to send a text to Dawson, forwarding both maps.

Kelly's here. I'm going in. Send backup. Sorry.

Because an immediate return message would come with an order for him to wait for backup, he silenced the phone and stuffed it in his pocket. He couldn't wait. Kelly might be out of time. He pulled on his FBI Kevlar vest, tightened the straps and buckled his hip holster. When he was finished, he readied his weapon and quietly opened the door.

He made his way along the perimeter of the house, pausing every few feet to listen for voices. The eerily familiar scent of a discharged weapon filled his nostrils, but he had to be imagining that. The silence amplified the sound of each step. He might as well have announced his arrival with a fireworks display.

When he reached the end of the building, he pressed his back to the wall and leaned around to get a peek. His breath hitched. Kelly sat on the ground, bleeding. A stocky older guy held a pistol to her head. How could he be at the same time desperate to gather her in his arms and furious enough to shake her for taking such a stupid risk? Without him.

He shifted back out of sight, swallowing the fear that he would never have the chance to do either of those things again. But as he prepared himself to engage with the suspect, he had the disconcerting sense that he'd been caught. The shout coming from around the corner confirmed it.

"Come out, come out, Special Agent Lazzaro. We've been waiting for you."

He slowly spun and stepped out from behind the building, planting his feet in a wide stance and aiming his weapon at the suspect, not thirty feet away. One he could have easily picked out in a crowded courtroom, let alone a regular police lineup.

"Judge Stevenson? What the hell?"

"At least one of you has a good memory. The trooper here didn't even recognize me at first."

"Maybe that's because she hasn't testified in your court as often as I have." He'd never been a fan of the minimum-sentence judge, but this he never could have predicted.

"She remembered eventually."

Tony longed to smack the smile off the judge's face.

Kelly looked like she'd been crying, her red-rimmed eyes contrasting with her unnaturally pale skin. Her hands were bound in front of her, and blood was congealing on her bare arm and plastering the short sleeve of her blouse to her skin. It was probably a surface wound, but he had to force himself to stand still rather than to rush to her and make sure.

As Stevenson combed his weapon through Kelly's hair in almost a caress, Tony's hands twitched against the metal of his Glock. Could he get off a shot without risking her life?

"But unless you arrived here in an Indy car, you were already on your way here when you received my text. Your girlfriend must have given you a heads-up after all."

"No. She didn't."

Stevenson raised one of those bushy eyebrows behind his crooked glasses. "Then how did you find out?"

"From the rest of the task force. They're all coming after you."

Tony considered for a second. Maybe it was better that the judge didn't believe him that the cavalry was on its way. Before he could backtrack on what he'd said before, Kelly shook her head, her eyes pleading.

"Run, Tony. You have to find Harper. He's already said that both of us are going to—"

The old man whacked the gun barrel against her open wound on her arm, her bound hands jerking as she was unable to shield the bloody mess. Her wail nearly dropped Tony to his knees. He didn't need her to complete her warning, anyway. The judge's weapon gave him a powerful hint of what he had planned.

Over his dead body. Literally.

Kelly had kept the suspect talking long enough for him

to arrive, but there was nothing to prevent him from ending them now. Nothing except Stevenson's widely known ego. He had to keep him talking about his crimes long enough for backup to arrive.

"You still haven't said what's going on here. And where's Cory Fox?"

Neither answered, but he followed their gazes to a spot just outside the woods. A body lay crumpled on the ground, one side of the head blown away.

Puzzle pieces shifted in his thoughts. He tested them for shape and size, for tabs and slots, turning and adjusting them until they fit into place. He didn't need all the answers. Just enough for now.

"Fox, I presume."

"I always knew you were a smart guy, Special Agent."

"And he was bad for business," Tony said. "Just like Kelly and me."

He didn't pose it as a question. There'd been so many hints of a larger local operation. Now, probably too late, he could trace those suspicions back to one common denominator: the judge who presided over so many similar cases.

"What did the notes say, Judge?" he continued. "'Don't ask questions' and 'Curiosity killed…' You had to protect your online business. You couldn't let anyone mess that up."

Stevenson smiled. "You have all these theories, Special Agent, but you're also smart enough to know that I can't let you keep that gun. Or do we need to end this right now?"

"I guess we're in no hurry." In fact, the suspect's threat gave him hope that they'd be able to stall a while longer. Stevenson still wanted to brag about his accomplishments, and Tony was happy to be part of his audience.

"Don't give it up, Tony," Kelly pleaded. "You can still…"

Tony shook his head when the judge raised the hand holding his weapon above her again.

"I'll drop it, but only if you don't hit her again."

"You're so cute. Look at you, making demands when you don't hold any of the cards."

He shifted the weapon slightly just the same. Then, and only then, Tony released the magazine, unloaded the round and tossed the weapon in a patch of trees in front of the house.

"Ankle holster."

"I don't have it." He lifted both pant legs to show him.

"Guess you weren't as prepared as you thought."

Tony gritted his teeth, forcing himself not to say something that would tempt the suspect to fire sooner. No matter what she'd done, Kelly needed him to keep his cool now.

"Phone, too."

Tony pulled it from his front slacks pocket and tossed it in the same direction he'd thrown the gun. He grimaced when it hit one of the trees and made a glass-cracking sound.

"You won't be needing that, anyway."

The judge chuckled in that same grating way he'd always done when Tony had been on the witness stand in his court. Tony followed Stevenson's instructions to lie on the ground and put his hands behind his head. He'd said it would be the same as Tony did in all his arrests, but Tony *never* forgot to cuff a suspect as Stevenson neglected to do.

"Uncomfortable, isn't it? Don't get any ideas about playing hero. It won't be as sexy as it is in the movies.

She'll just get to watch you die first instead of the other way around."

As Tony arched his back to lift his head, he bit his lip to keep from calling out. He lowered his head again but tilted it so he could still see them both. That was why Stevenson had held her until he'd arrived. He planned to force him to watch the woman he loved die. After that, he would be simple to kill. He might even beg him to pull the trigger.

"You two made this so easy."

Kelly asked the question before Tony could.

"How did we do that?"

She was trying to keep him talking, too, but she wasn't looking at him anymore. Stevenson was too caught up in his story to realize he was losing part of his audience.

"Oh, not at first, when you made me follow you both and then put GPS trackers on your personal cars, so I could plan your little accident."

"Just the personal ones? Not the rentals?"

Kelly looked in the direction he assumed hers was parked, then back the way he'd come.

"I already knew where you were at work." He pulled his cell from his pocket. "A burner. Besides, all the good electronics are at home. The signal's shoddy here, anyway."

Not weak enough that Tony and Kelly had failed to receive his texts. Tony could only hope that the one he'd sent to Dawson had reached him.

"I loved how much work you two put in trying not to be discovered, by the way. The park and ride. Hotel. You did *try*, anyway."

Tony managed to stay still, but Kelly startled over the revelations and then winced while staring down at her arm.

Stevenson was grinning now as if he was just warming up to his story.

"But now? This is great. You're both here. With the boy over there." He indicated Fox's body with a tilt of his head. "This place is perfect for a cemetery, though I'm afraid you won't have well-tended graves. Just dust-to-dust like the rest of the wildlife out here. In fact, the animals will probably help. Isn't that wonderful?"

Kelly straightened her shoulders and then blinked several times as if fighting tears again as she drew her tethered hands closer to her body.

"Are you telling me you think no one will miss us? That the rest of the task force won't be even a little interested in hunting for two team members who just vanished?"

"They might, but who's going to tell them where to look? I know I won't."

She opened her mouth as if to challenge him again but finally closed it.

"You see, that's the genius part." Stevenson held his hands wide. "You two have been keeping secrets from the rest of the task force, and the photos I'll send will prove that. Oh, yes, I have pictures. Steamy ones. I'll send them, old school, through the mail, so they won't be easily traced. Once these little gems come to light, every case the task-force lovers have investigated will be scrutinized."

Stevenson gestured toward Fox's body. "Including the one about a murder suspect who appears to have skipped town. In the end, no one will care if two police lovebirds seem to have taken off together, as well."

Kelly finally turned back to Stevenson. "You won't get away with this."

"Of course, I will. Just like my empire flew under the

radar for years. If not for a loser who took the game too far, only my friends on the Dark Web would ever have known that Soleil Enterprises existed."

The problem was that Stevenson was probably right. The task force could have searched for years and still never tied him to the random suspects whose depraved needs he served. Even if Tony had longed to transfer from the department, the thought of leaving this way and having the convictions he'd helped to secure brought into question made it tragic.

"The death of those girls was unfortunate, but they were collateral damage in an otherwise successful business model. Just like the two of you will be."

At Stevenson's words, Kelly straightened slightly, her chin lifted. Something about her move struck Tony as different, less submissive. His heart thudded where he'd pressed it to the ground. She only needed to hold on a little longer—at least he hoped it wouldn't be too long— but he sensed she was tired of waiting.

"And what about Harper?"

Her words were too low and measured.

Stevenson brushed away her comment with a wave of his hand. "Cory didn't tell me for sure, but I have to say, if she isn't dead already, she soon will be. That's probably best. Just one more loose end, all neatly tied and tucked away for good."

"You did this to them!"

Kelly came up off the ground in a fluid move and lunged for Stevenson, her wound forgotten in a rage-swallowed haze. Though she caught him off guard, her nails sinking into the flesh of his forearm, he curved the gun up over her with the reflexes of a much younger man and brought the grip down on her head in a sickening thud.

She seemed to fall in slow motion, as muscles, bones and determination collapsed in a downward slide. Blood colored her hair, the light brown quickly turning orange. Unlike its impetus, her landing was deafening in its silence. Was she unconscious? Or dead?

"No!"

Tony pushed up and off the ground and charged Stevenson without a weapon. Without hope. At the first pop from the other man's pistol, he remembered to at least run in a zigzag pattern. By the second, he was nearly on him. As the judge aimed once more at his throat, just above the top of his vest, Tony leaped forward.

He didn't care. He'd thought that he'd only let Stevenson hurt her over his dead body. Now he realized he'd really meant it. The odd click at his collarbone as he overtook the suspect and connected with the muzzle didn't make any sense at first. Shouldn't it have been louder? Shouldn't the pain have been sharper or hotter or *something*?

The wide eyes behind those glasses told him the weapon had failed to fire, but the thought barely registered as Tony pounded his fist into Stevenson's forearm until his grip released on the gun. Then he swiped it out of reach for either of them.

The pounding seemed to come from somewhere outside of him. Hard knuckles connecting with forgiving flesh, once, twice, one hundred times. Glasses flying off. Grunts. Pleas. More thuds. He didn't care. He couldn't stop. Didn't want to.

"Tony, stop! You're going to kill him."

Chapter 27

Kelly could breathe again when the glaze in Tony's eyes finally cleared. He couldn't seem to stop trembling, which made sense because neither could she. His knuckles were cut, Stevenson's nose still gushed, and though the blood on her arm was congealing, she figured it was covering her hair now, too.

"You're not—" He backed onto his haunches and looked down at the suspect. "Oh, my God. What was I...?"

As Tony crawled over to her, Kelly blinked several times, trying to force away the red and yellow spots still shimmying in front of her eyes. Even that didn't stop the conga drums that hammered in the back of her head, making her world shudder and sway. But something about Stevenson's hands moving to his face, where the blood continued to pour, wasn't right.

"You need to cuff him, Tony."

"Right. Wait. I don't have any handcuffs."

"He does." She lifted her bound hands slightly and indicated the direction of Stevenson's bag.

Tony told the judge to roll onto his stomach, and with

some painful shifting, Kelly kicked the bag his way. He pulled out zip ties, several pairs of disposable gloves, scissors and disinfectant wipes. He examined the blood on his hands, only some of which could have come from his cuts.

"Guess it's a little late for those."

"Have you ever heard of police brutality?" Stevenson called out as Tony bound Stevenson's hands.

While Tony repeated the Miranda warning from memory, he used some of the wipes on his own skin.

"Ever heard of self-defense?"

The man kept talking, but Tony left him and crouched next to Kelly instead and used the scissors to free her hands.

"Harper's here somewhere. I just know it."

"Even if you were in any condition to go into these woods and look for her, and you aren't, we can't move until backup arrives. For him."

"You called for backup?"

"Of course, I did. You should have, too."

He practically spat the words.

She shook her head as she used her good arm to push herself up from the ground. "I couldn't. You have to understand."

"Don't even talk to me about this right now."

The sound of crunching gravel drew her attention back to the driveway. A line of emergency vehicles—police, county sheriff, ambulance—showed through the low-lying branches. They'd come in on silent, but they'd shown up only because Tony had been the one to call for them.

Soon Kelly sat on the loading deck on the back of one of the ambulances while an emergency medical technician finished bandaging her arm and the cut on her head. He even rigged a sling of sorts to hold her forearm against her body.

As he waited next to the emergency vehicle, Tony waved over Dawson. Eric followed closely behind him.

"You two are in a world of trouble," Dawson said when they reached them. "What the hell were you thinking, coming here without backup? What happened to you? What happened to Fox? And, for that matter, who did that to Stevenson... I mean the suspect? He looks like someone beat the hell out of him."

Eric blanched as he looked from the body on the ground to the suspect being shifted onto a gurney. "Stevenson was connected to these cases? The *judge*?"

Tony spread his hands in a jerking movement as a signal for the questions to stop.

"No time for that now. It'll all be in the report. But we have reason to believe that the Toledo teen might be somewhere on this property. We need to conduct a full search. Would you call for the dogs, Special Agent Dawson?"

"Alive?" Dawson asked.

"Maybe." Kelly willed it to be true.

But Tony stomped on her words with his own.

"Probably not." He caught her sharp glance and then looked away. "We need to find out for sure."

His pessimistic prediction didn't stop him from rushing to the opposite side of the clearing and digging through the brush, where he'd tossed his weapon and his phone. He emerged about a minute later, carrying both. He handed Kelly his cell, its display glass crushed, while he tucked his Glock back in his hip holster.

Kelly returned his phone to him and slid off the deck to her feet, keeping her arm tightly against her.

"Where are you going?"

"I'm coming with you."

"Oh, no, you're not. You aren't even assigned to the task force anymore."

"How did you know that?" She looked back and forth between him and Dawson. "I was just informed."

"I was told before you were. Anyway, you can't go searching. You have that. And that." He pointed to the sling and then to the gauze pad taped to her head.

"You heard him say that one was just a scratch, and the head thing is tiny. Head wounds just bleed a lot."

"The EMT said you might have a concussion, too."

"So I won't go to sleep."

He crossed his arms. "When you declined ambulance transport, you agreed to take *yourself* to ER."

Kelly took a deep breath, but she couldn't keep from gritting her teeth. "I didn't ask for your permission to search for Harper. It's why I came here, and I'm not leaving until I do it."

She turned to their boss, suddenly aware that she might not need Tony's approval, but she would require the go-ahead from her superior, especially now that she'd been reassigned to the Brighton Post.

"Look, Special Agent Dawson, I promise I'll go to ER as soon as we're finished. I'll get a tetanus shot. Then I'll pack up my stuff and be back at the Brighton Post as soon as the doctors release me. But right now, I *need* to help. Whether she's dead or alive, please let me finish what I started. Let me give the girl's family some closure."

Dawson frowned, but when he turned to Tony, his mouth softened. He reached into his pocket and handed each of them a few pairs of disposable gloves.

"Fine. Just stay with Lazzaro. And only in and around the structures for now. The other teams will be taking on the woods as soon as they show up with the search-and-rescue dogs and their handlers."

She nodded. At least they were pretending there was some hope. Even if it was like telling them they could look for clothes at a discount store, but only in the shoe department, she would take what she could get. She had to do something.

Dawson instructed Eric, who still looked pastier than normal, to pull the map up on his laptop again so they could assign search areas once the teams arrived.

Tony started toward the cabin without her, putting on the gloves as he walked. "I won't wait for you."

"I wouldn't expect you to." Kelly scrambled after him, attempting several times to put a glove on one-handed. Finally, she stopped and tried again, using her arm in the sling for leverage.

"Here. Give me that."

He took the glove and yanked it on her hand, but he wouldn't look at her as he did it. If he could have done it without touching her, he probably would have tried that, too.

Still, he signaled for her to wait as he withdrew his weapon and entered the building.

"It's clear," he called from inside.

She pushed the door open to find the place in barely better shape than its weatherworn exterior. With only one window in the front and another one in the back that she hadn't seen before, the place was so dark that she had to use her phone's flashlight app just to see around. The retro-looking sofa with tapered legs and mustard-colored cushions looked like it had actually been around since the 1960s.

Someone had been living there, though. The bed was unmade, and clothes were piled in the corner. Bags of garbage had been dumped against the wall. The pantry's high shelves had enough nonperishables to feed at least one person for a few months.

It seemed odd that the shelves only went halfway down, and nothing was stacked on the floor, but she doubted there were many normal things about a suspect who was into princesses.

Tony emerged from the small bedroom after checking out the closet. "He was here, but it doesn't look like *she* was. No women's clothes. No *tiaras*."

Kelly couldn't help it. She shivered. "Do you think Fox lied about even knowing Harper? He knew about LITTLE BO PEEP. Police didn't tell anyone about that. Then he also said she *was* no princess. As in past tense."

"People lie. You know that. They do it all the time."

With that, he started out the door to examine the perimeter of the house. Kelly hurried after him.

"All right. That's enough."

"What's that?" He turned his head to the side but didn't look at her.

"You know what I'm talking about. I've already said I'm sorry for coming here without backup. Without *you*."

His gaze flicked to hers and away again. "You could have gotten yourself killed, all while trying to play the hero."

"I realize that now." She'd known when she'd decided to come, too. "Isn't that a little hypocritical? I'm not the only one who rushed in here like Dirty Harry. You're lucky to be alive, too."

She shivered at the thought of those rounds Tony had dodged as he'd raced to stop Stevenson. Especially the misfire, which would have been deadly accurate. At least she'd been unconscious for most of it and had to learn that story secondhand.

"Fine. We both screwed up."

"Don't you get it? I had to come alone. Stevenson hinted that he had Harper. He threatened everyone if I didn't come alone. I had no choice."

This time he trapped her in his stare. "Oh, you had a choice. You *chose* to lie. About your mother. You knew I would be happy for you that you'd turned a corner with her. You knew I would want to believe your story, even if it didn't ring true."

Having finished with the outside of the house, he tromped ahead and didn't stop until he reached the barn door. Kelly had to struggle to keep up with him. With each step, her arm burned, and her head throbbed. Her decision to skip even the ibuprofen from her purse didn't seem so wise now.

"It's not that simple," she said when she'd caught up with him again. "If I'd told you, there would have been no way you would have let me go alone."

"Hell no, I wouldn't have."

"That's just it. He said he would kill you *first*."

Even then, the thought of it gripped her chest and stole her breath.

"He was playing you."

"You don't know that. I couldn't take that chance. I also couldn't risk *not* going when there was even the slightest possibility that he might have Harper. That she might be alive."

"So, like I said, you made a choice."

He paused long enough to withdraw his weapon and ask for her to wait again while he did an initial scan to ensure the barn was empty. He waved her in.

"You made damn sure that I didn't get to choose. It's just like—"

"Now, you stop right there." She marched right up

to him for the face-off he deserved. "I might have kept something from you for your own safety, but it was nothing like what Laurel did to you. How can you even compare the two things? I didn't betray you. I was *protecting* you."

He turned away from her to holster his weapon and walked along the outside wall of the barn, which was barely a building at all anymore. Tall grass had reclaimed the dirt floor in the open area and between the horse stalls. The sky shone through several spots in the roof and the side walls. When he appeared convinced that the building was empty as well, he crossed back to her.

"Just like she did, you made your choice, and you took away mine."

"So that's it, isn't it? You've steered clear of relationships because you're terrified someone else will betray you. Now you're determined to see what I did as your self-fulfilling prophesy. It's your way of ensuring that no one will ever get close enough to hurt you again. Well, good job. You win."

Her eyes burning, she hurried toward the door, but when she reached it, she stopped. Questions that had played at the edges of her consciousness the past hour pushed closer, demanding answers. She spun to face him.

"Tell me, Tony, when exactly did Dawson tell you I was being transferred?"

"It was earlier."

"Earlier as in today? Yesterday? Last week?"

"It was yesterday."

"And why did he tell you first? Is it because you asked for my reassignment?"

He blew out a breath and lowered his head. "Yes."

His words were worse even than Stevenson's blow to her head. Starker in their cruelty.

"How could you!"

This time, he held out his hands, palms-up. "It was for your own good."

"I'm a big girl. Don't you think I should be able to determine what was *for my own good*?"

"Apparently not."

Heat rushed to her extremities, singeing her elbow, which already felt like it had been charred. She wanted to argue, but her jaw was clenched so tight she couldn't open it.

"You were too close to the cases. I knew it from the start, though I wasn't sure why. I should have asked for you to be transferred weeks ago."

She lifted her chin and stared him down. "How dare you. I told you those things in confidence. I even let them go."

"You haven't let anything go. You might have ruled out BIG DADDY, but you're still chasing ghosts. What you haven't figured out is that the root of your fear is inside you."

"Well, thank you for your analysis, Dr. Freud." She fisted her hands and winced when the arm in the sling protested. "Wait. Stevenson said you got here too fast to have been responding to only his text. How did you know I was going here because we both know I didn't tell you?"

He stared at the ground. "I tracked your phone."

Her hand automatically went to the waistband of her slacks, where she'd tucked her cell after Eric retrieved it from her car. "How did you…?"

"Companions Connect."

"What? When?" Her fingers fumbled as she held the phone in one hand, and she had to type in her passcode twice. Once inside, she flipped through the apps to one that permitted the phone owner to allow certain friends to see her location. She clicked on it. His name was the only one on the list.

"That's what you did when I gave you the code to look up some information? You *tracked* me? I can't believe you did that."

This time Kelly struck out ahead of Tony toward the third building they'd been assigned to examine before the other search teams arrived. Nothing he said could make his actions right. Anyway, the skeleton of a storage shed wouldn't require someone with a weapon to clear it first. She could see right through the structure, from one side to the other.

She'd already entered what was once its door when he rested a hand on her shoulder. Whirling around cost her in both pain and dizziness, but at least it knocked his hand away. An hour before she'd been terrified that she would lose him, and now she didn't want him to touch her.

Tony drew his brows together, but he lowered his hand to his side.

"It was just a precaution. I never planned to use it. You were in danger, and we still didn't know who we could trust. I would only use the app if he came after you. And he did."

"You can tell yourself it was just to be safe, but the truth is you spied on me because you didn't trust me not to go rogue."

To avoid seeing that knowing look on his face and being forced to consider that she'd done exactly that, she stepped through the nest of overgrown weeds, past rusted rakes and shovels. Beyond the two handles of an old wheelbarrow that stuck out in warning of yet another obstacle, she turned back to him, pulled out her phone and tapped its face.

"If it really was for my protection, then when did you launch the app to find my location? After the task force had information on Fox? The truth."

He shook his head.

"Then when was it?"

"It was when you first left. Something about your story didn't sit right with me."

"And as someone trained to know when people are lying, you had to check it out. Only this time, it meant checking up on your girlfriend."

He'd been bent over, examining some rotting hoses next to what had once been the wall, but he straightened suddenly, his gaze searching hers. They hadn't put labels on their relationship before, and now she was only doing it to hurt him.

"Don't you get it? I wanted to protect you because, well, I'm in love with you."

Kelly tried to swallow past the sudden thickness in her throat. Until then, she hadn't realized how much she'd longed to hear him say those words. Now that they'd filled her ears with sound, they rang hollow.

"Is that how you *loved* your ex-wife, too? By checking up on her and tracking her whereabouts? Because that sounds like control to me."

She was only saying these things to hurt him, but she couldn't seem to stop herself. "I've heard all about *her* betrayal, but that's only one side of the story. Maybe you need to admit that there might be two sides to it?"

He flinched as if she'd struck tender flesh. The instinct to take it all back struck her fast and hard. Had she even meant anything she'd said? Then his shoulders pushed back, and he trapped her with his stare.

"And maybe you need to get over everything that happened with Emily. Do you really believe you'll be able to make up for your mistakes by chasing down every missing victim now? I'm sorry to tell you that you won't be able to find them all. Even when you try, you'll learn that some will be recoveries instead of rescues."

He stared her down as if he was finished, but as she turned away, he added a parting comment.

"When you're unable to save one, will you use that as another excuse to never allow yourself to trust anyone, just like you've used Emily's abduction? You like to say you blame yourself, but that's not true. You blame everyone and everything for your inability to move on from the past instead of stepping up and taking responsibility for your own life."

At first Kelly could only stare at him, his comment searing in both its truth and its cruelty. When she found her voice, she returned fire in their war of words that would have no victors, only casualties.

"Well, it's good that I knew better than to trust you. Looks like I'm getting away from you just in time."

Then she rushed out of the final storage building, away from him, his hateful words and the disloyal part of her that questioned her certainty that he was wrong.

She picked her way through the minefield of discarded tools and broken equipment, blinking back tears she couldn't afford to cry there or anywhere. Not when it would confirm that Dawson was right to pull her from the investigation without even talking with her. She only lost her balance once because of her bandaged arm, but she regained it and kept going.

When she reached the cabin again, she opened the door with her gloved hand, slid inside and closed it behind her. Only a few more hours, or maybe several, and they would file their reports, allowing her to return to her life before the task force. Then she could pretend she hadn't messed up by getting to know Tony Lazzaro. And she could tell herself that loving him hadn't been the biggest mistake of all.

Chapter 28

Tony waited as long as he could before hurrying after Kelly back to the cabin, which was about a full minute if the clock was generous. He caught sight of Dawson on the way across the field, pointing to the cabin to indicate where Kelly had gone and gave a thumbs-up. Hopefully that would be enough to keep the admin special agent from catching up with her before he did.

What right did she have to run away when she was the one who'd just said unforgivable things? Well, at least he wasn't the only one. How could she say that he'd been trying to control her when he'd tracked her phone only to protect her? That she'd crossed the line by dragging his ex into the conversation proved just how wrong he could have been about a person.

Could she have been, even in the smallest way, right? At least about his decision to track her phone? No, he refused to believe that. Accepting it would rob him of his righteous indignation, and there was no way he would let go of that.

At the cabin, he paused long enough to slip on a fresh pair of gloves and then turned the knob. She was standing inside the bedroom, staring down at the unmade bed. Was she crying? Had he *made* her cry?

"Kelly?"

Slowly she turned around. Her face was dry, but her lashes were as damp as they'd been that last time that they'd made love. He tightened his jaw and gave the thought a push. It had been the last time, all right.

"What do you want now?" she asked.

"You can't just hide in here."

"I'm not hiding." She gestured toward the glove she'd somehow managed to get on her free hand. "I wanted to check this place one more time."

They both knew she was lying, so he could find no reason to point it out. If she could act as if everything was fine, he could play along, too.

She crossed to the threadbare sofa and pointed to the end table that was propped up with a brick. "Not only is there no TV and no power here, this place has no books, no magazines, no puzzles."

"You're right. He could have survived here a few months off the grid, but what would he have done here besides play in the woods?"

He swallowed as Kelly's gaze shifted to the door. Fox could have kept busy for a while out there, burying at least one body that they knew of.

Tony pursed his lips, considering. "I don't know. Maybe, in addition to chat rooms, he had a thing for bird-watching."

"See any binoculars or bird-identification books?"

"No. But he had to do something here. We're overlooking something." He crossed to the back wall and started knocking on it. "Maybe there were secret shelves that hid the guy's creepy magazines."

"Or there could be a hole in the ground outside or a

well. Something." She was working her way down the front wall, knocking like he'd been doing.

"Why don't you try the dividing wall to the bedroom?"

She nodded and took a diagonal path from the front door to that wall. If either of them had been talking, they might have missed it, but the squeak of one of the wood planks sounded strange, even for a place with more noises than a haunted house.

"What was that?"

Kelly asked the question, but she was already struggling down to the floor where the filthy rug covered the spot in front of the sofa.

"There's got to be something down there." He crouched at the end of the rug and started rolling. "A trap door. A storage area."

But nothing was there.

"Do you think we're hearing things?" she asked.

"Both of us? No."

Leaving the carpet rolled, they took turns walking across the floor in different paths, trying to recreate the sound from earlier. Outside, rumbling engines and barking announced the arrival of the search teams.

"Maybe it was just wishful thinking," he admitted finally.

"I was naive to think Harper would be okay after Fox confessed to killing Sienna and Madison. I just had to hope…"

"Yeah, me, too." He had hoped, but it was looking more and more like another victim had been lost on his watch.

"I just kept thinking he would have left some clue. Something that would jump out at me. Something… Wait." She held her palms flat in a startled gesture, though one was trapped in a sling at her side.

And suddenly that something that neither of them had remarked on earlier leaped out to announce itself to them both.

"The pantry," they called out in unison.

They rushed into the kitchen and Tony crouched just outside the open pantry door.

"Here. Let me."

Inside the storage area that Fox had left oddly empty, he started knocking on different spots as they had on the front wall. Kelly squeezed in next to him and started pushing down on the floor with her good hand.

Just when he was ready to conclude that they were wrong again, the flooring made a cracking sound and a whole section popped up. His gaze flicked to Kelly's before he slid his gloved fingers beneath it and lifted it a few inches. The rest required more wiggling and tilting, but finally he was able to remove the whole section that measured three feet by three feet.

"Well, that explains why the pantry had no lower shelves. What's in there? A storage compartment?" Kelly leaned closer and used her phone flashlight to get a better look. "No way!"

The illumination showed not a confined area at all but a narrow staircase. At the bottom was a steel door to a cellar, a sizable silver padlock laced through its security hasp.

"We need to call the others," Kelly told him when he lowered his foot to the first step.

"You're right."

Even if it was the last thing he wanted to do. He lifted his foot again, but as he started to back out, a sound reverberated in his ears. He came up so quickly that he nearly knocked her over. It might have been wishful listening, or his ears might have been playing tricks on him, but he could have sworn he'd heard muffled crying.

"Did you hear that?"

She shook her head. Had he only imagined it?

"She's down there." He said it as if that could somehow make it true.

"She has to be. You going to get Dawson?"

So why couldn't he move? He was faster than Kelly, at least right now. He should have been the one to go, but he was frozen there next to the opening. Was it that the life-or-death answers lay behind that locked door, and, like Kelly, he was too close to the case, too invested in those answers?

Kelly's gaze narrowed, but then she rushed to the door and threw it open. Once she stepped out on the porch, she stopped.

"Over here. We found something."

After several muffled voices responded to her shout, she called out again.

"We need bolt cutters. And bring a stretcher."

Kelly directed her phone flashlight down toward the open door through which Tony, Dawson and a male EMT had disappeared with their flashlights several seconds, or minutes, before. The broken lock had been discarded on the ground at the bottom of the stairs, and the long-handled bolt cutter they'd used to break off the lock lay propped against the wall.

It was all she could do not to rush down there to find out what was going on beyond that door, but she got it. She was hurt, and there was no reason for her to be down there when it was crowded, and she would just be risking further injury as well as getting in the way.

Finally, Dawson appeared at the opening.

"Do you think you can make it down here, Trooper Roberts?"

"But I thought you said— What do you need me to do? Is Harper down there? Is she, uh…?"

Then he smiled. "We think she's okay. I just asked her if she might be more comfortable talking to a female—"

"I'll be right down."

Getting there was more difficult than it looked, and she had to swallow a cry when she bumped her arm on the way down, but she made it to the bottom of the stairs and stepped inside the room.

At first, she didn't see Harper at all, the space overwhelming in its contrast to the stark setting upstairs. It looked as if a fashion doll's house had exploded, covering the paneled walls with hot pink and glitter. She blinked several times to allow her eyes to adjust to the brightness from several battery-powered lanterns. They hadn't found any tiaras upstairs, but in this room filled with pink tulle and lace, there were several, their rhinestones blinking whenever anyone's movement refracted the light.

"Kelly," Tony said in a low tone, and then tilted his head in the direction of the single foam mattress in the middle of the floor.

And there she was, curled into the corner, her dark hair a mass of tangles, her face tucked between her bent knees. Barefoot, she had on a pair of black leggings and a T-shirt that, from the filth on them, she'd been wearing for days.

"Harper?"

Though she'd said it in her softest voice, the girl still startled.

"We're all here to help you. We're going to get you out of here." She took a few steps closer and then gestured for the two men to move to the opposite side of the room.

Dawson had already started up the stairs to inform the others and, probably, to reach out to Toledo law enforcement officers, who would notify her parents.

"Is it okay if I sit next to you?"

Harper tilted her head and watched her for several long seconds, but finally she nodded. Kelly moved slowly, lowering herself to the floor beside her.

"Did he hurt you, too?" Harper said in a quavering voice.

A lump formed in Kelly' throat over that final word. Too. But the teen didn't need her tears or her pity.

"Well, something like that. He'll never get to hurt *you* again."

This time Harper looked up at her, those sad, dark-brown eyes seeking answers, most of which Kelly couldn't give.

"Promise?"

This one she could. "Yes, I promise."

"I want my mom."

Kelly started to explain that it would take a while for her parents to reach her, and she would have to be checked out at the hospital before she could be released to them. She didn't get the chance as Harper launched herself into her arms, an available female substitute for a mother who couldn't be there.

For several minutes Kelly held the girl, absorbing her sobs and rocking her in a way she guessed her mother would. She didn't want to allow her own memories to seep in, but she suddenly was grateful for that woman in the police car, who'd covered her with the itchy blanket and let her talk about blue slushes.

She couldn't look at Tony then, or wonder if he'd guessed what she was thinking about. He knew too many things about her, and he'd used them against her.

Only after the ambulance left with Harper, and more crime scene investigators descended on the property to cover both the house and the scene of the shooting, did Kelly finally head back to her car. Tony caught up to her as she reached inside to grab her purse.

"Finally heading to the ER like Dawson ordered hours ago?"

She shrugged, her arm throbbing more than it had all day. "I was a little busy before."

"Do you want me to drive you?"

She did. That was the worst part. Even after everything that had happened today, when she found out that her scratch was probably more than a scratch, she wanted it to be with him.

"That's okay," she said, instead. "Eric told me he would drive me since my car's kind of blocked in here. He feels terrible for letting Stevenson get details about the task force out of him. He didn't know. He thought we were all on the same side."

"So did I."

He didn't say more, and she couldn't risk asking, but she suspected his comment was about more than the colleague who had allowed Stevenson to get to them. She'd believed some things that weren't true, as well.

She took one last look at the old gray house, its exterior appearing more sinister now that she understood the sickness that had been contained inside.

"Do you think Harper wasn't the first person to be trapped in that cellar?" she couldn't help asking.

"Some of the CSI people seem to think there were others. Might even have been Fox when he was a kid, since he knew where it was located."

"His grandfather?"

"Guess we'll never know that for certain. But one

thing I've learned over the years is that some people aren't born predators. They're made."

She nodded and started away from him toward Eric's car.

"Hey, Kelly."

She turned back to him, at once hoping he would say something that could make everything right between them and knowing that it wasn't possible.

"I'm really sorry. About everything."

"Yeah, me, too." She turned away because she was determined not to let him see her cry, and her eyes were already burning. She might have lied to protect him, but he'd betrayed her trust. How could they ever come back from that? Did she even want them to?

She took a few steps away from him, and from the crunch of the gravel behind her, she realized that he was walking away, too. This was the way it had to be because sometimes sorry wasn't enough.

Chapter 29

Tony set the container on his kitchen table, his kitchen appearing a lot smaller than it had just that morning. His table seemed shorter, too, as he lifted items from inside the cardboard. He couldn't be sure since he'd never eaten at it, even before he'd stopped cooking lately. Instead of marveling over those things, he should have been reflecting on how easily he'd just fit six years in a box.

When his fingers brushed the loose sheet of paper he'd packed along with Carter's and Tabitha's framed photos and his spare dress shirt and tie that he'd always kept on hand, he pulled it out and lowered into one of the kitchen chairs to read it. His transfer. Not so long ago, it had been all he could think about.

So many things had changed, but a critical one had stayed the same: he was still longing for something—or in this case *someone*—he couldn't have.

His move to focus on identity theft was supposed to make his work life better. Apparently not. His heart just wasn't in it. Or in anything else.

His ringing phone broke up his building pity party. He hated that he was disappointed when his sister's name appeared on the screen again. It wasn't her fault she wasn't Kelly.

He clicked the button to pick up the call. "What's up, Angelena?"

"Just checking in. Was today your last day?"

"You know it was. Why'd you really call?"

"I need a babysitter. Miles and I really need a night out."

"Again?" He chuckled. "Besides, I've figured out your little plan."

"What plan? There's no plan."

"And I appreciate it. Really. Could I take a raincheck on the kid therapy tonight?"

She blew out an audible breath. "Fine. But you should call her."

"And tell her what?" He didn't bother pretending not to know who she was speaking about. They'd been having some version of this conversation for days.

"I don't know. That you're sorry you were such a boob. That you forgive her for lying while she was trying to protect you."

"Why do I always come out looking worse in your version of this story?"

"What are little sisters for?"

"But Angelena, how would I ever trust her when she went behind my back like that?"

"Do you love her?"

"Yeah." It felt good to admit it to someone else.

"Then figure it out."

"What if she can't forgive *me*?" Maybe that was his fear all along because he already knew he could forgive her. He already had. If their roles had been reversed, he would have lied, too. Anything to keep her safe.

"I guess you'll have to convince her, then. Don't let

pride or the mistakes you made with Laurel keep you from having what you want, okay?"

What if it's too late? The question rested on his lips, but he didn't say it.

His sister got off the phone quickly after that, as she must have realized she'd messed with his head enough for one night.

He considered stuffing the box in his closet with the kids' school desk, but when he entered the guest room, he started unpacking it instead. When he reached the file at the bottom of the box, he sat on the bed and opened it. The search had been almost too easy. He'd been trying to decide when to share with Kelly what he'd found, when his window of opportunity had closed for good.

Had it? Maybe it was too late for him and Kelly to be together, but that didn't mean he shouldn't at least try to give Kelly her life back.

Taking the file with him, Tony returned to the kitchen table where he'd left his cell. He opened the folder again and stared down at the number.

He would be lying to say he didn't secretly hope that this would convince her to give him a chance. Even if she didn't, though, even if she never came back to him, she deserved to know what he'd learned.

He took a deep breath and dialed. A feminine voice answered on the second ring.

"Hello?"

"May I speak to Emily?"

Kelly pinned on her shield, checked her gray tie in the mirror and carefully unrolled the sleeve of her dress shirt over her bandaged arm. Then she headed out of the women's dressing room.

"Look who's right on time today," Dion called out

from one of the desks that enclosed the Brighton Post squad room.

Per usual, Nick was at the desk right next to him.

"I guess someone's glad to be back home at her post. No traffic on your way to work today?"

"If you two need me to go back in there and waste ten minutes, I can do that, too."

She could still play along with the office banter since she'd returned two weeks before, but it wasn't effortless like she remembered. In fact, everything at the post seemed to have changed, from her fellow troopers to the daily second-shift briefings in the squad room.

Her patrol car probably smelled different, too, but she wouldn't know for sure since her doctor hadn't released her to full duty yet. That could have been the problem: she needed to get out on the road. But she sensed there was more to it. Maybe she was the one who'd changed. Loving and losing Tony had taken some part of her that she couldn't get back.

"Earth to Trooper Roberts." Dion waved a hand in front of her to get her attention. "Did you hear what I said?"

"No. Sorry."

"Lieutenant Peterson said to tell you there's a guest in the reception area waiting for you."

Something fluttered inside her stomach, and she didn't miss the look the two men exchanged. Could they be right? Could it be Tony out there, showing up to make some grand gesture? Did she even *want* him to do that? He'd betrayed her trust. He'd gone behind her back. Why did she have to keep reminding herself of that every time she clicked his name on her phone's contacts list?

She started down the hall to the lobby before her co-workers could ask. Once out of their sight, she had to force herself not to run. She paused next to the locked door that separated the lobby from the rest of the building.

"Someone was here to see me?"

The receptionist nodded and pointed toward the door.

Was she prepared to forgive Tony if he asked? Was she ready to take another chance with him? Kelly took a deep breath and pushed open the door.

The person on the other side wasn't Tony. Or any man. A plump twenty-something woman looked back at her, a long dark braid trailing down her back, her arms crossed as if she was cold, though the post's air-conditioning hadn't kept up in days.

"May I help you?"

"Are you…uh…Trooper Roberts?"

"Yes." Something about her eyes looked familiar, but everyone seemed to lately. She tried again. "Is there something I can do for you?"

"You don't remember me, do you?"

This time the woman smiled, and Kelly could picture those same front teeth, only with a split between them, pre-orthodontia.

"Emily?"

The woman nodded and grabbed her in a fierce hug that made her gasp from the pressure on her arm. When Emily stepped back, concern etched on her face, Kelly forced a smile.

"Just a little work injury."

"Sorry."

Someone cleared his throat, causing both women to turn. Ben Peterson stood at the open counter.

"I wondered if the two of you might want to continue your conversation in the interview room."

Kelly nodded, and he buzzed them back.

Inside the door, she paused. "Lieutenant Peterson, this is my…uh…childhood friend, Emily Nikolaidis."

"Barnard now," Emily corrected.

Ben, who knew more about Kelly's personal background than some of the others did, led them to the conference room and shut the door behind them. Kelly took a seat on the side of the long table.

Emily sat at the end. "I'm sorry. I shouldn't have shown up at your work."

"No. It's fine. Really. You just surprised me. You know. After all this time."

"I should have reached out to you forever ago, but you know how it is. We get caught up in our own lives."

At that, Kelly grinned. "We definitely do. You said you were married?"

"Two kids, too." She whipped out her phone and showed photos of little boys with dark hair and deep tan skin like hers. "I'm a nurse. Aaron's a firefighter. Our life is crazy sometimes, but we make it work."

"That's great. I'm so happy for you, Emily."

"And I'm happy for you. I was excited to hear you're a police officer. You get to help people every day."

Kelly tilted her head and studied her. "You *heard* that I'm a cop? Where did you…?"

"From your boyfriend, of course. Didn't Tony tell you he called me? He said he was helping you to reconnect with me. You didn't know?"

Kelly only shook her head since the lump forming in her throat made it impossible to speak. Had he reached out to her childhood friend as part of an apology? Perhaps. Still, he'd done it, even given the pain they'd caused each other. He'd made a grand gesture, after all.

"Maybe he wanted to surprise you."

"Maybe."

"What a sweet guy. He even offered to pay for my flight, but we couldn't let him do that. It was kind of him to offer."

Kelly couldn't bring herself to correct Emily's assumption that the two of them were a couple. Her own reasons for them not being together were becoming fuzzier with each new revelation.

"You seem really happy," she said instead. "I'm glad."

She could have stopped there, leaving the conversation with her childhood best friend in that safe place on the surface. But Tony had given her this chance, and though this probably wasn't the time nor the place, she would take that opportunity. Instead of continuing to chase absolution, it was time to ask for it.

She clasped her hands on the table in front of her. "I want you to know that I'm sorry for not being there for you, when, you know, everything happened."

"You mean when I was *abducted*? You can say it. Tony told me you might want to talk about it. Anyway, you *were* there for me."

"I wasn't." Her eyes burned, but she'd broken the seal that had held the words in place, and now she couldn't stop them. "I was confused and scared. You were different, and I was—"

"A kid," Emily finished for her. "We both were."

"That's not a good enough excuse for pulling away just when you needed me."

"It has to be." Emily reached across the table and took Kelly's gripped hands between hers.

"Can you ever forgive me?"

"For what?"

"For not screaming. For freezing when I should have been fighting him. When I should have stopped him." Tears flooded her eyes and escaped from the outside corners no matter how hard she tried to blink them away. Emily released her hands and grabbed the box of tissues always kept in the interview room for suspects and victims.

"There's nothing to forgive. I never blamed you. Never."

Kelly shook her head, Emily's freeing words clashing with a lifetime of self-loathing. Her friend hadn't blamed her, just like Tony had predicted.

Emily's eyes were damp now, too, so she grabbed a few more tissues for herself.

"In some ways, I think my abductor took more from you than he ever did from me. I never once blamed myself. But you did. You're still doing it."

She tilted her head to the side so her ear nearly touched her shoulder, her eyes sad.

"So stop. Please. For me."

"I'm trying."

"Try harder."

"I hate that there was never a conviction, or even arrest, in your case."

"Yeah, me, too. But a detective told me years ago that if no other similar abductions to mine were reported in the years after it, that could mean that the suspect might have been imprisoned on another charge. Maybe he even died there. I choose to believe that theory."

"I want to believe it, too," Kelly admitted. It was a departure from her determination to find him, but maybe it was time to let go.

"Enough about that," Emily said, smiling. "Tell me about this Tony. Are you two engaged? He seemed to be so in love with you."

"I think he does love me." Kelly cleared her throat, but she still couldn't keep the emotion from coating her voice. "I love him, too, but, well, I've never been good at relationships. And, you know, some broken things can't be fixed."

"Do you want to? Fix them, that is."

"I do, sure, but…"

"So fix them. Don't let what happened to *us* when we were kids keep you from living your best life or from being with the man you love. If you do that, the guy wins. We can't let him win."

Kelly didn't answer then. She couldn't. Why had she never considered before that by allowing her history to cripple her relationships she'd given him power over her?

Her friend took her hands again and smiled, despite the tears still shining in her eyes.

"That man of yours convinced me to come here, just so you would have the chance to put your past behind you. Sounds like a keeper to me."

Kelly couldn't help but to agree. In her heart, she'd always known that. After they'd made plans to meet at Emily's hotel later that night to really catch up, she returned to her desk assignment, but their conversation kept replaying in her mind. That and the truth that Tony had arranged this whole visit just for her.

She'd admitted out loud that she still loved Tony. Nothing he'd done or said could change that. He loved her, too. His plan to bring her and Emily together displayed that more clearly than any rooftop pronouncement ever could.

But was love enough for them to overcome their fear of trusting a second time when they'd already burned each other once? She didn't know the answer to that, and she wasn't positive that Tony's effort to help her reconnect with her friend was more than a parting gift.

It was like diving into a swimming pool in a pitch-dark natatorium, unsure of the water's depth or even if the pool had been filled at all. Well, she was tired of living cautiously and sick of being afraid. She didn't know about Tony, but she was ready to close her eyes, spread her arms wide and dive.

Chapter 30

The squawk of his doorbell caught Tony off guard as he was attaching wires to his new modem, and he whacked his head on the underside of his desk. He was still rubbing the side of his head and blinking back dots dancing before his eyes when he reached the front door and pulled it open.

Kelly was standing there, looking ethereal in a filmy, light blue sundress and silver sandals, her long hair left loose, its ends catching the breeze. He blinked a few more times, just to make sure she was real. He'd never seen her in a dress before, which was probably a good thing, given how hard his pulse pounded then.

"Hi," she said through the partial screen in the storm door.

"Hi?" His greeting came as a question, but how could it not when so much hope was crammed into a single word? Why was she there? Why now? Had she come because she was braver than he was, and she was ready to say that she wanted to be with him? Or had she come for the closure they'd never had?

She offered no answers as she stood there, shifting her feet and chewing her lip.

"What's going on?" he asked when he couldn't stand it anymore. "What are you doing here?"

She flinched, as his comment must have sounded harsher than he intended.

"I stopped by the task force office today. Eric told me everything."

She didn't ask to come in, but he pushed the storm door open, and she stepped inside. The scent of her shampoo struck him as she passed, and, as usual, he was helpless but to breathe her in. Images so sweet and so painful fluttered in his thoughts, but he pushed them away as he had each day since he'd seen her. The longest period of his life.

He gestured for her to have a seat on his replacement sofa as he sat in the new side chair. She did as he asked, but instead of saying more, she straightened her dress several times and crossed and uncrossed her legs. Randomly, he recalled she'd only been to his house once before, after Stevenson had wrecked it, but she wasn't looking around now. Clearly, whatever she had to say was important.

"I thought you'd just wanted a transfer out of the task force. Maybe to the Detroit field office. I didn't think you'd planned to leave the agency completely."

Was that it? Had she only come to discuss his career plans? Like an intervention or something?

"Plans change." Like when he'd tried to avoid falling in love with her.

She nodded, as if she at least understood that. Then she looked around, her eyes wide, as if seeing the place for the first time.

"You haven't started packing."

"Packing?"

Her gaze had been on the hallway that led to the bedrooms, but then she turned back to him.

"You'll be moving now, right? Since you left the FBI?"

Did she not want him to leave? Was that it? Hope tried to peek out from behind his determination to control it, but he couldn't risk that yet. "I hadn't thought about it. I guess Eric didn't tell you everything."

"What do you mean?"

"I've decided to become a consultant, helping schools, parents and kids learn how to be safe when online and to avoid online predators."

"That's amazing."

She must have realized she'd gushed, as she cleared her throat and started again.

"No, really, Tony. That's a wonderful thing you'll be doing. So many families will benefit from a program like that."

"I thought so, too. I've already booked appearances in several school districts, and community organizations are funding my presentations, so I don't have to work for free."

"Local school districts?"

He nodded, grinning. "It looks like I'll be staying in this area for at least the near future."

"That's good."

She wiped her palms on her skirt and shook her crossed leg in a fast, constant rhythm.

"Was that the only reason you came? To ask me about my choice to leave the agency?"

She shook her head. "I saw Emily yesterday."

So that was it. This was a thank-you call. "Oh, she came. I didn't know when she planned to do it. Was it a good visit?"

"The best."

Her face lit up, and he could only hope that after this meeting with her childhood friend, she would be free to experience that kind of delight far more often. That was all he wanted. At least, he told himself it was.

"You were right about her. She doesn't blame me. And she's happy and stable. She's really okay."

"That must be such a relief for you."

"It is. I'll never know how to repay you for reaching out to her. I wouldn't have done it, though I should have a long time ago. She said the same thing. It was the kindest thing anyone's ever done for me."

He leaned forward in his seat and rested his hands on his knees.

"I didn't locate Emily because I wanted you to feel indebted to me or tied to me somehow. That's not what I wanted at all."

She drew her brows together.

"Then what did you *want* to happen?"

"I wanted to free you from your past. You've been living with handcuffs tying you to a situation over which you had no control. I just wanted you to be free."

"Is my *freedom* all you want for me? Or from me?"

Her voice caught on the word that could mean so many things. It also couldn't begin to cover all he wanted with her in his life.

"What are you trying to say?" He held his breath, not knowing what was coming but finally allowing himself to hope.

"Can we at least try to be together? Can we try to rebuild our trust in each other?"

She paused, licking her lips, her eyes imploring.

"No secrets. No agendas. Just try."

He shook his head. "I'm sorry. I don't want to *try*."

The second that Kelly's tears spilled over her lower lids, Tony realized she'd misunderstood. Her elbows planted on her knees, she buried her face in her hands.

He scooted from his chair to kneel in front of her and gently pulled her hands away from her face. Her skin was damp with her tears.

"Don't you see? I don't want to just try anything. I want to risk *everything* with you."

Which one of them moved first, he wasn't certain, but suddenly she was in his arms, kissing him with the same desperation that flooded through his veins. He couldn't hold her close enough or kiss her deeply enough to show her just how he felt about her.

By the time that Kelly slid her mouth to the side and drew in a ragged breath, he had pulled her across his lap on the floor. When she pressed her cheek to his and chuckled, he could feel the rumbling of her contentment everywhere.

Careful so that he didn't squeeze too hard on her healing arm, he moved her back from him so he could look into her eyes.

"I'm in love with you, Trooper Roberts." Her beautiful smile, her already-swollen lips, only made him want to kiss her again.

"And I'm in love with you. Desperately."

"I want to be with you and marry you and, someday, make babies with you."

She blinked since a lot of this was new information for her, particularly the part about kids, but then she leaned her head back and laughed out loud.

"What's so funny?"

"Can we just be a couple first? For a few days? Three weeks, tops."

"Fine. But there's one more thing I have to ask you."

"Okay, but if you're asking what I want printed on the stone for our side-by-side burial plots, I'm going to say you're rushing it."

"No, this is serious."

"Okay." She straightened as much as she could while draped across his lap and used her hand to draw down her smile into a blank expression.

"I need to know if you can be with me now that I've left law enforcement and all of my job security to follow my heart."

She smiled again.

"Do you really think I fell in love with you because you were in law enforcement? That couldn't be further from the truth."

"No. I guess I didn't, but I just don't want you to be *disappointed* in me."

"I could never be disappointed in you, but just so we're clear here, I'm not in love with the badge. Only you. Whether you carry it or not. And the fact that you're choosing to help people to avoid becoming victims? I didn't think I could love you any more than I did, but I was wrong."

He covered her mouth with his again, kissing her gently, longingly, with every promise he could offer, every hope he could share from his heart.

This time when he lifted his lips away, she was smiling.

"When are you going to show me the rest of the house?"

"But you already saw it the day we were here getting—" He stopped as he got the true meaning of her request. She'd made a similar offer once at her apartment. "Oh."

"I need a better tour." She giggled this time as she scrambled from his lap and stood.

He climbed off the floor and reached out a hand to her.

"Please allow me to give you a tour, my dear."

Their fingers laced together, he led her down the hall to his bedroom.

He turned to face her as he crossed the threshold into the room and released her hand as she stood just outside the door.

"Are you ready for this?" He meant far more than just their lovemaking, and her smile signaled she understood.

She stepped through the doorway and slid her hand up his chest and around his neck. "I'm in. All the way."

The passenger door of the minivan popped open, and Nick's grinning face appeared in the opening.

"Ready to play the blushing bride, Miss Kelly?"

"Oh, knock it off, or I'll shoot you. And I have my ankle holster under this dress to do it."

That earned another laugh from her colleagues who'd crowded into one borrowed car so as many of them as possible could deliver her to the church. Or Mill Pond Park, where they'd planned their fall wedding, anyway. There'd already been enough one-liners in the car that she'd probably cried off most of her eyeliner.

"Here, let me." Dion elbowed his way in front of Nick. "He doesn't know what he's doing."

He held a hand out for her and even assisted in pulling the rest of her train from beneath the dash, signs he'd probably been an in-demand prom escort.

The park couldn't have looked more perfect, its trees all decked out for an autumn party. Even if it was a little chilly today, and everyone's hair would be more wind-blown than in other wedding photos. She wouldn't have done it any differently. This was the place she and Tony had begun to fall in love, and it was the place to make it legal.

The other car doors opened, and several fellow officers climbed out, all spiffy and shined in their dress uniforms. Another set of guests wore dress slacks and ties, along with their badges, anther uniform of sorts.

Ben took several steps ahead. "Looks like everyone else is already here."

Nick frowned at Trevor. "I wonder why. A whole carload of cops, and you couldn't push the speed, even a little?"

Trevor grinned. "Well, we're here, aren't we?"

Kelly took in the line of chairs arranged just beside the duck pond and then a group of people in suits and dresses near the playground area. "I see my parents. I'd better get over to them."

"You're going to need this." Delia, who'd just climbed out of the back seat, helped her put on her veil, which she'd managed to keep hardly mussed.

Kelly blinked back tears as Delia pulled the blusher down over her face.

"You make a beautiful bride."

"Yeah."

"Absolutely."

"Sure."

The others chimed in, suddenly awkward when all of them usually had a joke to tell. Particularly Vinnie.

"Thank you all for bringing me here today. I really appreciate it."

"You're welcome," Vinnie said. "Now go get married."

She made her way over to her parents and brothers. "Anyone seen Tony yet?"

Her brother Sam pointed, and whatever anyone else said fell away as she caught sight of her amazing groom, decked out in a smart black tuxedo, already pulling at the collar. He was watching her, too, and the look of love in his eyes could carry her through whatever joys and mishaps took place throughout the day.

"Could everyone take your places?" the minister called out.

Tony stood next to him, and Kelly stood at the end of the makeshift aisle, her arm tucked through her father's.

The rest of the events took place in a blur. Words spoken. Vows repeated. The only thing she would remember clearly was the feeling of approaching Tony, step by step, and knowing that her love was waiting there for her.

There would be a huge party later where they would celebrate with laughter, dancing and more than a few adult beverages, but the part Kelly looked forward to the most was the slush machine she and Tony had insisted on when planning the wedding. She would be enjoying her favorite flavor: blue.

* * * * *

Don't miss Dana Nussio's other
Harlequin Romantic Suspense story from her
True Blue miniseries:

Shielded by the Lawman

Available now wherever
Harlequin Romantic Suspense books
and ebooks are sold!

ROMANTIC suspense

Available December 3, 2019

#2067 COLTON'S RESCUE MISSION
The Coltons of Roaring Springs • by Karen Whiddon
The sudden spark of attraction toward his brother's former fiancée, Vanessa Fisher, takes Remy Colton by surprise. Seth's addictions and emotional distress have gotten out of control. Will Remy's desire to protect Vanessa from his brother be his own downfall?

#2068 COLTON 911: FAMILY UNDER FIRE
Colton 911 • by Jane Godman
Four years ago, Alyssa Bartholomew left Everett Colton rather than see him in danger. Now, when their unexpected baby is threatened, the FBI agent is the only person who can keep her safe.

#2069 DETECTIVE ON THE HUNT
by Marilyn Pappano
Detective JJ Logan only came to Cedar Creek to figure out what happened to socialite Maura Evans, but as the mystery surrounding her deepens, local police officer Quint Foster finds himself hoping she'll stay a little longer—if they get out of the case alive!

#2070 EVIDENCE OF ATTRACTION
Bachelor Bodyguards • by Lisa Childs
To get CSI Wendy Thompson to destroy evidence, a killer threatens her and her parents' lives—forcing her to accept the protection of her crush, former vice cop turned bodyguard Hart Fisher.

Get 4 FREE REWARDS!

We'll send you 2 FREE Books plus <u>2</u> FREE Mystery Gifts.

Harlequin® Romantic Suspense books feature heart-racing sensuality and the promise of a sweeping romance set against the backdrop of suspense.

FREE Value Over **$20**

YES! Please send me 2 FREE Harlequin® Romantic Suspense novels and my 2 FREE gifts (gifts are worth about $10 retail). After receiving them, if I don't wish to receive any more books, I can return the shipping statement marked "cancel." If I don't cancel, I will receive 4 brand-new novels every month and be billed just $4.99 per book in the U.S. or $5.74 per book in Canada. That's a savings of at least 12% off the cover price! It's quite a bargain! Shipping and handling is just 50¢ per book in the U.S. and $1.25 per book in Canada.* I understand that accepting the 2 free books and gifts places me under no obligation to buy anything. I can always return a shipment and cancel at any time. The free books and gifts are mine to keep no matter what I decide.

240/340 HDN GNMZ

Name (please print)

Address   Apt. #

City   State/Province   Zip/Postal Code

Mail to the **Reader Service**:
IN U.S.A.: P.O. Box 1341, Buffalo, NY 14240-8531
IN CANADA: P.O. Box 603, Fort Erie, Ontario L2A 5X3

Want to try 2 free books from another series? Call 1-800-873-8635 or visit www.ReaderService.com.

HRS20

SPECIAL EXCERPT FROM

H HARLEQUIN®

ROMANTIC suspense

*To get CSI Wendy Thompson to destroy evidence, a
killer threatens her and her parents' lives—forcing her
to accept the protection of her crush, former vice cop
turned bodyguard Hart Fisher.*

Read on for a sneak preview of
Evidence of Attraction,
*the next book in the Bachelor Bodyguards miniseries
by Lisa Childs!*

"What the hell are you doing?" she asked as she glanced
nervously around.

The curtains swished at the front window of her
parents' house. Someone was watching them.

"I'm trying to do my damn job," Hart said through
gritted teeth as he very obviously faked a grin.

She'd refused to let him inside the house last night.
From the dark circles beneath his eyes, he must not have
slept at all. Too bad his daughter's babysitter had arrived
at the agency before they'd left. He wouldn't have been
able to take Wendy home if he'd had to take care of
Felicity.

But even though his babysitter had shown up, the little
girl still needed her father—especially since he had full
custody. Where was her mother?

"You need a safer job," she told him.

"I'm fine," he said, but his voice lowered even more to a growl of frustration. "It's my assignment that's a pain in the ass."

She smiled—just as artificially as he had. "Then you need another assignment."

He shook his head. "This is the one I have," he said. "So I'm going to make the best of it."

Then he did something she hadn't expected. He lowered his head until his mouth brushed across hers.

Her pulse began to race and she gasped.

And he kissed her again, lingering this time—his lips clinging to hers before he deepened the kiss even more. When he finally lifted his head, she gasped again—this time for breath.

"What the hell was that?" she asked.

He arched his head toward the front window of the house. "For our audience…"

"You're overacting," she said—because she had to remind herself that was all he was doing. Acting…

He wasn't really her boyfriend. He wasn't really attracted to her. He was only pretending.

Don't miss
Evidence of Attraction *by Lisa Childs*
available December 2019 wherever
Harlequin® Romantic Suspense
books and ebooks are sold.

Harlequin.com

HRSEXP1119

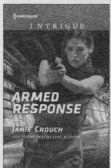  
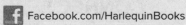
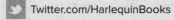
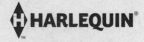

Love Harlequin romance?

DISCOVER.

Be the first to find out about promotions,
news and exclusive content!

 Facebook.com/HarlequinBooks

 Twitter.com/HarlequinBooks

 Instagram.com/HarlequinBooks

 Pinterest.com/HarlequinBooks

ReaderService.com

EXPLORE.

Sign up for the Harlequin e-newsletter and
download a free book from any series at
TryHarlequin.com.

CONNECT.

Join our Harlequin community to share
your thoughts and connect with other
romance readers!
Facebook.com/groups/HarlequinConnection

**ROMANCE WHEN
YOU NEED IT**

HSOCIAL2018